His Secret Side

Pamela Burford

Harlequin Books

TORONTO • NEW YORK • LONDON
AMSTERDAM • PARIS • SYDNEY • HAMBURG
STOCKHOLM • ATHENS • TOKYO • MILAN
MADRID • WARSAW • BUDAPEST • AUCKLAND

For my husband, Jeff Loeser

Special thanks to my dear friend Michelle Miranda, R.N., for graciously helping me with the medical details in this story; and to my sister Patricia Ryan, for her love and support.

ISBN 0-373-22360-9

HIS SECRET SIDE

Copyright © 1996 by Pamela Burford Loeser

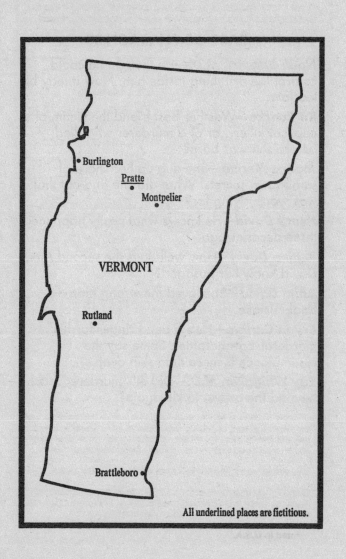

Burlington

<u>Pratte</u>

Montpelier

VERMONT

Rutland

Brattleboro

All underlined places are fictitious.

CAST OF CHARACTERS

Noah Stewart, M.D.—He thought he could control the evil thing inside him. Now it may be too late.

Kit Roarke—Was her best friend the victim of a copycat killer...or of a murderer who died before she was born?

Joanne Merino—She dug up her share of small-town secrets. What did she find out that was worth dying for?

Henry David—He knows what really happened three decades ago.

Bettina David—How well does the second Mrs. David know her husband?

Anita David—She loved the wrong man—a fatal mistake.

Bryan Carlisle—He's a dead ringer for his murderous grandfather. Some say the resemblance is more than skin deep.

Ray Whittaker, M.D.—Did this murderer reach beyond the grave, to kill again?

Chapter One

Even with her back to him, Noah Stewart knew he'd never laid eyes on the woman he caught plundering his file cabinet. He paused on the threshold of his office and listened to ten fingers furtively clawing through his patient records.

No question, this lady wasn't local. Everything about her screamed city. For one thing, Pratte, Vermont, had never seen hair like that. Long chestnut corkscrews *boing*ing willy-nilly from under a scrunched linen hat. He wondered if she meant it to look like that—the hat *and* the hair. His eyes didn't linger long on her head, though. From this angle as she bent over the files there were more interesting things to look at . . . like that round little bottom giving a delicious shape to her long, gauzy summer dress.

He leaned a shoulder on the doorframe and crossed his arms over the ever-present stethoscope hanging from his neck. He knew if he turned that instrument to his own chest, he'd hear the steady heart rate of a calm man.

Calm, hell; he was downright serene. No stampeding blood pressure, no adrenaline rush.

No Ray.

It had been ten years since he'd salvaged his sanity by learning the tricks that let him pull in the reins whenever the thing inside him wanted out. At this point those breathing and mind-set techniques were hardwired in, an automatic response to stressful situations—like watching a stranger rifle his file cabinet. He didn't even have to think about them.

When he had to think about them, he was in trouble.

She was scouring the *M*'s. For the third time. Frustration squeezed a low oath from her throat.

"Try *Z*," he advised, and had the satisfaction of seeing her jump. The startled glance she threw his way turned into a classic double take. Whatever she was expecting Dr. Noah Stewart to look like, he clearly didn't fit the bill. She gave him a cursory once-over, as if sizing up an adversary. He detected something else just then, and wondered if he imagined the flicker of interest in her soft brown eyes, immediately squelched.

For his part, he knew his own carefully controlled features wouldn't betray him—his command over his emotions was too well honed. He was capable of recognizing his instinctive response to this stranger's enticing bottom and wide, sexy mouth without letting it interfere with rational thought.

"Zimmerman," he clarified. "Etta Zimmerman."

Her frown revealed equal parts suspicion and befuddlement. She started to shake her head.

"Trust me."

She stared at him a long moment, then closed the file drawer and pulled open the one under it, squatting to locate Zimmerman, Etta. The long skirt of her oatmeal-colored dress puddled on the threadbare Oriental carpet.

He watched her back stiffen, heard her breath catch. Still squatting, she pivoted toward him, a folder clutched in her fingers.

Merino, Joanne.

She didn't ask how he knew. Just wagged the folder. "Zimmerman?"

Noah pushed off the doorframe and closed the door, then crossed the room to slump into the cracked green leather chair behind his desk. "Alice—" He cocked his head toward the door. "That's the pit bull you had to slip past to get in here. Alice always files Etta's boarders under her name 'cause she figures they're transients."

His visitor was on her feet once more. "Transient? Joanne lived in Pratte for nearly a year, Dr. Stewart." She opened the folder and started flipping pages.

"I never said it made sense. One of Etta's 'guests,' as she calls them, has been with her for thirty-four years." He shrugged and steepled his fingers. "That's Alice."

"I suppose that's the sort of thing irascible old ladies are expected to do in quaint little tourist traps like this," she muttered, scanning the pages. "Excuse me, I mean sleepy little hamlets, complete with kindly country doctors. You've even got the gestures down." She flicked a glance at his steepled fingers, which he was rhythmically flexing. "Very Marcus Welby."

The fingers froze midflex.

"You'll have to shake the Southern accent, though," she advised dryly, "and cultivate something a little more New England."

Noah regarded his own wavy reflection in the glass doors of the bookcase across the room, and found it all too easy to see a thirtyish poseur with short blond hair, a faded blue denim shirt and a bendable Bullwinkle the Moose figure clinging to his stethoscope. He yanked off the stethoscope and tossed it onto his desk blotter.

"Just for the record, Kit, there's more to Pratte than the handful of tourists we manage to attract. This is a vital small town with a sense of history, an unspoiled corner of Americana.''

It took a few moments for his use of her name to sink in. When it did, her eyes widened, then narrowed to lock with his. ''Someone in this unspoiled corner of Americana murdered my best friend, *Noah*.''

She redirected her attention to the file.

''Looking for anything in particular?'' he asked.

''Cause of death.''

''Didn't Jo's dad tell you? I called him when I got the toxicology report from the ME. I thought it might be better coming from me than Chief Jordon.'' He held out his hand. ''Give me the folder, Kit.''

She flipped a page and stopped dead, staring. She'd found it. ''God. Curare,'' she whispered.

He rose and pulled the folder out of her hands, then sat and nodded toward the green leather club chair in front of his desk. ''Sit. Maybe I can clarify some of this.'' He checked his watch. ''I have a few minutes before the après-lunch crowd descends.''

She sank into the chair, slowly. ''Sal told me what you said, but I just couldn't...'' She swallowed, suddenly pale. Seeing it in black and white seemed to have a sobering effect. ''Curare. Isn't that the stuff primitive tribes use to off each other?''

He nodded. ''South American Indians have used it for centuries. The Macusi tribe, for one, and the Zaparos, from around the Curaray River—hence the name. The deadly plant extract is mixed with appetizing stuff like ants and snake fangs. Then they dip a blow dart—or an arrow or spear, whatever—into the poison and shoot it at the enemy. Or dinner on the hoof. The 'flying death,' they call it.''

''Wouldn't it be easier to slip it into someone's food?''

"Curare's harmless when ingested—it's soluble. Has to be injected to kill."

"How does it work?"

He hesitated. The horror of Joanne Merino's last minutes was seared into the dark corners of his mind. At the most unexpected moments it emerged to taunt him. Indict him. He had no desire to coax the memory out of its hidey-hole... or to share it with Kit.

Nevertheless, he sensed her need to put a face to this thing that had taken her friend, if not to the killer himself—to get a handle on the why and how, if not the who.

He cleared his throat. "Curare is a neuromuscular blocking agent. The victim suffocates. The muscles of the chest and diaphragm—that is, the muscles necessary for respiration—are paralyzed."

She drew in a long, slow breath. He could imagine the scenario playing itself out behind her wide, haunted eyes. "Did she suffer?"

He wanted to say, *Don't do this to yourself.* His reluctance to answer had to be painfully eloquent, yet she met his eyes unwaveringly. And waited.

"Yes," he said. "But for a very short time."

Still she waited.

He made himself continue. "Curare poisoning causes chest pain, extreme shortness of breath and cyanosis—a bluish gray cast to the skin. The pulse rate drops. The drug doesn't affect the brain and central nervous system, so the victim..."

No. Not *the victim.* It was Jo. Beautiful, tormented Jo. More vital—more goddamn alive!—than anyone he'd ever known.

In his mind's eye he saw her lying where she'd fallen on a bed of pachysandra behind a stand of paper birches. The ground cover was torn up, having taken the brunt of her thrashing in the few moments before the paralysis had claimed her extremities. And still she'd struggled for life. He could have told her it was futile.

Ray had come out then, and watched her, too. Noah had never felt his presence so strongly.

"Jo was aware the entire time," he said, and added, "but it couldn't have been more than a few minutes."

She was silent for a full minute, staring through him. "The flying death," she whispered at last. Her face crumpled just before she lowered it. She made no sound, but her shoulders shook with silent sobs.

Almost immediately she straightened her spine and wiped her eyes with her fingertips. The face she raised was flushed with grief, but rigidly composed.

Noah slowly lowered himself into his chair, with no recollection of having risen.

"I'm sorry," she murmured. "I thought... I was done with all that."

"No need to apologize." The words sounded ridiculously formal to his own ears.

"So. You know who I am," she said. "Joanne must've mentioned me."

"You were very special to her."

Kit leaned back in the chair. She looked weary as hell. "We were like sisters. God knows Jo needed a sister. She was the only female in a house full of men."

"A widowed father on disability and two shiftless younger brothers, Frankie and Sal junior," he said.

Her eyebrows rose. The hint of a smile around the eyes. "That's right."

"Whereas you, Kathleen Roarke—Kit to your friends— are the only child of a single mother. Not exactly a June Cleaver clone. You ran away and moved in with Jo and her family when you were thirteen."

The smile was history. "You and she got to be bosom pals, I see."

He shrugged and met her hard, assessing gaze. Clearly she was wondering what else he knew about her. "It's the end of June," he said. "School just let out in Chicago, where you teach pampered kids in a snotty private school. Sixth grade, is it?"

"Fifth."

"Tell you the truth, I was half expecting to bump into you about now."

"Ransacking your office files?"

He shrugged again. "You're a pal of Joanne Merino's. Anything's possible."

That earned a wry smile, quickly squelched. "Let me assure you, breaking and entering wasn't on the agenda when I got into town this morning. I just flew out to go through Jo's things and have them sent to her dad and—" she flicked a glance toward a huge leather shoulder bag she'd dumped near the file cabinet "—you know, take care of everything. I couldn't get away till school was out. And Jo's father—"

"I know. He's wheelchair-bound. And one of her brothers is doing three years at Joliet, isn't he?"

"Sal junior. He's even worse at breaking and entering than I am. And Frankie...well, no one knows where Frankie is. Which, if you knew Frankie, is a blessing."

He laced his fingers behind his head and leaned back. "So. What happened in the two or three hours since your plane landed to turn you to a life of crime?"

"Tom Jordon."

Pratte's illustrious chief of police. He should have guessed.

"I went to see him first thing," she said. "It's been ten days since Jo died. A week and a half! Do you know what that nitwit told me?"

"Something along the lines of 'You just leave this nasty business to us, ma'am, don't worry your pretty little head about it'?"

Her expression told him he wasn't far off. "The same moronic, condescending runaround I got when I called him last week. He's got no suspects. Nothing. Zip. What the hell has he been *doing* for ten days?"

"Interviewing everyone who was at the party, for one thing. You know it happened at the town treasurer's annual garden party?"

Kit nodded.

"And following up on whatever leads he may have gotten, I suppose."

"Well, he won't tell me a damn thing. *If* there's anything to tell."

He leaned forward and started to steeple his fingers, then thought better of it. "And you figured the rest of Pratte is probably just as moronic and condescending, and if you wanted to find out anything—" he tapped the folder "—you'd have to dig it up yourself."

"Can you blame me?" She leaned forward, too, and something in the set of her shoulders gave him pause. "So tell me, Dr. Stewart. How do you come to know so much about curare?"

He held her unflinching gaze for a long moment, while mentally flaying himself for his renegade tongue. He wasn't usually so careless. "What happened to 'Noah'?" He flashed his most engaging grin, more Casey-Kildare than Welby. He hoped.

The lady was immune to his high-wattage charm. "Whatever. How do you know about the Zapata Indians and all that?"

"Zaparos." He dropped his eyes to fiddle with a pen on his desk. "I researched it when Jo's toxicology came back. It's not the sort of thing one sees every day."

"Unless you're a doctor."

He looked at her.

"Curare *is* used in medicine, isn't it?"

"Well, derivatives, yes, like Norcuron. Generally in anesthesiology. To literally stop a patient's breathing so a surgeon can work near the lungs. Or to relax the muscles and reduce the amount of other anesthetics needed. That sort of thing. A respirator takes over, naturally."

"Then it's available in hospitals."

"Depends on what you mean by 'available.' It's kept in the hospital pharmacy. It's not like your basic psychopath can just waltz in and borrow some."

He could almost see the gears turning in her mind. A damn quick mind, if he was any judge.

"You were there," she said. "At the party, I mean. You signed the death certificate."

"I was with Joanne when she died, yes. I didn't know what I was dealing with at the time. It looked like cardiac arrest. Or pulmonary embolism, perhaps. But it didn't make sense."

"A young woman with no history of heart disease."

"Exactly. It wasn't until the autopsy that they found the needle mark."

"Where was it?"

"Her right hip. It was a tiny puncture, and Frank Royce— that's the ME—probably wouldn't have even noticed it except there was a little bruising around the area."

"Were you there? At the autopsy?"

"Yes." That had been rough.

"Did they find the syringe?"

"No, but the police didn't even search the grounds or begin questioning the guests till after the autopsy. Remember, at first it was assumed to be natural causes."

"Did you get to the party before Jo?"

He forced himself to look her in the eye. "No, after."

"Oh." Kit tucked an errant reddish brown curl under her hat. He could almost hear the whirring and clicking of synapses as she located a mental compartment for this tidbit, fitting it in with everything else she knew about the circumstances of Jo's death. Which he hoped wasn't all that much.

"Why?" he asked, knowing the answer.

She shrugged. "I just, you know, wanted to find out who she arrived with."

Liar. "Sorry."

"I don't suppose you noticed if she was hanging out with anyone in particular at the party?"

"Nope. Just kind of circulating, like everyone else."

She pulled Jo's file closer and scanned the long list of office visits.

"Most of her problems were psychosomatic—brought on by stress and emotional factors," he said. "The standard therapies weren't too successful, but then again, Jo wasn't very diligent about following them. And she wouldn't even consider psychotherapy, so eventually I broached the subject of nonmedical alternatives."

"Like?"

"Yoga, TM, biofeedback."

Her head snapped up. "Transcendental meditation? *Joanne?*"

He smiled. "I know. I couldn't quite picture it, either, but I figured I'd give it a shot."

"What was her response?"

"Well, if there's anything to laugh therapy, her response was very healthy."

"I could've told you not to waste your breath." Her finger trailed down the chart. "May second, May fifteenth, May nineteenth. Ulcer, spastic colon, migraine. She's had the migraines for years, but the rest is news to me. Good God. Three visits in the first two weeks of June...for the same things that plagued her in May. Ah, plus a touch of menstrual irregularity to keep things lively."

"There are things we talked about that didn't make it into the chart," he said.

"Such as...?"

"Unexplained bouts of weeping. Recurrent nightmares."

"What did she have nightmares about?"

The same thing I do. "She didn't say."

"Any idea what had her so worked up?" she asked.

"I thought *you* might know."

An ingenuous half smile. "You did?"

Well, he'd lobbed that one out there, but she clearly had no intention of catching the thing and running with it. She let her gaze drift to her surroundings. If Pratte was an unspoiled corner of Americana, his office was one of its dust bunnies, freeze-dried in the sixties. Dark paneling, ponderous furniture, the requisite Norman Rockwell print.

While she perused the room, he perused her. Absently she adjusted the V neckline of her dress, his eyes following the movements of her graceful fingers. The dress was modest enough, but the supple fabric draped her high, softly rounded breasts in a way that made it hard to tear his gaze away. He didn't think she was aware of the effect.

Her eyes found him once more, alight with frank assessment. He liked the fact that Kit took no pains to hide her curiosity. He liked Kit, in fact, and was grateful for the mental discipline that enabled him to acknowledge his attraction with strict detachment, his hard-won emotional shields firmly in place.

"Your sign outside said family practice. You the only show in town?" she asked.

"I'm it. I do everything around here from setting bones to delivering babies."

"How long have you been in Pratte?"

"Two and a half years. The last M.D. left four years before that. In the interim the nearest doctor was a half hour away on dry roads. And he's a famous drunk—reeks of cheap wine, so Alice informs me. If you were sick, it was either Dr. Thunderbird or the emergency room at Wescott Community Hospital, even farther away."

"Not much of a choice when Junior's running a temperature of a hundred and four. The town must've been tickled pink when you came along."

"It works out well for all of us."

She squinted at a point on the wall above his head. "You got your medical degree at Emory, I see. Is that where you're from? Georgia?"

He nodded. "Roswell."

"Well, I'm not going to ask how you found yourself with a family practice in the Black Hole of Vermont," she said, rising. "I'm sure it's a hellishly long and tedious story, and unless my ears deceive me, your waiting room is full."

Noah restrained a smile. Suddenly it was easy to imagine this woman growing up with Joanne Merino—and holding her own. How had Jo put it? They'd raised each other. Absently she brushed another curly tendril of hair off her forehead, and it flopped back. Noah's fingers itched to lift the strand and tuck it back under her silly hat. He could almost feel the silk of it sliding between his fingers.

She lifted her cumbersome bag, slinging the strap over her head, bandolier style. He rose to see her out.

Her steps slowed as she approached the doorway. She eyed him hesitantly. "Just one more thing. Joanne was involved with someone here in Pratte. That's all I know. I don't know his name. I was hoping you might."

"You think I keep track of who my patients are dating?"

She stiffened and faced him fully. "Why *wouldn't* she tell you?" she snapped. "She told you about her kid brother stamping license plates in Joliet. She told you about my worthless mother, for God's sake!" She squeezed her eyes shut and dragged in a ragged breath. "Look. I'd just like to find out everything I can about her life here."

"Kit. Listen to me." Noah put his hands on her shoulders—a mistake. She twisted abruptly, shaking him off, her eyes flashing dangerously. He knew he was coming off as a condescending jerk. On a frustrated sigh he stuffed the offending hands in his back jeans pockets and said, "You came to Pratte to collect Jo's things. Do that. Do it and go home."

"No." Her voice was flat, brittle. She looked away for long moments. "I can't, Noah," she whispered at last. "I can't. I need to... I don't know. Tie up the loose ends. For Jo. For my own peace of mind." She faced him again, her expression so candid, so raw and wounded, Noah had to turn away to steady his shields against her.

He scrubbed at his jaw. Cleared his throat. "I know what you think of Tom Jordon, and I'm not about to defend his methods—or his personality. But he *has* been in the business a long time—"

"Maybe too long."

"Leave all this to him, Kit. I know you're hurting now—"

"Don't! Don't give me that 'I know what you're going through' crap. You sound like Jordon." Pure bulldog tenacity underlined the grief in her features, lending starch to her delicate jawline. He didn't want to admire her, but dammit, how could he not?

She pulled in a deep breath, composing herself. "You don't know me, Noah. You may have known Jo, she may have told you all about her old pal Kit, but you don't know *me*. Not if you think I can walk away from *this*." The last word was punctuated with a sharp yank on her shoulder bag.

With jerky motions she unlatched the bag and extracted a sealed brown cardboard carton, about the size of a shoe box but stumpier. She placed it in his hands—it was heavier than it looked.

"That's all that's left." Her voice cracked. "I stopped by the funeral home after I saw Chief Jordon."

Noah understood then. He knew that if he opened this box, he'd find a metal canister containing Jo's ashes. Just the way they packaged it at the crematory. Neat and tidy.

A sharp knock on the door startled them both. "Noah? The natives are getting restless," came a gravelly voice from the other side.

"I'll be right there, Alice," he called. When he turned back to Kit, he read the plea in her eyes.

"Help me, Noah. I need an ally here in Pratte. Someone who knows these people." Her voice became a whisper, her eyes searching his. "You . . . cared about Jo. I can tell."

"I don't know what I can do for you, Kit. What anyone can do at this point except the police."

"The police!" The starch was back. "If Jordon had anything on the ball, don't you think he would've contacted *me* at the beginning of the investigation, instead of my having to call *him?* Wouldn't he have asked if I knew anything, if Jo might've told me anything that could give them a lead?''

"Did she?"

She hesitated only an instant. "Yes."

He waited for details he already knew. She stared back impassively. So much for putting her trust in the kindly country doctor. He knew if this bright, resourceful woman chose to stay in Pratte and pursue the circumstances of her friend's death, she'd leave Tom Jordon's lumbering investigation in the dust.

And then, God help him, he might have to stop her.

"This information, whatever it is, did you share it with Chief Jordon?" he asked.

"What do you think? I cast my pearls before that swine, and look where it got me."

"Well." He aimed for a tone of finality. "That's all you can do for now, Kit. Go home. I'll personally keep track of Tom's progress and let you know when there's anything *to* know. That's a promise."

"Thanks, but that's just not good enough." She took the box from him.

"Does this mean you'll be staying?"

"I guess it does." Gently, almost lovingly, she tucked the box into her shoulder bag. "There's no one back home who needs me as much as Jo does."

Noah had no choice. If he couldn't dissuade Kit from staying and nosing around Pratte, he had to closely monitor her activities. And the danger she represented.

"All right," he said, forcing a smile. "Don't make a move without me. I'll do everything I can to help."

Kit's shoulders sagged in relief. Her face lit in a broad smile that transformed her features and made his breath snag in his throat. God, she was beautiful. It was the first time he'd seen her smile. Really smile.

He wanted to tell her he didn't deserve that smile, didn't deserve the naked gratitude in those beautiful brown eyes. A cold, hard weight settled in his chest as he asked himself, What have I become? What has Ray made me?

Impulsively she grabbed his hand in both of hers and squeezed it, her eyes misty as she beamed up at him. "Thank you, Noah," she whispered. "Thank you."

Chapter Two

The tiger stared at Kit with its one remaining eye, its body limp from decades of literally having had the stuffing squeezed out of it.

Tenderly she stroked the dingy, matted fur, recalling a time when Tiggy had been plump, two eyed and master of all he surveyed from the head of his mistress's bed. Joanne was ten when she won him at her neighborhood block party, having clobbered the competition in a sack race. The prospect of losing had never crossed her mind.

Kit was eight, and covetous. She'd gone home with a tiny baby doll that night, the cheap kind molded of brittle plastic that splits along the seams. Its hair was painted on. Jo's Tiggy was covered in fluffy acrylic plush. The tag said it was made from "all new material." Kit wasn't sure what the alternative was, but she was impressed nonetheless.

She knew it was just as well she hadn't won Tiggy. It had been hard enough finding a hiding place for the little doll. Irene Roarke saw no reason to allow her daughter that which Kit had stolen from her by her very existence—a childhood.

A cardboard carton was lying open on Jo's bed, where Kit sat with Tiggy on her lap. She laid him in it, on top of a well-worn dictionary and the other accoutrements of Jo's trade. She'd already bagged her friend's clothes. Jo's landlady,

Etta, had told her a school for troubled children in the next town was planning a rummage sale to raise funds, and could use the donated clothes. Kit thought that plan would have met with Jo's approval. If anyone knew what it was like to be troubled children, it was Kathleen Roarke and Joanne Merino.

She crossed to the window and put her back into the task of forcing the paint-choked frame another inch higher. An early-summer breeze carried the aroma of green living things. Nice view—the generous back lawn of the rambling white clapboard boardinghouse and the woods beyond.

She smiled. Jo wouldn't have appreciated the view. Not that it would have bothered her; it would simply have gone unnoticed, along with everything else that didn't directly pertain to the book she was working on—her current raison d'être, requiring a tour of duty in Pratte, Vermont. In any event, green stuff never rated high on Joanne Merino's list of priorities. Not even the folding kind.

The room itself was another matter. Try as she might, she couldn't picture the Jo she knew willingly spending one hour, much less eleven months, between these walls. No, she couldn't imagine her sitting at the wobbly white dressing table—sans the skirt that must have once adorned it—to write her book and her articles for the weekly *Pratte Citizen* on her laptop computer. Or sleeping under the prosaic floral bedspread that matched the faded curtains swagged over white sheers. Not exactly Jo's speed.

Her eye was drawn to the shelves filled with an appalling array of knickknacks—*chatchkas,* Etta called them. Figurines of Boston terriers, ballerinas and children with large, sad eyes; souvenirs of Etta's trips to Greece and Cincinnati; mementos of her daughter's Girl Scout days.

Jo must've had some burning need to write that book.

She looked at the dressing table, now bare but recently occupied by Jo's laptop, a stack of printouts and a caddy of three-and-a-half-inch computer disks, according to Etta. She wondered who had all that now, or whether it still existed.

Thinking about that brought her back to the day Jo died—the longest day of Kit's life. She'd spent most of that Saturday in staff meetings. Jo's father had called her at the school with the news just after three, when she was about to leave for the day. By the time Sal senior's sister had finally arrived from Florida and Kit had felt free to leave him, it had been after midnight. She'd climbed into her six-year-old Celica and had tried to remember driving from the Harrington Academy in Lincoln Park to Sal's little frame house south of the Loop near the old stockyards, but had drawn a blank.

She'd let herself in to her one-bedroom apartment, hauled the Stoli out of the freezer, dropped her keys and briefcase to the kitchen floor and slid into a corner, where she woke six hours later with a throbbing head and a stiff neck.

After most of a pot of coffee, she was able to orchestrate a hot shower. Only then did she reenter the kitchen and push Play on her answering machine.

Kit, someone broke into my room. They ransacked *it! They took my laptop. My disks. My hard copy and all my notes. My God, Kit, they're after my book! Listen...call me right away, okay?*

Kit's heart was thundering so violently she missed the beginning of the next message and had to rewind the tape. Jo's tone was less frantic now, more guarded. Kit remembered there was no phone in her room—she'd had to make her calls from the kitchen of her boardinghouse.

Me again. I've thought about it. I think...I think it's this guy I'm seeing. That took my book. I know, I know, I never told you about him. A gust of nervous laughter. *So call me a dirty name, but I knew you wouldn't approve. He's not...*

suitable. Well, maybe you wouldn't say it that way, but you'd think it. I know you would.

Anyway, I never thought I'd say this, but I think I'm in way over my head on this one. This guy, he found out about the book. And...well, that's not good. And he knew I'd be at the gym this morning, and that's when it happened.

God, where are you, Kit? You told me you check your machine. Call me!

She fast-forwarded past the next message, from her cousin Marc, and heard Jo's voice for the last time.

Listen, I'm leaving the house now. The town treasurer has this garden party thing she does every year. The entire staff of the Citizen *is invited. Counting the free-lancers, that's, like, a whopping eight of us.*

Jo sounded breezy...relaxed. Hell, she was going to a party, right? How better to forget your troubles? Kit lowered herself into a chair and cradled her head in her hands.

The sound of an indistinct male voice in the background of the tape yanked her head back up.

What? Oh. Jo laughed lightly. Kit could almost see her tucking the receiver under her chin to address her companion. *You think* you *need a drink! If Grace doesn't bring out the hard stuff, we'll pick up a bottle of Glenfiddich after.* More male noise, and the sound of Jo rummaging in her purse. *Be that way. I'll just sneak some of yours when you're not looking. Damn. I left my shades in the living room. Would you? I think they're on the TV. Thanks, hon.*

Softer now, right into the mouthpiece. *Sorry, Kit. Listen, I gotta run. It's just...I know how paranoid I sounded before, and I didn't want you to worry. Everything's fine. And listen.* A whisper. *I was so wired before, I forgot to tell you the book's safe, 'cause I saved it on a disk. Not with the others—*

Loud. *That was fast. Okay, I'm ready. Let's rock and roll!*

HE RECORKED THE BOTTLE of Glenfiddich and picked up the half-full jelly glass before pushing Record.

"Paul, it's two-thirty a.m. on the twenty-sixth . . . uh, the twenty-seventh, I guess. I know I told you I'd had it with these tapes—the midnight ramblings of Noah Stewart—but the hell with it, I'm not gonna get back to sleep tonight, and I can't face *Attack of the Fifty-Foot Woman* on the late late show, so you win. This time.

"This dream was a keeper—not as hazy as the others, a little crisper around the edges, if you know what I mean.

"He got closer, Paul. Closer than ever before. I was—he was—Christ, we were in bed. With Ruby. Asleep. The phone woke me up. I answered. I mean Ray, dammit, Ray answered. And it was her.

"Well, this part we've seen before, right? So it's the same as before, it's her and she can't breathe, she sounds real bad. I can hardly make out what she's saying, it's just this panicked wheezing. And I say, 'Anita, calm down, try to calm down, I'll be right there . . .' I almost say 'honey,' but I stop myself in time.

"Ruby's real groggy, and I tell her Anita's having an attack, I've gotta run over and give her a shot. And meanwhile I'm pulling on some clothes real fast—flannel shirt and chinos, no underwear. I sleep naked, by the way. Don't think I ever told you that. Ruby's always after me—after Ray—to wear boxer shorts or something in case Debbie has a nightmare and decides to crawl into bed with us. So I sleep naked just to rile her.

"Where was I? So I'm dressed now and—and, Paul, that's as far as I've ever seen before, right? But now I run downstairs, just flying down those stairs, and I run into the office and grab my black bag, and I know it's already packed, I have everything I need in there.

"My God. Think about that, Paul. I kept it in the damn bag, all ready to go. Just waiting. I'm a cold goddamn bastard.

"Okay, uh, so I jump into the Fairlane and—hah!—I'm thinking about the fight on TV that night. I watched a boxing match on TV. Won twenty bucks from Henry betting on some fighter, and that's what I'm thinking about as I tear down those dark back roads to get to his house—collecting that twenty from Henry when he gets back from Montpelier tomorrow. Not about his wife and how she can't breathe, not about the... thing I'm about to do to her. I'm thinking about the damn fight.

"And that's as far as I got. Thank God. The sheets are soaked with sweat. I think I scared the doggy doo out of Max, must've yelled or something, 'cause he jumped on the bed. Or maybe he woke me up. Good old Max.

"So there you have it. The latest installment in the continuing saga of 'Dr. Ray Whittaker—The Final Days.' Tune in next week for another zany episode."

He pushed Stop for a minute to collect his thoughts, and tossed back the last of the Scotch before reaching for the Record button again.

"Listen, I...need to talk to you, Paul. In person, not like this. Helluva time for you to go on sabbatical, buddy. Hold on to your hat—when you get back, I may finally let you put me under. You know...take me back. No, not thirty-two years, so don't even ask. The dreams are graphic enough, thank you. If I ever got the Cinemax version, crisp, clear and unabridged, I'd go over the edge for sure. No, I need you to help me tap into...more recent events.

"You know, Paul, you always told me nothing would happen, you always said I'd learned to control it. Him. And after a while, I guess I began to believe you.

"All I can say is, I hope to God we were right."

"THIS IS ALL JOANNE HAD on the Frigidaire."

"The Frigidaire?" Kit accepted the little pile of papers Etta Zimmerman handed her.

"My guests tack their papers and whatnot on the fridge with magnets. You know." Etta indicated the refrigerator with a toss of her bewigged head. The appliance was festooned with all manner of "whatnot"—receipts, invitations, business cards, picture postcards, fliers, newspaper clippings.

The first item in Kit's hand was a pink ticket from Sparkle French Cleaners. Jo had left a jacket and slacks. "Oh, great," she muttered. "More clothes." And she thought she'd bagged them all.

Etta Zimmerman was about four-ten and, at seventy-nine years of age, trim and well dressed. Unfortunately, the refined elegance of her wardrobe failed to divert one's attention from the thing perched on her head. Big and blond and brassy. The hairline was implausibly low, and the netting clearly visible beneath the perky curls.

Jo's next piece of whatnot was a schedule of exercise classes at Valkyrie, a health club in a neighboring town.

"Expensive place, that Valkyrie," Etta volunteered. "Very chichi, you know what I mean? Not like the Y. Henry's wife got her to join there."

Strange Jo joining a fancy place like that, Kit thought. The Y was more her style. "Henry?"

"Joanne's boss, Henry David. Owns the *Pratte Citizen*."

"Oh, yeah. I wanted to get over there to talk to him today, but I got wrapped up in going through Jo's things, and then...well, I guess the day just got away from me. It'll have to wait till tomorrow." She'd call Noah after dinner and ask him to accompany her. Would he be free in the morning? She admitted that she hoped so, but chose not to peer too closely at her reasons for wanting to see him again. This was about Jo, after all. Only Jo.

The last item was an appointment reminder, the kind that doubled as a business card. Jo was supposed to see Dr. Noah Stewart at 10:30 a.m. on June 21. A few days after she died.

"Poor girl. Always at the doctor," Etta clucked. "One thing after another, it was with her."

Kit flicked the card with her thumbnail. "Did she seem any different in the days or weeks before she died? More...anxious, maybe?"

Etta shrugged. "Anxious, who knows? She was like a little hummingbird, that one, always buzzing around. So much energy, you young people have. Coffee?"

Kit grinned. "You said the magic word."

She planted her bottom on the beige vinyl seat of a well-worn dinette chair and dropped the papers on the table, which was draped with a plastic tablecloth sporting fat fruit. She watched the tiny landlady fill the old-fashioned steel percolator and plug it in, then open the oven—avocado green like the other appliances—and poke around. The aromas of meat loaf and roasting potatoes filled the enormous kitchen.

"I don't suppose you have a safe in the house?" Kit asked.

That earned a puzzled frown. "What would I put in a safe?"

"Would there be any place other than her room where Jo might've stashed something?"

She pondered that for a moment. "Not that I can think of. Why? Something missing?"

"A computer disk. A little one, three and a half inches square."

Etta pulled off her oven mitts. "Those were all stolen, no?"

"All but one. I'd like to chase it down if I can." Kit didn't elaborate. She was certain Jo's landlady knew nothing about the book her boarder had been writing.

"Well, feel free to go through the garage, the basement, closets, wherever. Such a hodgepodge, they are. I can't even find things I *know* I have."

"Thanks," Kit said, though she doubted such a search would bear fruit. Jo wouldn't have kept her valuable backup disk in the house. In Chicago, where she'd been a free-lance writer, Jo always farmed out duplicate disks of important material to Kit and her father for safekeeping. Neither she nor Sal had received anything like that. Jo's personal papers included no record of a safe-deposit box, though Kit intended to check with the local banks just to make sure.

She watched Etta tear open a bag of Cheez Doodles. "I can't say how long I'll be here, Etta."

"So? You have Joanne's room as long as you like."

"I assume she paid through the end of the month. If I stay longer—"

Etta waved a hand dismissively. "If you stay longer, you stay longer. I won't take your money."

"Etta—"

"Eat." She shoved the bag closer to Kit.

Kit shook her head, grinning, but she obeyed. "Well, we'll talk about it later. You're a good person."

"Huh. You sound like Noah. Good karma, he says I have. Says I must've been a saint in a former life. Sure. Etta Zimmerman. Now, there's a good saint's name." She munched in silence for a minute, then said around a mouthful of Cheez Doodles, "It hit that boy hard when Joanne died. I was there. I saw."

"You were there? At the treasurer's party?"

"Gracie Drummond, I've known since she was a twinkle in her daddy's eye. Sure, I was there. Me and about a hundred other folks."

Kit spoke softly. "Tell me what happened, Etta."

The landlady sighed and closed her eyes for a few moments, as if summoning the strength to respond. Kit hated to ask it of her, but she needed to picture it in her mind's eye, to begin fitting the pieces together.

Etta spoke at last. "Less than an hour into the party, it was. I'm talking to my friend Carol La Rosa from my book club when that Carlisle boy, Bryan, comes tearing across the lawn, yelling something about Joanne. Nobody paid much attention at first, such a hubbub, it was, everyone drinking and laughing and loosening up. You know.

"And he's hysterical, all red in the face. He grabs Al Drummond and knocks him down practically, shaking him. 'Somebody help her!' he's screaming. 'She can't breathe!'" Etta paused. "Back behind some birch trees, she was, at the edge of Gracie's lawn. Not five minutes before, I was talking with her. Not five minutes!"

Etta's face looked ashen. Kit remembered Noah's reluctant description of Jo's death.

"She was still alive. Al ran to call 911, but the rest of us, we're looking for Noah, he's nowhere in sight. It seemed like forever before someone found him in the solarium. But I guess it was less than a minute, really."

"In the solarium? Was anyone else with him?"

"No. All alone, he was, sitting on one of Gracie's new wicker armchairs, sipping a schnapps."

Etta must have seen something in Kit's expression, because she added, "Which doesn't surprise me. He was exhausted, poor boy. Dead on his feet. Hadn't slept in two days. Little Andy Kramer got hit by a car riding his bike. No helmet. Noah wouldn't leave the hospital, Wescott Community, till he was out of the woods. I knew 'cause Alice called me to cancel my blood pressure checkup. Tell you the truth, I never expected him to show, but there he was, at

Gracie's party. Not that he was able to do anything for Joanne.''

She took a deep breath. "She...passed on in Noah's arms." She looked at Kit, her eyes moist. "There was nothing he could do, Kit. He tried.''

"I know." She laid her hand over the old woman's. It felt as insubstantial as a baby bird, the bones prominent under papery skin.

Etta squinted into the recollection, as if trying to make sense of the senseless. "So...*agitated* he was. I don't know how to describe it.''

"Agitated? You mean like distraught?''

She shook her head. "He wasn't himself, Kit. There was this look in his eyes. Cold. He was holding her, wouldn't let anyone else near her. Even when she was...gone. He...well, he scared me, I won't deny it. It's like something snapped inside him.''

The aroma of coffee now competed with the cooking smells. Kit rose and located two mugs and the milk. She thought about Noah's lively hazel eyes, framed by dark lashes and eyebrows in striking contrast to his pale hair. Cold? It was hard to imagine. But then, grief could do strange things to people, so they said. "They must've been very close," she murmured, pouring the coffee. "Noah and Joanne." She carried the mugs to the table and sat.

"Sure. They were good friends right from the first.''

Kit schooled her features. It wasn't hard to make the mental leap from "good friends" to something more. Knowing Jo, anything was possible. He was her doctor, yes, but he was also tall, handsome and powerfully built. With a yummy Southern accent, to boot. No, Jo wouldn't have hesitated, Kit knew. But as for Noah...well, who could say? Were doctors even allowed to mess around with their patients? She knew that kind of thing was a major no-no for shrinks, but what about regular M.D.'s? In any event, it was a cinch he wouldn't want to advertise such a liaison. Not in this teeny "slice of Americana."

"Did Jo have visitors?" Kit asked. "Like a boyfriend?"

"She never brought anyone here that I saw. That kind of visiting is done in the living room—the bedrooms are strictly off-limits, you know what I mean? That kind of trouble, I don't need."

Kit looked at the wall phone—avocado, of course. "The day...the day Jo died, the day her computer was stolen, she called me from here. Called my answering machine, that is." How many times since then had Kit wished to God she'd checked her messages that day? She'd thought about it at lunchtime and decided not to bother. If she had . . .

She sighed harshly. Hell of a lot of good *ifs* do Jo now. "Anyway, someone was with her then—I heard a man's voice. Do you know who that might've been?"

Etta shook her head. "Saturday mornings I run errands. I went straight to Gracie's from the video store."

"Perhaps one of your board—guests might know." Kit lifted the mug to her lips.

She shrugged. "You can ask. Malcolm might've heard something." She let loose with a high-volume screech. *"Malcolm!"*

As the hot brew flushed Kit's sinuses, she grabbed a paper napkin and turned to see a man amble into the kitchen from an adjacent corridor.

"Coming, Mrs. Z." He was tall and heavyset, with thinning gray hair, dark-rimmed eyeglasses and a light accent that sounded vaguely British. He carried a small glass ashtray and a lit cigarette, which immediately overwhelmed the cooking odors.

"I can't remember, dear," Etta said. "Were you home the day of Grace Drummond's party? The Saturday before last."

Kit anticipated the usual response when one is asked to search one's memory: a thoughtful pause, a brief study of the ceiling, perhaps an *um* or *uh* for good measure.

But Malcolm answered immediately, his eyes never straying from Etta's. "I was at the Thackeray from ten forty-nine till three twenty-three. I made forty-seven dollars and fifty-five cents in tips." He flicked the ash off his cigarette and brought it to his lips.

His accent wasn't British, Kit now realized, but Australian.

Etta explained. "Malcolm parks cars at the Thackeray Inn on weekends when they have an affair. Weddings and christenings and whatnot. Elizabeth Murray gave herself a birthday party that day, didn't she, Malcolm?"

"Yes. A brunch buffet with a string quartet. Floral centerpieces with lots of balloons. Light green and lavender, and some Mylar ones that said Happy Sixty-Fifth Birthday. I haven't met this lady, Mrs. Z."

"Oh! Where's my head?" She waved her hand in introduction. "Kit Roarke, Malcolm Ryder. Kit's a friend of Joanne's, Malcolm. From Chicago."

The bespectacled stare Malcolm turned her way was unnerving. "Joanne doesn't get many visitors. What's Kit short for?"

A giant fist squeezed her chest, stealing her voice. Thankfully Etta had no such problem.

"Malcolm." The landlady beckoned him closer and laid a hand on his beefy arm. She spoke gently. "We talked about what happened to Joanne. You remember."

He just looked at her a few moments, then his face deflated. "I'm sorry, Mrs. Z. I forgot."

"No need to apologize, dear." She patted his arm.

"I forgot."

"It's all right, Malcolm," Kit assured him with a smile.

"Did I hurt your feelings?" He never blinked or shifted his gaze from Kit's eyes. It was the kind of stare that screamed *unhinged*. Other than that and his interest in the social life of a corpse, he appeared normal enough.

"Not at all. And since you ask, Kit is short for Kathleen."

Etta said, "Well, I better go get my permanent-press things out of the dryer." She opened the door to the basement, flicked a light switch and slowly descended the stairs.

Malcolm took another drag of his cigarette—unfiltered, Kit noticed. *Is all of Pratte caught in a time warp?* she wondered.

"Are you going to live in Joanne's room now, Kathleen?"

"Uh...well, I am, yes. Just for a little while. A few days, maybe. And please, call me Kit." No one called her Kathleen. Not since her mother.

"I don't want to."

"Oh."

"And please don't call me Mal. It means bad. Also abnormal and inadequate. I looked it up in Joanne's dictionary. *Merriam-Webster's Collegiate Dictionary*, tenth edition. She wrote in it."

"Uh-huh."

"You're not supposed to write in books."

"Well, no, that's true. But I guess Jo needed to make notes or something."

"Joe is a man's name."

Kit took a deep breath. "So. Your room's right over there?" She nodded toward the corridor, grateful for a respite from The Stare.

"Yes."

"I guess you hear a lot that goes on in the kitchen."

"Yes. May I have some Cheez Doodles?"

"Oh. Of course. I'm sorry. Help yourself." She held out the bag, and he took a handful.

"I don't suppose you heard anything that morning before you left for the Thackeray," she asked. "Jo's—Joanne's room was broken into early—nine, nine-thirty—when she was at the gym." She indicated the exercise schedule lying on the table. "The Valkyrie."

"I was here until ten thirty-two, but I didn't hear anything. It takes me exactly seventeen minutes to get to the Thackeray. They only need me on the weekends, when there's a party. Monday to Friday I work at the Fine Food, on Linden Road. I maintain the physical plant."

He sweeps the floors, Kit surmised.

"Sometimes I assist the security officer. Sometimes I bag groceries."

Her gaze went to the back door, off the kitchen, with its curtained multipaned window, right above the lock. After she'd played her answering-machine tape for Chief Jordon, he'd told her the "perpetrator" had simply broken a pane of glass and let himself in. Malcolm's room was at the back of the house. If he was here, he should have heard *something*.

"Have you lived here a long time, Malcolm?"

"Thirty-four years and seven months."

That rang a bell. "Noah—Dr. Stewart—mentioned you when I spoke to him earlier."

"I don't like Dr. Stewart."

"No?"

"He told me to quit smoking." Malcolm took one final puff, clamping the butt between thumb and forefinger. He ground it out in the ashtray and delicately plucked a fleck of tobacco from his tongue.

She smiled. "Yeah, well, that's—"

"And he told me to lose weight."

"Uh…" His girth attested to an appreciation of Mrs. Z.'s home cooking.

"He said hypnotherapy might help me, and he knows a good hypnotist, but he's on sabbatical right now. I don't want to be hypnotized. I like smoking."

What was it with Noah Stewart and voodoo medicine? Kit wondered. TM, hypnosis. Was that what they were teaching in med schools nowadays?

"Am I fat?" Malcolm asked.

"No," Kit lied.

"I like Dr. Whittaker," he said. "He doesn't tell me to quit smoking or lose weight."

For the second time in as many minutes Kit was tonguetied. True, she'd expected the townspeople to talk about Ray Whittaker—counted on it, in fact. But to hear Pratte's most notorious former resident discussed in such benign terms— and in the present tense, no less!—rattled her. Then again, she had to consider the source.

Once more, the landlady rescued her. "Nobody was telling folks to quit smoking in the sixties," Etta grumbled, reentering the kitchen with a full laundry basket. "Leastways, not too many were. And why would anyone in their right mind tell you to lose weight back then, Malcolm? Like a stick, you were."

He took the basket from her and set it in a corner, his expression clouded in perplexity. "The sixties?" He extracted a pile of neatly folded sport shirts from the basket, juggling them carefully to avoid contact with his dirty ashtray. "Was it really that long ago?"

"Thirty-two years, it's been," she confirmed. "Thirty-two years since Ray died." She looked at Kit. "Do you know about our Dr. Whittaker?"

Our Dr. Whittaker. The grudging possessiveness of the statement struck Kit. She began to comprehend what Joanne had somehow intuitively known.

Ray belonged to Pratte. He was the boil on the town's butt, the crazy aunt locked in the basement. The inescapable thing that was as much a part of this "unspoiled corner of Americana" as church suppers and strawberry festivals and overpriced ice-cream cones for the tourists.

"Yes," Kit said. "I believe Jo mentioned him."

Chapter Three

Henry David propelled himself through the water with enviable brawn and stamina. The lush head of silver hair seemed out of place atop such a youthful physique.

Kit stepped out from the shade of the patio awning into the dazzling sunlight, her patience at an end. She'd already watched Henry swim about thirty laps, and Lord knew how long he'd been at it before she'd arrived.

"He could be in there all morning," Noah drawled from a patio chaise, where he was thumbing through the latest issue of—what else?—the *Pratte Citizen.* "Unless you have all day to wait, I suggest you make your presence known."

Noah had gone extra early to Wescott Community to check on his patients that morning. He was bending his schedule to accommodate her. The least Kit could do was speed things up a bit. She crossed about fifty feet of broadloom lawn and sauntered onto the tiled pool deck.

Henry executed another perfect turn, tucking his body and springing off the pool wall. His fluid crawl stroke faltered slightly when he noticed Kit, and he grinned at her through a sheet of water before taking his next breath. When he reached the end this time, he pulled off his goggles and tossed them onto the deck, then hoisted himself up and lithely hopped out.

For a man in his sixties, he was something. Tall and trim—he even wore one of those stretchy little Speedos, and he looked good in them. The welcoming smile never left his handsome, tanned face as he raked fingers through his hair and grabbed a towel from a chaise.

"How long have you been out here waiting for the old fart to finish his laps?" he asked. His speech held the hint of an accent Kit was at a loss to identify. Something vaguely Continental, but coarser.

His grin was infectious. "Too damn long," she said, "but I'm not complaining. You're pretty impressive for an old fart."

A sandy chuckle escaped, and the laugh lines framing his pale blue eyes deepened in appreciation—of both the compliment and her spunk, she suspected. He vigorously toweled his face and head, followed by his arms, legs and the mat of gray hair on his chest. Now that she was closer, his age became more evident. His bronzed skin failed to hug those lovely muscles with the same youthful snap it must have once had.

"A couple more comments like that and you won't need a résumé *or* tear sheets," he said, flipping the towel over his shoulder. "Shameless flattery is the key to self-promotion." He extended his hand.

Uh-oh. "Mr. David, I'm Kit Roarke." She shook his hand. "From Chicago."

Comprehension gradually dawned. She watched the jovial light in his eyes fade and felt his firm grip slacken. He gently squeezed her hand before releasing it. "I'm sorry," he said. "I didn't realize...I put an ad in the paper...."

"I understand," she said, and almost wished she didn't. He was looking for a replacement for Jo. "I'm Joanne's friend...an old friend of hers...." Why was this suddenly so hard?

"Come on." He laid his large palm on her back and started toward the house. "Kit, is it?"

"Yes. Uh, did Jo mention me?"

"Not that I recall." His attention went to her companion then, rising to greet him. "Noah."

"Henry." The men shook hands.

Kit thought an explanation was in order. "I asked Noah to...to..."

"To introduce her to Jo's friends in Pratte," Noah supplied smoothly.

Henry grinned. "Looks like she doesn't need you. The lady's doing just fine on her own. Let's go inside for something cool." He dropped his towel on a patio chair and slid open the glass door through which the housekeeper had ushered Kit and Noah a few minutes earlier.

They reentered Henry David's impressive home and were once again ambushed by the nippy bite of central air. It wasn't even that warm outside—high seventies, maybe—though Kit supposed that constituted a scorcher for central Vermont. She chided herself for her depression-era mentality, a product of her upbringing. It was none of her business how this man chose to burn his money.

"We swung by your office first," she said. "Your son said you wouldn't be in today, so we decided to ambush you here."

"Just as well. Can't hear yourself think in the newsroom—the place is a zoo."

Henry's home answered the question she'd asked herself the day before. No, all of Pratte was most assuredly *not* trapped in a time warp. This was an enormous, ultramodern structure with all the amenities, occupying five hilly, wooded acres on the outskirts of town. The newspaper business must be more lucrative than she imagined.

Even as the thought formed, she rejected it. The *Pratte Citizen* was a local weekly, for heaven's sake. Jo had told her it was supported entirely by advertising and mailed free to the townsfolk. How much of a profit could such a business provide?

Her host led her through the breakfast room and living room, with its high, canted ceiling studded with huge skylights. The walls were white, the floors bleached oak adorned with imported rugs in pastel shades, each one of which probably cost more than Kit's car. Central stone fireplace. Leather, lacquer and glass. Art by people she'd actually heard of. The room was straight out of a magazine spread, one of those that tells the reader how to copy a million-dollar layout on a budget of only four hundred grand.

Henry didn't stop until they were in a den, as richly furnished as the living room, but cozier. Lower ceiling, more books. A touch of wood. A picture window offered a spectacular view: lush formal flower gardens in the foreground, wooded hills in the background. He circled behind the wet bar and opened a small refrigerator. Kit propped herself on a bar stool and watched him slap a can of diet soda on the bar.

"I make a deadly frozen margarita," Henry offered, pulling an ice bin out of the freezer. He flashed those ivories again, with an impish shrug and a wink to match. "It's almost noon."

Dear Lord, this man must have been painfully sexy when he was younger, Kit thought. The kind of guy you can't look at for long without your brain seizing up.

She made a show of checking her watch. "It's nine-forty."

"Close enough." A bottle of Cuervo 1800 materialized on the bar top.

"Thanks, I think I'll pass. But if you have another one of these..." She tapped the soda can. "Regular, not diet."

"I think that can be arranged. Noah?"

"Nothing for me, thanks."

Henry filled two tumblers with ice and poured the drinks, his expression softening, those laugh lines deepening again. "Jo would've taken the margarita."

"No, she wouldn't." Noah chuckled. "Two or three straight shots, maybe."

Kit clinked glasses with Henry. "Beats Froot Loops any day."

From her perch across the bar from her host, it was easy to imagine she was tossing back a cool one at a nudist colony. His casual state of dishabille was a delicious contrast to the elegantly appointed room, and his relaxed, irreverent manner was disarming.

Noah strolled to the huge window and stood staring out, his hands in his jeans pockets, his stance casual. Still, she sensed an underlying disquiet. It was nothing she could put her finger on. The sunlight pouring in emphasized the strong angles of his face, the thrust of his solid jaw, and turned his hair to polished gold. His eyes captured the fire, as luminous now as a clear, bottomless lagoon. In his office he'd been handsome, but here, gilded by sunlight, he was positively breathtaking. She had to force herself to look away.

Henry leaned a palm on the bar and downed most of his soda in one long pull. "When did you arrive in town, Kit?"

"Day before yesterday. I'll be staying a few days to make sure everything is, you know, packed up and settled."

He nodded. "Let me know if I can help in any way."

"Thanks. I appreciate it."

"I mean it. If you get any trouble from anyone, come up against any roadblocks—insurance, banks, government agencies, what have you—give a holler. After more than forty years in the newspaper business, I've got contacts everywhere. There's almost no one I can't reach—" he paused, grinning "—and apply the thumbscrews to if need be. Ask Noah. He's seen me in action."

"A force to be reckoned with," Noah agreed dryly. He began a slow trek around the room, idly perusing the books and furnishings. His manner said, *This is your show, Kit. I'm just along for the ride.* The repressed energy she sensed, crackling like electricity just under the surface, said something else.

Kit smiled her thanks to Henry. "I hope the offer's sincere. I have a feeling I may take you up on it at some point."

"Have you talked to anyone else since you arrived?"

"Chief Jordon."

He winced. "And that wasn't enough to drive you to drink? You're a strong woman, Kit Roarke."

"Doesn't it bother anyone else that the man's at a dead end?"

Henry sucked an ice cube into his mouth and crushed it with his molars, staring into his glass. "It bothers everyone that the police haven't been able to come up with a suspect. And the more time that passes..." His shrug was accompanied by a disgusted sigh. "Joanne was a wonderful girl. You know that. I know that. So does Noah. She was bright. Funny. And a solid reporter. The best I ever had. God knows what she was doing in Pratte."

Kit was tempted to tell him. *Listen, Henry, your pal Joanne, that "wonderful girl" and your best reporter, was using you from day one.*

"'Course, that doesn't mean she charmed the socks off everyone in town," he added with a raised eyebrow.

Noah emitted a snort of agreement as he inspected a framed lithograph over the sofa on the far wall.

Kit allowed herself a rueful smile. "What a shocker." No one knew better than her how abrasive Jo could seem to those who didn't share her audacious outlook and her bent sense of humor. Which was most people. Henry, however, appeared to be a rare exception. Clearly he and Jo had been simpatico. Just how simpatico? she couldn't help wondering.

"But my point is," Henry continued, "it doesn't matter what people thought about her, who liked her and who didn't. Her murder stunned everyone. Everyone. There isn't a person in Pratte who doesn't want to see it solved."

Noah read her mind. "Well, maybe one," he murmured.

"Jordon's a horse's ass, it's true," Henry went on, "but I don't know if I'd go so far as to call him incompetent." He said to Noah, "You've only been here a couple of years, Noah, so you might not be aware, but Tom's always done a decent job for Pratte."

"How many murders has he had to solve?" Kit asked.

The instant the words were out of her mouth, she wished she could suck them back up. This was the wrong person to say that to. Something in his expression hardened ever so slightly, and suddenly he looked all of his sixty-something years.

"I'm sorry," she said. "I didn't think."

He pulverized another ice cube in his mouth, his gaze penetrating. He flicked a cool look to Noah. "You know more about Pratte than I imagined, Kit."

She chose her words carefully. "Just the basics. Just what Jo told me. I know that Ray Whittaker murdered your wife thirty-two years ago. Your first wife."

"Anita."

"Yes." Out of the corner of her eye she saw Noah become very still. Inexplicably her palms began to sweat. "And I know that Ray died before it went to trial. That's it, really. I don't know the, um, circumstances or anything."

"Not even that Ray and Anita were having an affair?" Henry asked.

"No," she answered truthfully, followed by a shameless whopper. "I'm not here to pry."

Henry leaned over, resting his forearms on the bar top. "Kit, it's been three decades. Don't worry. You're not about to scratch open any raw wounds." He met her eyes. "Ray Whittaker was my best friend. The man was like a brother to me."

"Sounds like he took brotherhood a little too far," she murmured.

That eyebrow rose again and he shook his head, smiling sadly. "You might say that. I didn't have an inkling what was going on behind my back." He finished his drink. "He killed her one night when I was out of town. I was a reporter for the *Burlington Free Press* back then. I was in Montpelier when she died, covering some stupid political sex scandal that never panned out.

"Anita was severely asthmatic. She used to get these violent attacks where she couldn't breathe. It was goddamn scary, I'll tell you. Usually I'd drive her over to Ray's or he'd come to us, and he'd give her a shot of epinephrine. A few times she had to be hospitalized. Anyway, that night it seems she had one of these attacks and called Ray to come give her a shot."

He lapsed into silence, and she realized he assumed she knew what happened next. Jo hadn't given her a blow-by-blow, and she'd never asked.

Noah finally spoke up, from so close behind her that she flinched. "I don't think Kit knows the rest, Henry."

Kit felt the hairs on her nape tingle as she saw Henry's eyes widen, his shoulders stiffen. "Jo never told me," she said.

Henry's voice was barely audible. "God. I guess not." He studied her face for a long moment, his brow furrowed, all traces of bonhomie gone. "He killed her with curare."

The impact of his words slammed into her like a fist, stealing her air. She heard the whimper of surprise—of denial—and belatedly recognized it as her own. "I don't—I don't believe it."

She was on her feet now, gripping the edge of the bar. Raw anger swelled within her as she recalled her conversation with the police chief. "Jordon didn't mention this. That bastard never said word one about it." Not even when she told him why Jo was in Pratte!

Kit had handed over her answering-machine tape to the police chief, and watched his face as he listened to it. That patronizing smile said it all, even before he spelled it out. Everyone in town knew that Joanne Merino, girl reporter, was high-strung and excitable. Surely Kit knew it, too. And what was all this about a book?

She'd told him, and watched his expression ice up. Gone was the indulgent hand patting. Jordon had actually cussed, and bestowed a wealth of vulgar epithets on her dead friend. At the time it seemed a refreshing change.

Well, Jordon was, as Henry had pointed out, a horse's ass. More difficult to swallow was Noah Stewart's complicity in this seeming conspiracy of silence. He had to realize she'd assumed Jo was Pratte's first and only curare murder, and he'd chosen not to enlighten her. Irrationally, she felt a sting of betrayal. She studied his impassive expression and sent a silent message: *We have some talking to do.*

"You're assuming the two murders are related," Henry said.

She let her expression of incredulity answer for her.

He raised his hands in appeasement. "Hey, I'm not saying it's coincidence. I think this is some sick copycat thing. I know Noah agrees with me. I'm sure Jordon does, too. What else could it be? Think about it. Ray Whittaker's been dead and buried for thirty-two years."

What else could it be? Kit sat on the bar stool again, thinking about the book Jo had moved to Pratte to research in secret. The book destined to be the next *In Cold*

Blood. The book no other author had ever gotten off the ground because of a dogged lack of cooperation by the locals.

Jo had been determined to outmaneuver the close-mouthed town and reconstruct—in the nittiest, grittiest detail—the murder of Anita David, the decades-old crime that had become an obsession with her. She would take up residence, become one of them. Shake their cookie jars and turn their pockets inside out.

And they wouldn't find out what she was up to till it was too late.

Except someone did. *This guy, he found out about the book. And, well... that's not good.... God, where are you, Kit?*

What cookie jars had Jo shaken? Kit wondered. Who found out about Jo's project? Who was she so afraid of at the end?

Noah asked, "What kind of weapon did you think Ray used?"

"I figured he, um—" she swallowed around a sudden knot in her throat "—shot her or something."

"Not a chance," Henry said. "This was no crime of passion. It's not like he suddenly went crazy. He planned it out, bided his time. He knew he wouldn't have long to wait—just till her next attack. The fact that I was out of town at the time was an added bonus he hadn't counted on."

"So he gave her curare instead of epinephrine."

"That's right. She died and Ray called for an ambulance and said she'd suffered heart failure related to the asthma attack, and that he was too late to save her."

"The perfect crime," she said.

"It would've been, if the son of a bitch could've held his booze. He got roaring drunk a few days later and mouthed off about it."

"To you?"

His eyes glittered with hatred. "Yep. He told me he'd had an affair with my wife, and he told me what he'd done to her."

"And you told the police," she said.

"Damn right I did. We had to have Anita exhumed so they could do an autopsy and test for curare. It was there, all right."

"Why did he kill her?"

"The way I figure it, Anita fell in love with him," Henry said. "To Ray, she was just another conquest, I'm sure of that. One of many. She must've been ready to blow the whistle, make it public. It would've destroyed his marriage, for starters—and he sure as hell didn't want that. Not to mention what I'd have done to him if I'd known. Plus, if it ever came out how many of his patients he'd seduced, his medical license would've been in danger."

Kit squirmed, suddenly wishing she hadn't asked Noah to accompany her. "He really did it with his patients?"

Henry snorted. "Ray was one horny bastard. And a master at exploiting their trust, abusing the doctor-patient relationship. He used to brag about it—how he worked them, wore them down, used their personal divulgences to manipulate them. Listen, the guy was my buddy, like I said. That doesn't mean I approved of his behavior."

Kit wasn't sanctimonious enough to condemn Henry for his friendship with Ray. Her relationship with Joanne had borne similar strains.

"How long was Ray married?" she asked.

"Ten years. To Ruby. They had a little girl, Deborah. Poor kid was six years old when all this happened. She's a contract attorney in Boston now, done quite well for herself. She's married with four kids of her own."

"What's her married name?"

Henry hesitated, obviously wondering why she wanted to know. "Carlisle."

Kit straightened. Why was that name familiar? Bingo. "Is she related to a Bryan Carlisle?"

Henry shot her a surprised glance, looking as if he'd just caught a whiff of raw sewage. "Did you meet that little creep?"

Noah muttered, "For God's sake, Henry, don't get started."

"No," she answered, wondering what she'd just stepped into. "Etta Zimmerman mentioned him. She said he's the one who found Jo." *That Carlisle boy, Bryan, comes tearing across the lawn, yelling something about Joanne.*

A hint of pain crossed Henry's face. "That's right. He did." He sighed. "Yeah, Bryan is Deborah's oldest son. Must be eighteen or nineteen now. Been bumming around Pratte for the past year, since he graduated high school."

"I wouldn't say 'bumming,'" Noah offered, with more feeling than he'd shown all morning. "He earns his way. That kid's a hard worker." Henry's response to this was a derisive grunt.

So. Ray Whittaker's grandson discovered Jo in her death throes. There was a chilling irony in that.

"Why do you hate him?" she asked Henry.

"Bad blood. The kid's no better than his grandfather. Leave it at that."

She cocked her head as if to say, *Fine with me.* She looked over her shoulder at Noah, who stood close enough to touch. Close enough to detect his masculine scent. She wondered if Jo had liked the way he smelled, too. A high-pitched beeping sounded, and he glanced at the contraption hooked on his belt as he turned it off.

Henry said, "There's a phone down the hall in Bettina's study."

Noah nodded. "Excuse me."

Henry watched him leave, then cocked his head toward the doorway. "Looks like you've been busy since you got to Pratte."

She shrugged. "I wanted to get all the facts straight, and I figured the town M.D. was a good place to start. It helps that he was her friend, too." Kit wasn't about to apologize for being nosy. God knew Jo wouldn't have left a stone unturned if it had been Kit's mortal remains in that little cardboard box at Etta's.

She straightened and met his gaze. "I'm not going back to Chicago till I've answered all the lingering questions to my satisfaction. And who knows? If I dig up anything enlightening, maybe it'll help jump-start Jordon's investigation."

"Jo was fortunate to have a friend like you, Kit."

She looked away for a moment and swallowed hard, determined not to let Henry hear her voice crack. She'd failed Jo; no syrupy platitudes could change that. "Yeah, well..." With a glance to the open doorway, she said, "About the party. Etta said it took a while to find Noah when...when Jo..."

"He was in the solarium. I'm the one who located him, as a matter of fact. He was sitting there all by his lonesome, if you don't count the fifth of Scotch nestled in the crook of his arm." He grinned.

"Etta said he was exhausted from a medical emergency."

"I don't know about that. I just figured he was the only guy with the nerve to do what the rest of us wanted to—at least me. Get away from that white-glove crowd and toss back a few in peace and quiet."

"Were you there—I mean right there—when Jo died?"

The flesh around his eyes tightened fractionally. "Yeah, I was there."

"How did Noah handle it?"

One eyebrow rose. "You heard about that, huh?" He paused, as if weighing his words carefully. "I think something snapped in him. Just for a little while. Maybe he was exhausted, like you say. Maybe the booze had something to do with it, though he seemed sober enough.

"He was pretty much in control at first. Took one look at her and tossed his car keys to someone—Bryan, I think—and sent him running for his medical bag. He started working on her right away, or trying to. But it was so goddamn hopeless." His features had hardened. "Sorry. Anyway, that's when he seemed to change. When it was clear he couldn't do anything for her and she was . . ." He hesitated.

"I know she suffered," Kit said quietly.

Henry leaned on his elbows and scrubbed at his face with his palms, as if by doing so he could eradicate the memory. He lifted his head and stared out the picture window. "Yeah. She suffered." He cleared his throat. "At that point Noah just wasn't himself."

The same phrase Etta had used, Kit remembered.

"His face, his eyes . . . It was like I'd never met this guy. Even his body language was different." He gave a mirthless half laugh. "Strange as that may sound."

"His body language?"

"Every expression, every movement. Suddenly Noah was a stranger to me. To all of us. He was down there in the ivy with her, and she was . . ." He took a deep breath. "Well, she was still alive, but going fast, you know. And I tried to help. I mean, I don't know that much about CPR, but I sort of caught on watching him, and I got down there with him and reached for her."

He met her eyes. "Kit, he backhanded me, and I mean, I went flying." His hand arced in illustration. "That was one hell of a wallop. I guess it was all that adrenaline or something—all that frustration." He shook his head. "All I know is, I hurt like hell for a full week."

Another peek at the doorway. "What do you think of Noah? In general?"

Henry shrugged. "He's a solid guy. I always thought so. I'm not gonna hold one strange episode against him. It was a ... bizarre situation, to say the least. He didn't remember belting me, but when he found out about it, he apologized." He shrugged again. "It was no big deal. Hell, I suffered a lot worse growing up in Montreal. I was always in one scrape or another."

"Aha!" she crowed. So *that* was the accent she'd been trying to identify—French Canadian. "Henri David," she said, giving his name the full Gallic treatment. *Dah-veed.*

He chuckled—she liked the raspy way he did that. "Aha! Kit Roarke." He'd turned the tables by slathering on a thick brogue. "I'll be thankin' ye not to remind me o' me humble origins, begorra."

As long as you don't remind me of mine, she thought. She looked around the sumptuously furnished den. "Nothing humble about where you've ended up."

"I guess I've done all right for a poor, skinny, scrappy kid from the East End. I got my start bundling papers for *Le Journal de Montréal.*"

"I stole a copy of the *Pratte Citizen* from Noah's waiting room. Pretty impressive." If you were into puff pieces from local businesses and politicos, photo spreads of school concerts and the Memorial Day parade, and editorials about such gripping issues as whether the twirling team should wear fringed pink leotards or lime green hot pants.

"It's all right for a small-town weekly. I'm proud of it. So you were in Noah's place, huh? What did you think of it?"

"That it's trapped in the sixties."

"Well, it hasn't been altered at all since Ray Whittaker lived there."

The shock must have been plain on her face, because Henry took one look at her and said, "You didn't know?"

Noah's voice jump-started her heart and brought a prickle of heat to her face. "It's the only place in town with an existing medical office," he said, closing the door. "Ray grew up in that house—a fourth-generation M.D. There was one other owner after Ray died, and he left a few years before I arrived."

"And neither of them so much as changed Ray's wallpaper," Henry added, chuckling. "But I guess that's to be expected with bachelors."

"I didn't know Ray's family was from Pratte," Kit said.

"The Whittakers were founding fathers," Henry explained. "They've been on easy street since about 1890 when Great-Grandpa Sam hit it big with a couple of hot patents."

"What did he invent?"

"Medical instruments, of all things. He had that house built around the turn of the century."

"Eighteen ninety-seven," Noah volunteered.

She remembered being intrigued by the outside of Noah's sprawling old home, which housed his practice. Brick and stone, with a slate roof, gables, latticed windows and a profusion of eccentric masonry work.

Henry said, "A fascinating old place, really, inside and out, if you can forget who once lived there." He had the unfocused look of someone peering into the past. "I spent a lot of time in that house when Ray was alive. When Ray and Anita were alive."

Kit was peering into a more recent past. She was thinking about her dead friend and the obsessive project she'd undertaken—the long-held secrets she'd planned to unearth. Where would *Kit* go if she wanted to find out everything she could about someone's life? She'd start at his home, of course. *Neither of them so much as changed Ray's wallpaper.*

She thought about Joanne Merino's information-gathering techniques. *The end justifies the means, kiddo.*

She thought about her first surprising glimpse of Noah Stewart, M.D., when he'd caught her pawing through his files. Yeah, shoulders like that always did it for Jo. The object of her musing had wandered back to the far side of the room and settled on a cream-colored leather sofa that looked butter soft. His arm was thrown over the back, one ankle propped on a knee.

"I assume that wasn't an emergency," Kit said, referring to his phone call.

"Nope. But we can't stay much longer—I start seeing patients at ten-thirty."

"No problem." She turned back to Henry. "Listen, before I go, let me ask you one more thing. Joanne's social life. Nobody seems to know who she was dating."

Henry's expression was unreadable as he tipped back his glass. After a thoughtful, ice-chomping pause, he said, "She did get phone calls at the office, of course. Some of them sounded more than a little chummy from her end."

"She didn't tell you about him? Didn't mention his name?" She heard the note of incredulity that had crept into her tone, and consciously stifled it. "I don't know, it just seems like you two were probably on the same wavelength...."

"That we were, but you know Jo. When she decided to keep her lips zipped..." His expressive shrug said the rest.

She remembered Jo's words. *You wouldn't approve. He's not suitable.* She could think of few paramours less suitable than one's personal physician. She avoided looking at Noah.

"Did you get to the town treasurer's party before Jo?" she asked Henry.

"Yeah, Bettina and I were there about ten minutes when I saw her saying hi to Grace."

"Did you happen to notice who she arrived with?"

"No... but people were just sort of drifting into the backyard in groups, from around the house, you know. We all parked in front. You think she came with someone?"

"I know she did. Her car was still at Etta's—it hadn't been moved since that morning when she got back from the gym." *And found her room ransacked.*

Then she'd left for the party in the company of the mystery man who'd fetched her sunglasses while she was talking to Kit's machine. If Chief Jordon knew who that man was, his lips were sealed. He'd refused to answer her questions about the investigation. Nothing would make him happier than to have her pack up her dead friend's ashes and wing her way back to the Windy City posthaste.

"I don't suppose your other employees would know who she was seeing," she said.

He shook his head. "She wasn't that friendly with anyone else at the *Citizen*. Wasn't in the office that much, anyway, except to file her stories and write some of the regular columns."

"So she wouldn't have left anything of her own there?" Kit didn't think Jo would have risked keeping the backup disk of her book at the office, but anything was possible.

"Not that I know of, but if I come across anything, I'll drop it off at Etta's." He looked at her. "How did you know she was seeing someone?"

The door swung open, saving her from having to lie. She wasn't prepared at this point to disclose Jo's fears to anyone except Tom Jordon—and she almost regretted having confided in him.

The woman standing in the doorway was as beautiful as Henry was handsome, but younger. She looked to be about forty, slim and elegant—even in her sweaty workout clothes—with dark hair worn in a sleek French braid. She stood transfixed, staring at the cozy scene at the bar, obviously unaware of Noah's quiet presence. Her eyes settled on her seminude husband, and foolishly Kit felt her face grow warm once more.

"Bettina!" Henry's now familiar smile flashed, along with something else Kit failed to identify, some kind of unspoken communiqué to which she was not privy. Spousal telepathy. Probably something along the lines of *This isn't what it looks like.* He reached out to lift and turn Kit's wrist, the better to read her watch face. She sensed the repressed strength in his warm, dry hand, as muscular as the rest of him. His touch was casual, almost paternal, putting her at ease.

"I wasn't expecting you back for another half hour," he said. "Finish your workout early?"

"Not really. I decided to skip the sauna, and shower at home." She smiled and began to back away. "Excuse me, I didn't mean to disturb your interview." Noah rose to greet her. "Oh! Noah. I didn't see you there." They exchanged greetings and a quick cheek peck.

"You're not disturbing anything." Henry waved her inside. "Kit Roarke, my wife, Bettina. Kit's a friend of Joanne's. Just got into town day before yesterday." He pulled a small bottle of grapefruit juice out of the fridge, shook it and twisted the cap off.

Bettina's smile froze and she glanced quickly at her husband and Noah before taking the hand Kit offered. With her handshake came a clean athletic scent, a blend of fresh sweat and Chanel No 5. "Oh. I..."

Kit sympathized with the other woman's discomfort. To her knowledge, Emily Post had never covered "Meeting the Best Friend of a Murder Victim."

"I'm...so sorry," Bettina said, releasing her hand. "It was..." Another glance at her husband. "Everyone was so shocked. I'm so sorry," she repeated.

"I know. Thank you."

"You'll have to excuse my appearance," Bettina said, looking down at her sneakers, bike shorts and crop top, loosely covered by a baggy lavender tank-style T-shirt. She was tanned and toned. Apparently fitness was a family affair in the David household. She accepted the bottle of juice from Henry, smiling her thanks. "I just came from the health club."

Something clicked. "Valkyrie, right?"

Bettina's eyes widened.

"Joanne joined Valkyrie," Kit said. "Her landlady said you introduced her to it."

"Oh. Yes. She wanted a place to work out, and that's the nicest club in the area." She took a healthy swig of juice.

Noah interpreted. "It's the nineties version of the smoke-filled back room, is what she means," he said, a sardonic gleam in his eye. "Women only. Grace Drummond, our treasurer, is a regular. Plus every other female town officer and selectman, most of the female business owners in Pratte and just about every other woman with a six-figure income."

Henry sighed with mock wistfulness. "I pine for the good old days, when the movers and shakers were potbellied, cigar-chomping, suspender-snapping men." He pounded his chest. "Hombres, dammit! Real guys who like red meat and never heard of the StairMaster."

Bettina paused in midgulp, swallowing around a wicked grin. "You'd be surprised how much moving and shaking you do on the StairMaster, love."

"It's hard for me to picture Jo joining an expensive place like that," Kit said.

"Well, she seemed to think it was worth it," Bettina said. "I saw her there at least three times a week."

"Perhaps I should ask *you*, then. Henry said he didn't know who Jo was dating. Maybe you do...?" When Bettina didn't answer immediately, she added, "You know, steam-room chitchat. I thought she might've—"

"No." A quick, dismissive smile. "I don't remember her mentioning anyone." Bettina turned away and reached across the bar to chafe her husband's bare arm. "Aren't you cold, love? It's like a meat locker in this house."

"I like it cool. You know that." He wasn't smiling.

But Bettina was, a little too brightly. "Well. It wouldn't hurt you to throw something on." Before he could respond, she asked, "How many laps did you do?"

"Eighty or so."

Her concerned gaze studied his face. She looked pointedly at Noah and asked, "Did he eat anything?"

"I'm fine," Henry said.

Bettina began to cross behind the bar. "A piece of fruit?"

"I'm fine, Bettina," he snapped. "I'm not hungry. But perhaps Kit—"

"No. Thank you. I had Etta's waffles for breakfast." Kit patted her stomach. "That should hold me for a few days." She rose and picked up her purse. "We've monopolized you long enough, Henry. I'm grateful for the brain-picking session."

He laid a hand on her back. "Remember my offer, Kit." A couple of affable thumps on her spine. "Anything I can do."

"Well, I do have just one more question. Ray Whittaker died while out on bail, right?"

Bettina stiffened at the mention of the murderer.

"That's right," he said.

"Jo didn't say, but I'm assuming he committed suicide...?"

Three sets of eyebrows shot up.

"He didn't commit suicide?" Kit asked.

"Hell, no!" Henry roared good-naturedly. "*I* killed the son of a bitch!"

Chapter Four

Kit and Noah had taken separate cars in case he was called away on an emergency. On her way out to Henry's earlier, Kit had passed a dairy farm. Her gaze had strayed from the pasture full of cows doing their cow thing—the very picture of bucolic indolence—to the distant Green Mountains, doing their mountain thing. Here was Vermont, she'd thought, doing its Vermont thing, and she'd been happy to let it.

Now, on her return trip, her eyes never wavered from the road. It wasn't asphalt she saw, but the face of a long-dead murderer. Before letting them leave, Henry had hauled out a box of old snapshots, black and white for the most part, dozens of photos of the Whittakers and the Davids, or combinations thereof. Henry and Ray fly-fishing. Anita and Ruby ice-skating. Little Debbie with her ax poised to chop down a Christmas tree.

Why she'd always imagined Ray Whittaker as a man in his middle years, gray haired and age thickened, she couldn't say. The photos showed a young, slim man, shorter than Henry, perhaps five foot ten or eleven. But the full impact didn't hit her till her host produced a color snapshot. There was Ray flipping steaks on a charcoal grill, with Anita and Ruby at his side, highballs in hand. All three were laughing into the camera. It was easy to imagine that Henry, behind

the lens, had just told a wickedly funny joke, and managed
to catch that charmed instant when the punch line kicked in.

"He looks like a teenager!" Kit had said. Red hair.
Freckles.

Freckles, for God's sake!

"He was thirty-six in that picture," Henry had responded, "four years older than me. It was taken a few
weeks before he died."

A few weeks before he cold-bloodedly murdered one of
the women standing there laughing with him. Anita David
looked to be in her thirties, too, with a wavy blond pageboy
and a full, womanly figure. Ruby Whittaker, on Ray's other
side, was darker and smaller than her friend. Kit wondered
if she'd known about her husband's extramarital activities.

Ray's youthful build and features were offset by intelligent brown eyes and a pockmarked complexion. The de-
fect, rather than detracting from his looks, lent an
interesting cragginess to his boyish face.

Henry's account of Ray's death was succinct. Ray's high-
priced lawyers get him released on bail, and now he's mad.
That kind of ice-cold mad he'd get sometimes. That scary
too-goddamn-calm mad. He comes out to the house—to
talk, he says—and Henry takes one look at Ray and knows
that new Walther of his, that slim .380 PPK, is tucked into
his waistband somewhere, under his windbreaker.

Was he drunk? Kit asked. Not this time, Henry said. And,
sober, Ray was a dead-on shot.

Seems odd, doesn't it? she wondered aloud. Here Ray had
painstakingly planned the "perfect" murder, even pa-
tiently waited for the victim's next asthma attack. Why
would such a man do something so rash, grab his semiautomatic the instant he's out on bail and go after the guy
who blew the whistle?

That was Ray, Henry said. It was cold calculation or
reckless passion with him, never an in-between. Nothing

existed for him at that moment except the driving need to empty that .380 into his old pal.

But the edge Henry had in size and strength—not to mention raw rage over his wife's murder—made the struggle that ensued an uneven match. In the end Ray bled to death, gutshot with his own weapon. Henry was held blameless in an indisputable case of self-defense.

In downtown Pratte now, Kit found a parking space for Jo's light blue Corolla in front of Ye Olde Video Shoppe. At Pratte Hardware Emporium next door she bought packing tape for the boxes she was mailing back to Sal. Rounding out the usual array of utilitarian merchandise were picture postcards, camera film and maps, not to mention mugs, bumper stickers, key rings, gimme caps and T-shirts all sporting the green Pratte, Vermont, logo for those requiring tangible proof that they'd been to a Quaint New England Town.

She strolled the main drag, watching the tourists and scoping out the layout. At the heart of town, like the hub of a wheel, was the requisite white, steepled church. Staring at it, Kit could only marvel at the stark contrast between this sweet, simple town and the rough neighborhood where she grew up.

But then, Jo had survived the rough streets of Chicago. She had to come to this sweet, simple town to get murdered.

Kit turned away from the soaring steeple and made a beeline for the Corolla. She needed answers, and God help the good doctor if he tried to pull the kind of evasive crap he'd ladled out the day she arrived.

Kit negotiated Pratte's hilly, twisting residential side streets and turned onto an overgrown uphill driveway marked by a rural mailbox on a post. Noah Stewart, M.D. Family Practice. Gravel rattled around in the Corolla's undercarriage as she pulled in next to Noah's dusty black

Cherokee. Two other cars were parked near the side entrance to his practice. Patients, no doubt.

Kit checked her watch as she climbed out of the car—11:20. She had no intention of waiting out the next forty minutes or so under the watchful eye of Noah's trained pit bull, Alice. Besides, the day was too sunny and warm to spend even one minute of it sitting in a doctor's waiting room with sick people hacking in her face.

She looked around, more attentive to detail than she'd been two days ago. The house appeared to be in decent repair, but the grounds of the onetime Whittaker homestead had a look of calculated disorder, as if the days of meticulous landscaping were long gone.

From behind the house came the whining roar of a gasoline engine. The sound rose and ebbed at intervals, disabusing her initial impression that it was a lawn mower. She began walking in that direction.

As she passed the open window of an examining room, a toddler's high-pitched wail drowned out the roar of the motor. Vaccination time, no doubt. She peeked in and saw a young woman cuddling and crooning to her daughter, whose squalling dropped off to a tear-streaked scowl punctuated by hiccups. Noah's back was to Kit as he disposed of the syringe, then deftly affixed a Band-Aid to the girl's arm and commended her bravery.

She caught herself smiling as she rounded the house. She'd always been a sucker for displays of male tenderness toward children. Probably because she'd never had a dad, she figured, though God knew Sal Merino had tried his hardest to fill that particular void.

The large backyard was as unruly as the front, choked with untrimmed trees and shrubbery, as if the nearby woods were intent on reclaiming it. She looked toward the source of the racket and saw, about thirty feet away, a squat paper birch studded with dry brown leaves. Small branches littered the ground at the foot of a folding ladder.

Someone stood behind a large lower limb, which began to separate from the tree at its base. The branch fell away and Kit stumbled to a stop, gaping at Ray Whittaker.

Ray wore only cutoffs and held a rumbling chain saw in his right hand. He stepped back to study the tree, sparing her barely a glance as he selected his next target.

"Doc's office is over there." He gestured with the saw. "The door with the big sign on it."

She commanded herself to breathe. The freckles were there, but not the pockmarks. Ray Whittaker probably hadn't worn his coppery hair in a long ponytail like this young man, and he almost certainly didn't have a tattoo of a hawk in flight on his right biceps.

"I'm not looking for Noah. I mean, I'm waiting for him to break for lunch," she said.

This earned a second look. His eyes flicked over her and returned to the tree. He was much younger than Ray, too, she now saw, with the lean, sleekly muscled build of an athletic youth. Fine sawdust clung to the light mat of russet hair on his chest. She'd enjoyed quite a rousing display of male flesh today, and it wasn't even noon.

The saw yowled to life and he began severing a huge branch in front, his biceps popping, the hawk twitching as he worked.

She ambled closer, shouting to be heard. "Is the tree dead?"

He jerked at the sound of her voice so close just as the limb came away. "Look out!"

Kit yelped and darted to the side as the heavy limb crashed down right where she'd been walking. She didn't need his sardonic smirk to feel like an idiot, but it helped.

"Is the tree dead? Is that what you asked?"

She gave a weak half laugh. "Stupid question." Kit waited for sarcastic agreement, but none came. With a wary glance at the homicidal tree, she approached him, hand extended. "I'm Kit Roarke."

He hefted the saw into his left hand and dried his right one on his cutoffs. "Bryan Carlisle." His palm felt hot, callused and a little sweaty despite the wipe-down, his grip firm. He didn't return her smile.

"Bryan. Oh. You're Bryan." At least she wasn't losing her mind. There was a reason for the resemblance to Ray.

Something clicked in behind his brown eyes then, something hard. "What've you heard about me?"

The kid's no better than his grandfather. Leave it at that.

"Nothing."

"Bull." He turned back toward the birch. She'd failed some test, and he was dismissing her.

"You're right, it's bull," she conceded, "but I don't think people really want to know everything that's said about them."

His back to her, he ran his hand over the trunk of the dead tree, flicking off curls of papery bark. "It doesn't matter. I know what you heard." He threw a grin over his shoulder, and it was Ray Whittaker she saw at that moment, flipping steaks and sharing a joke with the ladies.

"I got the bad genes." Laughing, he turned and spread his arms in a see-for-yourself gesture. "I roll into town last year and the yokels do, like, this giant double take. It was Creature Feature time, man." He gave his words a Boris Karloff spin, with wagging eyebrows. "The Evil One returns from the grave."

The chain saw roared for a second and Kit jumped with a yip she was helpless to stifle. She muttered a low curse. "Very funny."

Apparently Bryan thought so, too, but his obvious self-consciousness redeemed him. He seemed to be laughing more at his juvenile sense of humor that at her response to it.

Frenzied barking drew their attention to a large golden retriever loping across the lawn from the direction of the screened-in porch, with its built-in dog door. The animal was headed straight for Kit, whether to lick her face or tear out her jugular, she couldn't say. Bryan quickly moved to intercept him and grab his collar. "Easy, Max."

This could have been the set of *Nightmare at the Kennel,* she thought. It was all there: a dog, a chain saw and a half-dressed, tattooed youth with bad genes.

The instant Bryan released him, the beast was all over her, drool spraying, tail swinging, warm dog breath in her face. It was all she could do to keep her balance.

"Max! Get down!" Bryan commanded, hauling him off her. "Sit!" Max sat. "Stay!" With one eye on Bryan's admonishing finger, the dog scooted toward Kit on his haunches, his tail rhythmically thwacking the ground. *"Stay!"*

She backed up, and the dog scooted forward again, practically vibrating in canine rapture. Bryan seized his collar, and Kit petted him, earning his slobbering gratitude.

"Where's your pride, man?" Bryan asked him. He turned to Kit. "I think he's in love."

Something live rocketed down a tree at the edge of the woods, cutting short Max's slavering devotion. He tore off into the trees.

"Well, at least he lasted longer than my last boyfriend," she observed.

"Bryan! I told you I'd give you a hand with that," Noah scolded from the steps of the porch. "Why didn't you wait for me?"

At the sound of his master's voice—that Georgia drawl so charmingly out of place at this latitude—Max bounded out of the woods and charged across the lawn. By this time

Noah had noticed Kit standing with Bryan. His eyes were mostly on her even as he knelt and roughhoused with Max for a few moments, effortlessly wrestling the big animal to the ground as if he were a puppy.

"I'm doing all right," Bryan answered.

She figured Noah was six foot two or three; that, along with a solid, muscular build and masculine grace, explained his imposing presence. He started across the lawn toward them, Max at his heels. "I can see that," he said, "I just—"

"When I finish taking it down, I'll get rid of the brush and start splitting up the logs."

Noah joined them and nodded politely to Kit before turning his concerned gaze to the younger man. She could see him taking in the flushed face and incipient sunburn. "Knock off for a while, Bryan. Doctor's orders. You've—"

"Save it, man." The saw whined into high gear as he resumed his work.

Noah's features tightened in frustration and he turned to Kit. She sensed he would have liked to push the issue but didn't want to embarrass Bryan in front of her. "I've gotta get back in there, but I'll break for lunch in about twenty minutes."

"That's okay, Bryan and I have been having a real interesting chat." Let him chew on that, she thought, giving in to a wicked impulse to tweak him a bit for withholding information from her.

A muscle in Noah's cheek twitched and his eyes cooled to a pale greenish amber as they flicked from her to Bryan. It struck her like a slap. He didn't want to leave them alone together! Their private tête-à-tête bugged the hell out of Noah, and she didn't know why.

Unless it was because he was afraid of what Bryan might tell her. Of what she might learn. That possibility crawled up her spine with icy little fingers and tickled her scalp. She didn't care to speculate on what it was Noah might not want her to learn.

"Well," she said, with a casualness she didn't feel. "Don't let us keep you. I'll be here when you break for lunch."

The saw idled in Bryan's hand and he glanced at the dog, now lying in the shade of a nearby spruce. "You know, my grandfather had a dog named Max, too," he said. At the sound of his name Max raised his head, and finding nothing more exciting than three pairs of eyes staring at him, let it drop again. "And get this," Bryan continued. "It was a golden retriever! Just like this guy. That's something, huh?"

Kit thought so. She turned to Noah to find his look of uneasiness had hardened into something else. Something...well, scary. A cold-eyed intensity that made those icy fingers tighten on her scalp and squeeze, even as she told herself she was being silly. He caught her eye then, and something in her expression must have alerted him. As she watched, the muscles in his face relaxed, his heightened color returned to normal and his eyes darkened fractionally. All that in about five seconds.

She blinked. No. It couldn't have been a conscious thing. No one could willfully control the size of his *pupils*, for heaven's sake!

Noah's smile was wide and genial as he said, "It was sort of a joke."

A joke? "The dog's name?" she asked. "You did it deliberately?"

"Well, sure. When I realized my new puppy was the same breed as the dog that lived here thirty years ago, I gave him the same name." He shrugged, the smile still in place. "Had to call him *something*, right?"

"Guess so," Kit murmured, though she guessed nothing of the sort. Admittedly, she didn't know him very well, yet somehow Noah didn't seem like the kind of man to bring home a puppy and give it another dog's name.

"I better get back in there before Jack Cantor decides to draw his own blood sample." Still smiling, Noah turned and ambled back to the house.

"So." She turned to Bryan. "You do yard work for Noah."

"And anyone else that doesn't mind having their hedges trimmed by the Bad Seed." He looked around the neglected lawn. "I should be able to do something with this place before fall."

"How'd you get by during the winter?"

"I taught the tourists to ski at Stowe. How come you're so nosy?"

She shrugged. "I got the bad genes."

One side of his mouth curved up. "It's the red hair."

"I prefer to think of it as chestnut. It's more brown than red." She shared his lopsided grin.

"It's more red than brown. It's really beautiful, too. Wild, you know?" With his free hand he reached for the untamed thatch of corkscrew curls that fell to her shoulder blades. "How do you get it to do that?" Idly he pulled one long ringlet and watched it recoil as he released it.

"How do I *get it* to do that? After a couple of decades of battling the stuff, I finally threw in the towel and let it have its own way, that's how I get it to do that."

"I bet Noah can't keep his hands out of it."

The image invoked by Bryan's offhand comment swamped her senses in a dizzying rush. It took an effort of will to force her thoughts away from Noah's long, warm fingers sliding through her hair, over her scalp. She gave a light chuckle as she felt her face burn, then said, "It's not like that. I only met Noah yesterday."

"Tourist?"

"No. I'm a friend of Joanne Merino's."

Now it was Bryan who seemed to slam up against the unexpected. His eyes grew round and he suddenly looked about twelve. Then his features tightened and he looked away, his chest rising and falling rapidly. He glanced at the chain saw he still held, idling with a low rumble, as if he'd never seen it before.

"I know you found her," she said gently.

He lifted his eyes to hers. They looked weary, defeated. He cleared his throat. "Listen, I gotta finish taking down this tree."

"We can talk while you work. I promise to stay out of the way."

There was one more limb to remove, then the bifurcated trunk. Bryan swiftly dispatched the limb and pulled the ladder up to one of the skewed boles.

Kit did some quick arithmetic as he climbed the ladder and began to lop off the top two feet of the trunk. The ripe green fragrance of the nearby woods blended with the tang of fresh sawdust spraying from the whirring chain. She shouted to be heard. "You graduated high school last year, so that makes you, what? Nineteen? Twenty?"

"Eighteen." He kept his eyes on the chunk of tree as it thudded to the ground. The sun was nearly overhead, and his face and chest were sheened with sweat. "I skipped a year."

So he was smart. She supposed it ran in the family. What's a bright kid like this doing mowing lawns and giving skiing lessons when he should be in college?

"Your mom must've gotten married young," she said, remembering that Henry told her Debbie was six when Ray died, making her thirty-eight now. Of course, there's young and then there's ridiculously young. Kit's mother was only forty.

"Your nosy genes are showing," he said. "I was an accident."

"Join the club." He shot her a quick look. Good. She'd managed to chip away a bit of that belligerent pride. "Most of the world is an accident, Bryan."

He descended two steps on the ladder and carved another hunk of tree. She watched the play of muscle in his gleaming back and shoulders and wondered if she was turning into a dirty old woman at twenty-six. His skin had taken as much of a tan as a redhead could expect, and was beginning to turn pink on the high spots. He let the log fall.

"Were you and Jo friends?" she asked.

He didn't answer right away, but his expression was eloquent. Painfully so. Where Jo was concerned, this boy's emotions were close to the surface. Too close.

Good Lord. Joanne had been ten years older than Bryan. Kit hoped to God her friend had exercised self-control, a rare commodity for Jo under such circumstances.

"I *thought* we were friends," he said sullenly.

His answer surprised her till she realized what it probably meant: Jo hadn't responded to his crush. Perhaps her friend had finally begun to develop a sense of propriety and good judgment.

You wouldn't approve. He's not suitable.

Then again, perhaps she hadn't.

Bryan pulled a red bandanna from his back pocket and wiped his face, then tied it around his forehead. He continued cutting pieces from the first trunk till he reached the crotch of the tree. The ground was littered with the debris of the once-live thing he was methodically dismantling. He turned off the saw and set it on the ground, then stretched his back to loosen the kinks.

With no tree parts crashing down around her, Kit felt safe approaching him once more. "Bryan, did you and Jo arrive at the treasurer's party together?" She held her breath.

He laughed. "You think I was *invited* to that thing?" He leaned against what was left of the tree and said, "I crashed that sucker. Grace Drummond has no use for me."

"Did you see Jo before she...? I mean, you know, did you speak with her?"

"Tom Jordon asked me the same thing. He's our police chief. Have you met him?"

"I've had the pleasure," she deadpanned.

Bryan grinned. "Guy's a prime bozo, huh?"

At least Henry and Bryan agreed about something. "Yes, indeed, and he's not playing nice," she said. "Won't share. So, did you talk with her?"

"I *wanted* to. I wanted to...explain some stuff, you know? Clear the air." He started picking at the paper bark again. "We'd had, like, this fight. A disagreement, I guess. Anyway, she wouldn't talk to me."

"What did you argue about?"

"Betrayal."

His expression said, *Don't ask,* so she didn't, though it was killing her.

"Did you notice who she *was* talking with?"

He shrugged. "The Drummonds, of course—Grace and Al. Some of the local bigwigs and the people Jo worked with..."

"Henry David?"

"King Henry, sure. And his wife, Lady Nip and Tuck." His eyes narrowed. "Gotta suck up to the boss man, right?"

So the hostility was mutual. But *Lady Nip and Tuck?* "I met Bettina David this morning. She looks like a natural beauty to me."

"She ought to. She's spent enough of her daddy's money on the wonders of modern medical science." With both hands he stretched the skin of his face back into a rictus intended, no doubt, to emulate the results of cosmetic surgery.

"Her father's rich?"

He snorted. "Carter Sheridan? What do you think? Owns, like, this humongous multinational conglomerate."

"Sheridan hair-care products?" *That.* Sheridan?"

"Bingo. Plus he owns a few other little companies you might've heard of. Emerald Valley drink mixes. Conti-Meeker Pharmaceutical. Et cetera, et cetera."

"Wow. Talk about deep pockets. Kind of a hodgepodge, though, huh? I mean, what do those companies have in common?"

He laughed. "Chemicals."

Kit thought of the Davids' lavish life-style and absence of gainful employment. The pieces began to fit together. "Henry could've done worse than marry into that family," she observed.

"That's how he started that rag of his, the *Citizen*. With the old man's money. A wedding gift, can you beat that? Bettina asks, Daddy gives."

Something about that didn't sit right. Then it came to her. "Bryan, the *Citizen* was started the year after Anita died."

"Yeah, so?"

"So...so Henry couldn't have had Sheridan's money back then. He couldn't have been married to Bettina back then, 'cause she would've been... Let's see, she's about forty now."

Bryan's bark of laughter stopped her short. Again he performed that grotesque finger face-lift and announced, "Bettina'll be fifty-two next month, Kit."

"No!"

"She was nineteen when she married Henry. His first wife wasn't even cold. They'd been carrying on for, like, a year behind her back." His hatred was palpable.

"What do you have against Bettina?" she asked.

"If it wasn't for that bitch, my grandfather would still be alive."

Chapter Five

My grandfather would still be—

"Bryan, what are you saying?"

"I said it. He'd still be alive." There was a mulish set to his features.

What could he mean, except maybe that if Bettina hadn't had an affair with Henry, then Anita might not have taken up with Ray, and Ray wouldn't have killed her and—

Good Lord, could it get more complicated?

"Bryan—"

"Forget it." He picked up the saw. "I shouldn't have said anything. I'm not gonna say anything else till I have the proof. Then I'll show everyone."

Proof. So the kid was conducting some sort of investigation of his own. Pratte had a sudden infestation of amateur sleuths. Kit knew she wouldn't get anywhere badgering Bryan for details, and decided to back down gracefully. For the moment.

He started to turn back to his work, and she stopped him with a hand on his arm. "Bryan, I need to know some things about how it was when you found Jo." She felt him stiffen. "Can you tell me about it?"

The depth of emotion in his glittering eyes rocked her. It might have been anguish she saw, or loathing. Maybe even remorse. Possibly some unholy mixture of all three. He'd loved Jo, she was pretty certain. Had he hated her, too?

"No," he said. "I don't wanna talk about it."

"Please." Her grip tightened. "I loved her, too, Bryan," she whispered. "She was like a sister to me. Closer. I need…I just need to hear it all." She released him. "I know you hurt, but I hurt, too, and I need to hear it."

When he met her eyes now, the world-weariness she saw shocked her. His resemblance to his grandfather was startling. She saw his Adam's apple rise and fall. His eyes bore a suspicious sheen. He cleared his throat and fiddled with the chain on his saw.

"After Jo wouldn't talk to me, I stuck around long enough to get half-crocked. I kinda…I guess I kinda just hung around to ride her case, you know, like glare at her and stuff from a distance when she was trying to talk to people. Let her see me getting sloshed. You know. Rattle her." He shrugged, then smirked at the memory. "Real mature, huh? Well, so anyway, I went to snag one last beer, and that's when I lost sight of her."

"How long had the party been going on at that point?" Kit asked.

"Hour, maybe a little more. So I couldn't find her and I figure the hell with her, I'm outta here, only I didn't want to cut right through the party and run into Grace Drummond, so I sorta skirted around the edge of the lawn, through the trees. That's when I found her."

He wouldn't meet her eyes. "She was on—" He swallowed convulsively. "She was on the ground, behind a bunch of these." He slapped the birch trunk. "No one would've seen her from the party. Which I guess was the point, huh? And she wasn't…making a sound."

A shudder raced through Kit. "But she was conscious, right?" According to Noah.

He took a deep breath. "Yeah. She was fighting hard to breathe, turning, like, blue. You could see she knew what was happening to her."

"But she couldn't tell anyone who did it."

A long pause, then a whispered "No."

"Bryan." She waited for him to look at her. "Who do you think did it?"

A subtle change came into his eyes. He was staring at her but seeing something or someone else, she knew. Finally he said simply, "The same one that did the first."

"The first?" He couldn't mean the same person who killed... "Anita David?" She swallowed hard. "Bryan, your grandfather murdered Anita David."

His smile was one of gentle tolerance, and a shiver scuttled down her spine. "People ignore what's, like, right in front of their eyes when it goes against what they think they know," he said.

Jo used to say the very same thing. What was he trying to tell her? That Ray Whittaker didn't murder Anita David?

Bryan powered up the chain saw. "People are lazy, Kit. Up here." He tapped his head. "Afraid of new ideas when they think they know what's what. Afraid to shake up the status quo, you know?"

It was like running full speed into a wall. The sick suspicion that she'd never find the answers she needed, because she was asking all the wrong questions.

"Bryan. Why did you move to Pratte?"

He flashed a Ray Whittaker grin and said, "To shake up the status quo. Why else?"

Max alerted them to his master's divine presence just then, and they turned to see Noah crossing the lawn.

"So, what did you want to see me about?" he asked, all business.

"Do you mind if we get out of the sun? My Irish complexion has reached its limit." *And I want to see Ray Whittaker's wallpaper.*

Noah stared unblinkingly just long enough to let her know he wasn't fooled for an instant. "Come on." He turned and led the way back to the house. Max trotted along with them as far as the porch, then took off toward his siesta spot again. Noah opened the screen door and held it so she could precede him.

"Does Bryan always drive himself like that?" she asked.

"He's a hard worker, but he's really been overdoing it lately."

"Since Jo died?" She glanced over her shoulder, and caught something unguarded in his eyes before he shuttered them. Something at once wary and menacing. Something that made her nape prickle.

"You two have yourselves a nice little confab?" he asked.

She turned to face him squarely. "Was Bryan in love with Joanne?"

The question didn't seem to surprise him. "Yes."

"Was she in love with him?"

"No." Just like that.

Go for it, girl. You're on a roll. "Were they lovers?"

He smiled. "That's so quaint. I like that. 'Were they lovers?'"

Something about the way Noah said "lovers," wrapping that Southern silk around each syllable, made her insides clench. Way down low. And that irritated the hell out of her.

He moved around her to cross the slate-floored porch and hold open the door to the house. Walking through, she found herself in what looked like a breakfast room, with a round, glass-topped table and caned Breuer chairs. Apparently not *every* furnishing dated from the sixties.

He led her past the huge, old-fashioned kitchen into a parlor. Threadbare Oriental rug, sofa and love seat, age-darkened wainscoting, and—she smiled—faded green floral wallpaper. The room even smelled old, underneath the lemon oil. She waited as he crossed the room and opened a door adjacent to his medical office. He called to Alice.

"Would you bring Bryan a pitcher of something cold and some sunblock? I think there's a tube in the blue bathroom." He started to close the door and turned back. "And harass him till he uses it, okay?"

Kit heard Alice's nicotine-rusted "No problem, Noah," and knew Bryan didn't stand a chance. He'd probably be given a choice between wearing that sunblock and eating it.

She followed him into the kitchen. The glass-fronted cabinets were knotty pine, the small black-and-white floor tiles worn and chipped, but clean. He opened the squat, rounded refrigerator and pulled out a pizza box.

"Lunch around here isn't exactly haute cuisine," he said, detaching a slice from the congealed, half-eaten pie, "but you're welcome to join me." He took a bite.

She patted her midsection and reminded him, "Etta's waffles."

He grunted. Enough said. "Free cholesterol test with every fill-up." He pulled off a second slice, grabbed a paper napkin and led her out of the kitchen and back to the roofed-in porch. "It's too nice to stay indoors. Your complexion'll be safe out here."

She sat on a wrought-iron chair whose ornate curlicues were softened by multiple layers of white enamel, while Noah settled himself on a matching cushioned chaise that let him stretch out his long legs. He knew precisely what he was doing to her, the bastard. He'd given her a taste of the interior, but just that. Kit was itching to explore. She just knew Jo wouldn't have been put off this easily. But then, Jo had her own methods. Which led Kit to the next order of business.

"You didn't answer my question," she charged.

He paused midbite, his expression asking her to jog his memory.

She wasn't about to go through the "lover" thing again. "Were Jo and Bryan sleeping together?"

"Sleeping?"

She itched to choke that impish twinkle out of his eyes. "Were they having sex, goddammit!" She shot a quick look out to the lawn, but apparently her outburst hadn't carried to Bryan's ears.

He shrugged. "Beats me."

All that for a *Beats me?* "So. Jo didn't return Bryan's affection. And we don't know if they were *lovers*," she said defiantly. "You wanna know what I figure, I figure it's a good bet she had a thing going with you."

There. She'd said it.

He looked downright amused, damn him. He swallowed his mouthful of pizza and said, "Why didn't you ask me when we first met? I know you were thinking it."

"I did ask you when we first met."

"You asked if I knew who she was seeing. That's not the same thing, is it?"

She leaned forward, a surge of blood pressure lending bite to her words. "I'm trying to find out the most basic things about my friend's life in this town, Noah, and you're sure as hell not making it any easier for me. So if you're through playing your little games, I could use a straight answer."

His amusement evaporated. "I don't date my patients, Kit."

"'Date'? What a quaint term for what we're talking about."

His gaze snapped to her face, and she was irrationally pleased to see a glimmer of respect in his eyes.

"And would you admit it if you had 'dated' Jo?" she persisted.

He took his time answering, and she could tell he was giving the question serious consideration. "It would depend who asked, and why. Since it's you who ask, and under these exceptional circumstances, I would have to say yes."

"Oh," was all she could think to say for long seconds. Then she added, "But lemme guess. She wanted to."

He stared at her a long moment, then tossed the pizza onto the table, his appetite apparently gone. Kit wondered if the Southern gentleman in him was hesitant to answer truthfully and besmirch a lady's reputation. "She wanted to, yes. But for the wrong reasons."

Her breath caught. How could he know Jo's reasons for getting close to him, unless . . .

This guy, he found out about the book. . . .

The door to the house swung open and Alice bulled through, carrying a sweaty-cold liter bottle of root beer and a tube of SPF 30 sunblock. She barely acknowledged them on her way outside. Kit and Noah watched Bryan's grateful acceptance of the soda as he drank straight from the bottle, and his grudging use of the cream after Alice's hectoring.

Kit returned her attention to the porch, with the idle thought that this patio furniture must have dated from Ray's tenure. Then it came to her.

"What's wrong?" Noah asked, watching her face.

"Nothing, really. It's just that I recall seeing this table and a couple of these chairs in one of those old snapshots Henry showed us this morning." She decided to get to the point. "Why didn't you tell me about Ray when I spoke to you yesterday?" Assuming Noah hadn't discovered Jo's real reason for moving to Pratte, he couldn't know the significance of his omission.

He watched Alice make her way back empty-handed, and thanked her as she trudged through the porch and back into the house. Finally he answered, "I asked you to go home, Kit, to leave this business alone, remember?"

"So you just decided I was better off not knowing about the parallel murder. Even after you'd agreed to help me!"

"Parallel?"

"An accurate term, I'd say. Henry said you agree Jo was the victim of a copycat killer."

"That would seem the only logical explanation."

She spent a few moments pondering this "logical" explanation. "Am I the only one who just doesn't get it?" she asked. "One of Grace Drummond's guests, some well-respected member of the community, suddenly takes a notion to duplicate the most notorious event in Pratte's history? After thirty-two years?"

Her gaze was drawn to Bryan, sitting on the tree stump drinking his root beer. What was it he'd said? People ignore what's right in front of their eyes. Was she still asking all the wrong questions?

"If that's the only *logical* explanation, maybe we should start looking for *il*logical ones," she said. At Noah's curious look she added, "Bryan said Jo was killed by the person who did the first murder."

He stiffened, his hazel eyes boring into hers. She'd struck a nerve. He slowly turned that cold gaze on the youth outside. "Bryan has his own agenda," he said.

No kidding. "Which is . . . ?"

"I wish I knew," he murmured, still studying the boy. "He's been nosing around a lot since he came to Pratte. I figured he needed to come to grips with his heritage."

His heritage. "Must be a mindblower to learn you're descended from a cold-blooded murderer. Maybe he thinks his grandfather was innocent."

Noah turned back to her. "In that case he's in for a rude shock. Ray Whittaker's guilt is an indisputable fact." His statement reflected fierce conviction.

"Maybe he just needs to find that out for himself."

The interior door swung open and Alice stuck her head out. "Noah, Carol La Rosa's on the line. She says her mother fell down some steps. You better talk to her."

"Excuse me," he said to Kit, before hurrying through the door.

She sat for a minute watching Bryan clearing brush from around the tree stump, with Max supervising. She wondered how long Noah would be occupied with this phone call, and stared at the door through which he'd disappeared.

Without letting herself reconsider, she rose and went into the house. As she slipped past the parlor, she heard Noah's voice through the open doorway to his office, patient but firm as he attempted to extract details from the agitated woman on the other end of the line. "Take a deep breath, Carol. Sit down. Is she bleeding at all?"

Silently Kit peered into a large living room, with the same stuffy, time-worn decor as the parlor. She doubted Noah actually used either room. Ditto for the formal dining room with its humongous, gleaming cherrywood table and...two, four, six, eight...twenty chairs!

Down a short corridor was a smaller room that appeared to be a library or study. Here he'd clearly made his own mark, decades-old wallpaper notwithstanding. The southern exposure admitted plenty of sunshine through large, latticed windows. Ceiling-high Scandinavian-style blond wood bookshelves occupied all wall space not claimed by windows or the door. In one corner was a cozy reading nook—armchair and cluttered lamp table.

Here's where Noah lived.

It was as if he'd carved out his own private little enclave within the hostile borders of another man's domain. She had no business being here. It was Ray's environment she wanted to study, she reminded herself as she tentatively stepped through the doorway. Not Noah's.

She walked the perimeter of the room. The contents of the bookshelves reflected a varied and voracious appetite for the written word: hardcover bestsellers, beat-up paperbacks, books on history and science. Plenty of medical tomes, naturally, along with stacks of AMA journals. A book on transcendental meditation caught her eye, and she pulled it out, remembering he'd tried to get Jo interested in TM. The pages were dog-eared, with stripes of yellow highlighting and notes scribbled in the margins. Malcolm wouldn't approve.

She tucked it back in place and ran her finger over its neighbors: books on Buddhist and Hindu teachings, including the *Bhagavad-Gita;* a study of the Cabala, Jewish mysticism; a book on Wicca, the ancient Celtic witchcraft religion. The next one stopped her in her tracks. *The Search for Bridey Murphy.* What was he doing with that! As a young girl, she'd been fascinated by this story of a woman's discovery of her past life through regressive hypnosis. Kit had outgrown her juvenile interest in the paranormal about the time she'd tossed out her training bra.

Her eyes wandered back over the books on philosophy and religion. On reflection, *Bridey Murphy* wasn't so out of place here. From her studies at Northwestern and her own readings, she knew that the concept of reincarnation enjoyed widespread acceptance in Eastern religions and in the ancient and obscure roots of Western religion. Just as it suffered nearly universal rejection by modern men of science. Men like Noah.

What was it he'd told Etta? She must have been a saint in a former life. *Good karma, he says I have.*

She scanned the book titles as she began to retrace her steps toward the door. A good deal of space was devoted to medical books, which didn't surprise her. A family practitioner must be something of a jack-of-all-trades. She saw volumes on a multitude of specialties and subspecialties. She'd seen still more in his office, probably those he consulted most frequently.

Poisons.

The word drew her eyes. She didn't consciously reach for the book, but found it in her hands nonetheless. She flipped through the pages; it was a scholarly directory of every known poison, including relative toxicity, sources and properties. She slid it back onto the shelf and pulled out the one next to it, a physician's guide to diagnosis and treatment of poisoning. Before returning it to the shelf, she riffled the pages, stopping where a slip of paper had been tucked into the pages as a bookmark.

"Neuromuscular Blocking Agents." That was the term Noah had used when discussing Jo's death. She scanned the pages. Pavulon...Tubarine...Norcuron. He'd mentioned Norcuron, she recalled, as a curare derivative used in medicine.

Well, he did say he'd done a little research into curare after Jo's death. Of course, there was no mention here of Zaparos Indians or blow darts. She glanced at his makeshift bookmark—a cash register receipt from the local five-and-dime. He'd spent $3.12 on January 31.

She slapped the book closed, shoved it back on the shelf and left the room, retracing her steps down the corridor.

January 31.

She stopped in her tracks. Five months ago. Either Noah had grabbed an old receipt just lying around or...

His interest in curare predated Jo's demise.

She returned to the study, pulled out the book again and flipped open to the bookmark. The date was January 31, sure enough, two years ago! This was a two-and-a-half-year-old receipt, for items purchased shortly after he'd moved to

Pratte. She checked the copyright page of the book—it was published four years ago.

Kit shoved it back on the bookshelf with trembling fingers and pulled out the other book on poisons. If Noah had barreled into the room just then, she'd never have heard him over the pounding of her heart. This one was published seven years ago. No bookmarks here, but a quick flip through the pages bore fruit. Yellow highlighting directed her attention to two sections: true curare, under poisonous plants, and curare derivatives like Norcuron, under medical poisons. Noah had marked various words and sentences dealing with such issues as toxicity, symptoms and reaction times. The rest of the book was untouched.

She returned it to the shelf and quickly looked around, to make sure she'd left everything as she'd found it, then quietly made her way back through the house. The door to Noah's office was closed, and her pulse raced anew as she realized he'd finished his phone call. She took a deep breath and nonchalantly walked out onto the porch.

He wasn't there, and automatically her eyes scanned the lawn. Bryan was nowhere in sight, but Noah was there by the tree stump, hefting the logs into a rough pile. He looked up as she approached, and smiled, but something in his eyes slowed her footsteps.

"The emergency get resolved?" she asked.

"There was no emergency. Carol overreacted. I spoke to her mom—·she said her foot slipped on the last step and she landed on her well-padded rump. No harm done. Where were you?"

"Bathroom."

"I assume you found the yellow one all right."

She hesitated. Every instinct screamed, *Trick question!* "Uh...I used the blue one." Where he'd told Alice to find the sunblock. There probably was no yellow bathroom!

"I hope the lack of running water in the blue bathroom didn't inconvenience you. We've had some plumbing problems there."

He looked at her expectantly, awaiting a response, the swine. Plumbing problems, huh? Right then his smile took on a very Ray-like quality. Just for a split second. Long enough to make her wonder if she was imagining the murderer's face everywhere she turned. When she got back to the boardinghouse, would Malcolm have freckles and pockmarks? Would Etta be sporting a red wig and a hypodermic?

She had no hope of outmaneuvering Noah in the what-color-is-my-bathroom game. "Where's Bryan?" she asked.

"In the barn—" he cocked his head toward an outbuilding at the rear of the property "—getting an ax to split up this wood."

She imagined Ray Whittaker's look-alike wielding an ax in one hand and a chain saw in the other.

"Did I say something funny?" he asked.

She bit back her smile. "I'm just getting a little giddy. Must be the sun." She started across the lawn, heading for her car—well, it was her car now—and Noah walked with her.

"Where to?" he asked.

"The Pratte Public Library. My chat with Henry showed me just how ignorant I am about what happened here thirty-two years ago."

He didn't say anything until they'd reached the car. "And here I thought you were interested in the last eleven months—Jo's time in Pratte."

She couldn't say, *Jo's time in Pratte had more to do with what happened thirty-two years ago than the past eleven months.* But then, could be he already knew that.

"If Jo's death was some sick reenactment of Anita David's murder, then it makes sense to look back thirty-two years," she said, retrieving her car keys from the pocket of her baggy pink jeans. "For one thing, maybe I can find out why the killer targeted Jo. Did she and Anita have anything in common, for instance."

Noah had the strangest look on his face. A little sad, perhaps. Or resigned. "Still looking for logical answers, Kit?"

She shrugged and opened the car door. "Can't help it." The alternative was to buy in to Bryan's enigmatic mental meanderings, and she wasn't that desperate. Yet.

She slid behind the steering wheel, and Noah leaned on the open doorframe. "How can you be so sure Jo was targeted? Maybe the killer's so twisted, he just needed a victim—a surrogate Anita—and she was . . . convenient."

"In the wrong place at the wrong time."

"Something like that."

"Ah, the triumph of absurdity over cold reason. You're beginning to sound like Bryan."

That seemed to amuse him. He closed the car door. "Good luck at the library, Kit."

Chapter Six

Kit stared into the dresser drawer for a full minute without touching anything. Her clothes were all there—blue jeans and a couple of tops, a nightgown and underwear. Just as she'd left them.

Or were they? Her nape prickled. Slowly she reached toward the drawer, and stopped herself, racking her brain. Something was different.

She lifted the neatly stacked T-shirts, and that's when it hit her. The neatness of the stack. As opposed to how she'd left these items, folded but askew when she'd quickly yanked out the clothes she was wearing. Kit wasn't a slob, but she wasn't exactly meticulous, either.

Whoever had gone through her things was giving her too much credit.

Kit's breathing quickened as the impact hit her. Someone had searched this room. Jo's frantic message replayed itself in her head.

Kit, someone broke into my room. They ransacked *it!*

Well, this wasn't exactly ransacking, and as far as she could tell, nothing had been taken, but . . .

Could she be mistaken? She did a slow-motion turn in place, peering at her surroundings, trying to ascertain whether anything else had been touched.

The closet door was slightly ajar. Had she left it like that? Maybe. Kit pulled open the door and looked at the skirt and blazer she'd hung in the closet after clearing out Jo's things. She raised her eyes to her battered old green vinyl suitcase lying on the closet shelf, the top edge just visible. She hadn't pushed it so far back, she was certain. She yanked it out and opened it, glanced at the empty interior, then dropped it. No way to tell if it had been tampered with.

It was nearly dinnertime, and Kit had just returned to the boardinghouse for the first time since breakfast. Plenty of time for someone to sneak in. She had a good idea what the person had been searching for, and it could fit almost anywhere. Such as . . .

She stalked to the bed and tossed back the bedspread at the edge of the mattress. Was it her imagination or was the bed skirt bunched in places—as if someone had knelt and shoved an arm between the mattress and box spring, groping for something? Like a three-and-a-half-inch computer disk.

Damn. Maybe she *was* losing her mind.

From downstairs came the sound of Etta's voice, welcoming Malcolm home from work.

Etta.

Of course. She allowed herself a tentative sigh of relief. Etta must have come in and straightened her clothing. Maybe that's the sort of thing boardinghouse landladies do, she reasoned. Tidy the dresser drawers. Straighten the closet shelves.

And Etta had a key. Not that the ineffectual little lock on the bedroom door would discourage a determined prowler. Ten seconds with a hairpin could open any door in the place, Kit knew.

She went down to the kitchen. Two other rooms had apparently been occupied over the weekend, but now, at midweek, only she and Malcolm remained. Over roast chicken, rice pilaf and spinach salad, she thanked Etta for tidying up her room. The landlady's look of bewilderment wasn't the response she'd been hoping for.

"But didn't you—" Kit started.

"My guests' rooms, I don't bother with." Etta gave a negligent wave of her fork. "You're on your own as far as that goes."

Kit didn't share her fears that her room had been searched. Etta didn't need any more stress, and what if Kit was mistaken? She shook a bottle of ranch dressing and decided to try a different tack. "Did you have any visitors today?" she asked both Etta and Malcolm.

"I was at work today, at Fine Food," Malcolm said, carving the chicken. "I didn't get home till five twenty-three."

Etta shrugged. "People always pop in. You know. Everyone knows where to find me on a day like this. Out back, I was. Working on my roses and mulching the veggies."

"Who came by? Anyone I might know?"

The landlady thought a moment. "Did you meet Henry's wife when you talked to him this morning?"

"Yeah, Bettina came in for a few minutes."

"Well, she called after lunch and said she wanted to see my peace roses—she's thinking of putting some in on her property."

Kit remembered the elaborate gardens at the Davids' home. "Does she care for her own flowers?"

"I never thought so, but maybe she wants to start. Or maybe she just wants to know what to tell the gardener to put in. Huh. Me, I couldn't afford a gardener, and even if I could, I wouldn't hire one. Making things grow keeps me young."

Kit became aware of the aroma of new-mown grass drifting through the screened windows. "But you don't do the heavy work, do you? Like mowing and trimming bushes?"

"A coronary, I don't need. That Carlisle boy comes once a week. Bryan. He does all that."

"Wednesday afternoons," Malcolm said.

So both Bettina David and the Bad Seed were here this afternoon. She took a deep breath, steeling herself. "Noah didn't happen to drop by, did he?"

"No. Why?"

Kit shrugged. "Just curious." She was relieved until it occurred to her that anyone who knew that Etta was out back gardening could have slipped into the house without her even knowing. She had to wonder if anyone in Pratte knew Jo had saved a computer disk of her book. Or, indeed, if anyone in Pratte even knew she was working on the book.

Not for the first time, she wished Jo had disclosed the location of the backup disk she'd referred to in her message. Kit didn't relish the prospect of scouring Etta's garage and basement for it, but at this point those were the only places she could think of. She'd checked with the local bank that afternoon—as well as those in neighboring towns—and sure enough, none of them had any record of a Joanne Merino renting a safe-deposit box.

Earlier she'd spent a couple of hours at the Pratte Public Library, researching the history of the Whittakers, and the Anita David murder in particular. Henry's account jibed with the public record. It was all there, in decades-old newspaper accounts: Anita's death, Ray's arrest and his death during a struggle with Henry. Kit realized Jo must have had copies of all those old newspaper articles, stolen along with her computer, the hard copy of her book in progress and the rest of her research notes.

After checking the banks, she'd gone to Wescott Community Hospital and talked with the pharmacist there, Nina Shore, about curare. Wescott used the derivative Norcuron, Nina told her. The usual procedure was to start a patient with an injection from a vial, followed by a regulated IV drip. A respirator is used, naturally, as curare paralyzes breathing.

When Kit questioned her about security, Nina assured her that access to all medications was strictly controlled. It simply wasn't possible for the general public—including the more homicidal elements—to walk in off the street and snatch their poison of choice.

She remembered the way Noah had put it. *It's not like your basic psychopath can just waltz in and borrow some.* Of course, Noah was a member of the medical staff at Wescott, Kit knew. She assumed that restricted access didn't apply to him.

Leaving the pharmacy, Kit passed a nurses' station. A young male R.N. was on the phone, discussing a patient's postoperative care, and referring to a folder open on the desk before him. As she passed, Kit noticed an open doorway behind the station, leading to a storage closet of some sort.

Even from a distance, she could see shelves lined with small boxes. She recognized the brand names of various common analgesics, along with other, less familiar drugs. Clearly this was where prescribed medications waited to be dispensed.

Her steps slowed as she approached the elevator. Distractedly she stabbed the Down button.

She knew precious little about hospital organization. Was there a medications closet on each patient floor, behind each nurses' station?

She searched her memory for what Noah and Nina had both told her about the medical use of curare. A respirator is needed. Where did they use respirators?

The elevator arrived and an orderly stepped out, pushing an empty wheelchair. "Excuse me," Kit said. "What floor is the Intensive Care Unit on?"

"Fourth."

She found herself taking the elevator up instead of down. On the fourth floor the ICU was easy to find. She entered the area through well-marked double doors, passing two R.N.'s on their way out, clearly leaving for the day. The changing of the guard.

The unit was quiet. She saw a few patients in the glass-enclosed rooms, with a nurse tending to one of them. Keeping out of sight, she observed the nurses' station. A middle-aged woman in white was at the desk, putting away her purse, scanning paperwork, getting settled in. She'd obviously just come on duty.

Kit watched for a couple of minutes, until the nurse left the desk and entered a patient's room.

The station was deserted for the moment, as the new shift made their rounds. How long it would be empty was anyone's guess.

Silently Kit approached the desk, her eyes on the backs of the two nurses as they monitored vital signs and saw to the gadgets and tubes and other accoutrements of the ICU. She slipped behind the desk, making a beeline for the open doorway to the same kind of medications closet she'd seen on the second-floor hall.

On the shelves were various drugs, same as downstairs. A rolling cart sat under the shelves, with a multitude of tiny plastic drawers, each labeled with a patient's name. A small refrigerator held more vials, she discovered. And she saw a locked box, presumably for narcotics.

A large plastic bin sat on a shelf. Kit peered inside and saw two IV bags, with labels that had apparently been generated in the hospital pharmacy. One was filled with a nitroglycerin solution.

Wrong deadly substance, Kit thought with a wry smile. She was looking for poison, not explosives. The other bag was lying label side down. Taped to it was a small drug vial, the kind doctors use to fill a syringe.

She hesitated for a fraction of a second, to peek out the doorway and make sure she was alone. She turned over the heavy bag and swallowed the gasp that rose in her throat.

Norcuron. There on the label, along with the name of the patient it was intended for. This bag contained one hundred milligrams in one hundred cc of saline solution. And here it was, just waiting to be picked up.

Just waiting for that basic psychopath to waltz in and borrow some.

She crept out of the closet and around the nurses' desk just in time to avoid another R.N. coming on duty. First Noah's office files, she reflected, then his home study, and now this. If she ever decided to give up teaching, she might make a passable prowler. Kit Roarke. Sneak thief.

Well, so much for security at Wescott Community. And so much for the question of how the killer could have gotten hold of curare. She'd just proven that one of the most potent poisons known to man was available to anyone with enough ingenuity—and motivation—to sneak around this hospital.

It was the motivation part that kept Kit awake at night. Why kill Joanne Merino, after all? Noah seemed to think she'd been the random victim of a copycat killer. If that was the case, the murderer might never be found. But if it wasn't random, then it must have had something to do with Jo's book. Jo had said she was afraid of the man she was seeing—once he'd found out about the book.

Her friend had spent eleven months turning over rocks in this town. What had she uncovered that was worth dying for?

"YOU SURE YOU DON'T HAVE something more pressing to do today?" Kit asked, opening the trunk of Noah's Cherokee and watching him toss in two bulging garbage bags.

All of Jo's clothing was in these bags—all except for whatever Jo had brought to the cleaners. Kit remembered the pink dry cleaning ticket she was carrying around in her purse. One of these days she'd get around to picking up the cleaning. She knew why she was putting it off. She wasn't ready to see her dead friend's clothes freshly cleaned and pressed, stuffed with tissue paper and shrouded in clear plastic bags. Just waiting for their owner to wear them.

"No problem, Kit. I told you, this is my day off." Noah shoved the last bag into the trunk and slammed the door shut. He crossed to the driver's door as Kit settled in the passenger seat. "And I told you I'd help you out while you were in town."

"Well, still, you didn't have to come with me today. But...I'm grateful. I wasn't looking forward to this."

As he pulled out of Etta's long driveway, he turned and met her gaze. *I know,* his eyes seemed to say. *I want to make it easier for you.*

"So," she said. "This is a school for disturbed children we're going to?"

"Emotionally disturbed, most of them. From troubled backgrounds. The Powell School does a lot of fundraising—like this rummage sale. That and a modest endowment from the founder are all that keep it afloat."

She watched his hands as he steered. They were well muscled, long fingered, tanned, with a dusting of blond hair on the backs. These hands had tossed those heavy birch logs as if they were kindling. But she also recalled peeking into his exam room and watching him give the booster shot to his young patient. As powerful as these hands were, they were capable of great tenderness, too, she knew.

But then, Noah Stewart himself was a man of contradictions. All Dixie charm one moment; downright forbidding the next. Warm and cold. Candid and secretive.

Good and evil.

Kit shuddered and chafed the gooseflesh from her arms. She wanted to deny the undercurrent she'd sensed within this man. The fleeting glimpse she'd caught of something... unholy. A secret shadow something—or some *thing*—as malevolent as an open wound. But it was there.

It all added up to one inescapable fact.

Noah Stewart, M.D., was not what he seemed.

Which was why she hadn't told him about her room being searched. If she told him that, she might as well tell him about Joanne being robbed the day she died. But perhaps he already knew that. Some man had stood in Etta's kitchen with Jo when she'd made that last call to Kit's answering machine—presumably the mystery man she'd been involved with. Kit wanted to believe Noah's denial that he was that man, but...

Something kept her from trusting him.

After a twenty-minute drive, they arrived at the Powell School. The director, Hannah Aaronson, gratefully accepted her donation to their rummage sale and showed them around the school, which was in the quiet lull between the end of the spring session and the beginning of the summer session. When Hannah discovered Kit was a teacher, she became animated, detailing their teaching philosophy and the progress they'd made with their emotionally needy students.

Kit was impressed with the Powell School. She couldn't help comparing it to the Harrington Academy, the private school where she'd taught for four years. Harrington had the costliest state-of-the-art teaching tools, from the latest politically correct textbooks and workbooks to Pentium computer systems with CD-ROM.

Powell had well-worn supplies and old secondhand equipment, but it was clear, as Kit gazed at the children's artwork and reports hanging on the walls, and listened to the dedicated director, that they received plenty of warmth and support from the staff. She couldn't say that was always true at Harrington, where the emphasis seemed to be split between attracting well-heeled families and maintaining the highest test scores and college admission rates.

Kit responded on a visceral level as Hannah told of some of the troubled children the school had worked with and helped. She thought of her own childhood, shared with a too-young mother incapable of fulfilling—or even recognizing—her child's physical and emotional needs. She thought of the rage and desperation that drove her to run away from that hell at age thirteen and move in with Joanne's family—a move her mother, Irene, never contested.

She felt her chest tighten, and her throat constrict. Remembering. Yes, she could have used a place like the Powell School.

"I'm not going to beat around the bush," Hannah said as she led them back to the parking lot. "I want you to teach my fifth graders this summer, Kit."

Kit skidded to a halt, gaping at the other woman. Noah laughed at her reaction. Apparently Hannah had spent the past forty minutes interviewing Kit for a job, with the interviewee none the wiser. She raised her palms as if to ward off the offer. "Hannah, I'm not—"

"I know. You're not in the market for a summer job, and I don't care. I need a teacher, and I've been in this business long enough to judge people pretty quickly. Though I'll tell you right off the bat, I can't pay much, not what you're used to."

Hannah smiled and gnawed her bottom lip as if searching for the right words. Kit felt as if the older woman were peering into her past. "This is right, Kit," she said softly. "A good match. Tell me I'm wrong."

"You're not wrong." Kit felt her face grow warm. She felt irrationally exposed. To Hannah—and to Noah. As if the needy child she once was were standing there in her stead. "You're right—it's a good match—but I'm leaving in a day or two. Going back to Chicago."

She turned to look at Noah, seeking confirmation of her statement. He wanted her to leave, after all. He'd said as much. Go home. Leave the investigation to the authorities.

She wasn't prepared for what she read in his expression. Something suspiciously close to... anticipation. His lively hazel eyes searched hers for an answer. Those thick, dark eyebrows rose fractionally. *Well?* they seemed to say. *Will you stay?*

"I..." She swallowed hard, and made herself look away. She faced Hannah. "I can't. I'm sorry." Chicago was where Kit belonged. It was where she'd made her life. Pratte belonged to Jo.

Hannah accepted defeat more or less graciously. "Well, think about it, Kit. If you change your mind, classes start on the twelfth. There'll be staff meetings the week before."

As they drove back toward town, Kit surreptitiously studied Noah. His expression, so open minutes before, was now shuttered, revealing nothing.

"Why did I get the feeling," she asked slowly, "that you wanted me to say yes to Hannah?"

He was silent a minute, his eyes on the road. At last he said, "I know you have to do what you came here for, Kit."

"But you want me to go home."

He took a long, slow breath, his expression never changing. "I did. Maybe I still do."

"You don't know?"

He gave a half laugh. "You'd be amazed at what I don't know."

Kit let that enigmatic statement hang there.

"How'd it go at the library?" he asked, breaking the silence.

She shrugged. "I went through the old newspapers and the town history. Maybe there's some way I can locate the police reports from thirty-two years ago."

"I thought you were looking for similarities between the victims."

"Well . . . I am." *I'm looking for whatever Jo found that got her killed.*

After a long pause Noah said, "I have copies of all those old police reports."

"*What?* What are you doing with—" She stopped abruptly, not at all sure she wanted to know the answer.

"And the old autopsy reports—from Anita and Ray. I've got all of it. It's sort of a . . . special interest, you might say. I live in the man's house, after all."

And you named your dog after his. How far did the similarities go?

"I also have a ton of Ray's old photo albums, business papers, personal correspondence . . . even his grammar school notebooks, for God's sake. His widow, Ruby, left it all in the attic when she moved."

"Why tell me?" she asked. "You know I'll just hound you till you let me look at it."

"You don't have to hound me. It's all yours. After all, Bryan's pawing through it. Why not you?"

She hesitated only a moment before asking, "And Jo? Did you let her 'paw through it'?" Kit knew without asking that her friend would have sniffed out Noah's cache of memorabilia in a heartbeat—and done whatever was necessary to get to it.

He took his eyes off the road for an instant, long enough to shoot her a crooked smile. "Now, what on earth would Jo want with a bunch of musty old papers? They have nothing to do with the *Pratte Citizen.* Jo wrote about things like park renovations and the annual town meeting. You know that."

He was teasing her! He knew all about that goddamn book!

This guy, he found out about the book. And... well, that's not good.

Kit licked her suddenly dry lips. "When did you find out?"

"When she got desperate." Noah turned off the highway onto a two-lane road leading into town. "She held out as long as she could." He chuckled. "It took her no time at all to figure out what kind of goodies were entombed in the Whittaker attic. I knew she wanted the stuff, I just didn't know why."

"And that's when she came on to you," Kit guessed.

His smile disappeared. "That's right."

"But you didn't take advantage because of your high moral and ethical standards." At the moment she didn't care how bitchy she sounded. Noah held all the cards, and she sensed he'd share only the information that suited his purpose. Whatever that was.

He stopped for a red light, and turned to look at her. She almost regretted her big mouth. This was the cold Noah.

"I told you before, Kit, I don't date my patients. And I don't really give a damn whether you believe me or not." He turned away from her, waiting for the light to change.

Despite his protests, Kit sensed that he did give a damn what she thought of him. "I can't say I'm surprised at her methods... knowing Jo like I did."

"She was..." He scowled, remembering the Jo they both knew. "I don't think she had such a healthy self-esteem."

"I guess it's safe to say that someone willing to barter her body for a peek at some old papers suffers from low self-esteem," Kit said. She'd never deluded herself about Jo's faults before, and she wasn't going to start now. Her friend had been a survivor, like Kit. They had just chosen different survival strategies.

At the green signal, Noah turned in the direction of his home, not Etta's. "When seduction didn't work," he said, "Jo tried honesty as a last resort. She told me about the book she was writing and swore me to secrecy. And I let her have full access to all that crap upstairs."

After a few moments of silence he added, "I was Jo's friend, Kit. Probably the only real friend she had here."

Kit couldn't speak around the sudden lump in her throat. The simple sincerity of Noah's words struck her like a hammer blow. She laid her hand over his on the steering wheel and let her touch say what her voice couldn't. Slowly he looked at her, his eyes dark and intense, exposing more of himself than she'd ever seen. At last she found her voice, harsh and unsteady as it was.

"Jo needed a friend, Noah. I'm glad she had you."

"THIS PLACE IS a gold mine."

Noah watched Kit thumb through an album of black-and-white snapshots, pictures of the Whittakers and their friends and relatives. She stood between him and the lone window in the hot, stuffy attic room where Ray's things were stored. She was wearing that long, gauzy oatmeal-colored dress again, same as earlier this week, when he'd found her plundering his office files. Only this time she was backlit by shafts of sunlight arrowing through the dingy windowpanes.

Remarkable thing, light, he mused, studying her. It can make the invisible visible—all those dust motes pirouetting around her like snowflakes, for example—and turn an otherwise opaque dress transparent. At the very same time.

Remarkable.

He commended Kit's practicality in eschewing a slip on this warm day. Such a sensible girl.

Reluctantly Noah crossed behind her to raise the window, knowing that if he stood there much longer trying to read the label on her panties, he'd only succeed in raising something else.

"Those boxes over there contain personal letters and business correspondence," he said, grunting with the effort of budging the old window. "The ones behind them are mostly souvenirs and such, Debbie's artwork, that sort of thing. And over there—" he turned and pointed to the cartons piled on the other side of the room "—are Ray's books. Most of these boxes are labeled. You'll find it's all pretty organized."

She gazed around, clearly awed by the sheer volume of material available to sift through. Noah's attic consisted of three huge rooms, and the largest was crammed with the Whittaker family's personal papers and memorabilia, just as he'd promised.

"Those police and medical reports are in my study," he added. "You can look at them later."

"It would take me...weeks to go through this stuff," she said, squatting to open a cardboard carton filled with boxes of photographic slides.

"Jo spent about seven months at it, actually." He looked around for the light box he'd lent her to view the slides.

Kit gaped up at him. "Seven *months?* Up here?"

"Two or three hours a day. She needed to be meticulous, don't forget. Her book demanded it. She set up at this desk." He indicated the beat-up old oak desk and chair near the window, flanked by a sixties-style floor lamp.

"You didn't let her take any of this out of here?"

"Only to use the copier in my office—she wanted copies of some stuff to take back to Etta's and study at her leisure."

Kit opened her mouth to say something, then snapped it shut again. *Go ahead,* he was tempted to tell her. *Say it.* All those photocopied pages, along with her laptop, disks and everything else pertaining to the book, are gone. Stolen the day of her murder. He knew the internal battle Kit was waging over whether to trust him with these details. She didn't know how much he already knew, and it had to be killing her.

Kit was smart. Too smart for comfort. If he let on that he knew about the theft, it would take her about a nanosecond to figure out how he knew. And to link him with Jo's murder, snapping the fragile thread of trust he sensed developing between them.

He cursed the insane impulse that had made him bring her up here. He should be trying to keep her in ignorance, dammit, not foster her trust. He propped a hip on the desk and watched her hold slides up to the window, peering intently at the tiny images.

What would happen to that trust when she found out he was responsible for Jo's death?

Kit turned to him, smiling broadly. "I'm going to be a real nuisance, Noah. Think you can stand to have me haunting your attic for a few days?"

"You told Hannah you'd be leaving in a day or two."

"I know, but that was before..." Her eyes swept her surroundings and she shrugged.

"I told you, Kit. My junk is your junk. Of course, you may have to share this space with Bryan on occasion—he's still poring over this stuff. But at least you won't have to sneak around anymore, or pretend you were looking for the john."

Her gaze snapped to his. Then she smiled crookedly. "So tell me. Is there running water in the blue bathroom, or what?"

"Not a drop. I wouldn't lie." He couldn't suppress a grin. "I hope you found something interesting for your trouble."

He could see her hesitation. She tucked the slide she'd been examining into its storage box, then looked at him directly and said, "I found you have an impressive assortment of books."

That gave him pause. *Ah. The books.*

"Do you believe in reincarnation?" she asked.

"Yes. Do you?"

"No. I figure it's wishful thinking." She replaced the box of slides in the cardboard carton and closed the top. "An attempt to rationalize away the finality of death."

"Haven't you ever had an unexplained memory? Some talent or knowledge, perhaps, that came out of nowhere?"

"Never. And I must admit the last person I'd expect to believe in that stuff is a doctor—a man of science."

"It's nothing that can't be explained scientifically, Kit. Think about it. What'll happen to your energy when your physical body dies?"

She frowned. "My energy?"

"Your life force. Personality. Your soul, if you will. That's what it is, in essence—an energy field. Where will it go?"

"Well, it'll...go somewhere else. Becomes another form of energy, I guess."

"Because..." he prompted.

"Because energy can't be created or destroyed."

"Right. It's indestructible. It can be transformed, as you said—changed into other types of power. But it never dissipates entirely."

She gave him a wry smile. "The man of science twisting the laws of physics to serve his own—"

"Wishful thinking?" He grinned, not expecting her to believe.

She crossed the room to stand in front of him. He was still half sitting on the edge of the desk, and they were practically eye-to-eye.

"So tell me, who was Dr. Stewart in his last life?" she asked.

She was so near, the fresh, sweet scent of her hair floated over him like a veil. If she took one more step, she'd be bracketed by his thighs. He stared at her brown eyes and watched the ring of golden highlights change shape as her pupils widened.

The urge to touch her was overpowering. Noah struggled to control his response to her, to govern his breathing and heart rate in the way that had become second nature over the years—his techniques for keeping Ray from emerging.

Kit was studying his face, her expression attesting to the conflicting emotions warring within her, her warm brown gaze like a caress on his brow, his jaw and chin. His eyes.

He'd learned long ago how to maintain his hard-won control when he was with a woman. It was a skill he'd mastered, of necessity, along with all the others. He knew how to look, touch, want... how to drive his need into a woman's body and spill it in a blinding torrent of physical release...

While never once relinquishing his precious control.

So why couldn't he simply look into this woman's eyes without feeling the untamed part of him rattling its cage?

"Who were you, Noah?" she whispered, leaning forward with a teasing smile, her warm breath tickling his lips and stealing inside him to turn the key of the cage.

The thing he'd been in his last life wrapped its arms around her and crushed her to him, seizing her head in his long fingers to tilt it back. In the instant before he brought his mouth down on hers, he saw her passion-darkened eyes widen in fear.

But it was too late.

Noah no longer knew where he ended and Ray began. He didn't know who was ravaging Kit's mouth with this brutal kiss, and he didn't care. Because he wanted her as badly as Ray did.

She was stiff in his arms at first, from shock and fright. A whimper escaped against his mouth. She'd seen something in his eyes in that last instant, he knew. Something that had nothing to do with Noah Stewart, M.D.

The feel of her lips crushed under his sent a shudder of raw desire ripping through him. He invaded her mouth with his tongue, appeasing his primal need to be inside her.

Kit felt Noah's strong, demanding tongue slide deep within, exploring the sensitive interior of her mouth... touching, stroking, tasting. Claiming her. The primitive rhythm he set urged her to surrender, to abandon her fears.

For a few short moments she relaxed against him, drunk with the savage eroticism of his kiss. For a few short moments she gave in to his unrestrained hunger and her own repressed desire. She clung to his shirt, savored his fierce possession, felt its heat shoot to the deepest, neediest part of her.

Stunned by her own response, she tried to break away, pushing on his chest, arching her back. Still perched on the edge of the desk, he clamped his legs around her hips, pinning her between his thighs. She felt his strong fingers tighten against her scalp as he intensified the kiss. Finally, in one violent motion, she managed to twist her head to the side.

"Noah!" she gasped. "Please...you're scaring me." She despised the pleading tone in her voice. She'd never felt so helpless. "Don't do this. Please," she whispered.

He became very still, and she turned to look at his face, inches from hers. What she saw rocked her to her toes. She'd never met this man.

Good Lord. Wasn't that what Henry David had said? *His face, his eyes . . . It was like I'd never met this guy.*

He was breathing hard, his expression at once fierce and clouded with uncertainty, as if some battle were being waged within him. Beneath her palms pressed to his chest she felt the violent hammering of his heart. Tentatively, as if he were trying to make sense of his own actions, he looked down at his arms, at his legs, still imprisoning her. His hold began to relax. He stared at her disheveled hair and slowly untangled his long fingers from it.

He swallowed hard and turned to stare out the window, his features tight with shame and regret. He was trembling. When he spoke at last, his voice was hoarse. "I'd never let him hurt you, Kit."

His arms fell away and she stepped back, still reeling from their kiss, her body still throbbing with need.

Without looking at her, he pushed off the desk and crossed the room in three seconds, pounding down the stairs. She heard his footsteps on the next flight down and then the sound of the front door slamming.

She stood at the window and watched him jump into the Cherokee, his movements stiff and agitated. Max leapt around the Jeep, barking excitedly.

"Sorry, boy," Kit murmured from two flights up. "Your master's not in the mood for company."

Tires spitting gravel, the car disappeared down the tree-lined driveway.

Chapter Seven

I got closer last night.

Noah mentally corrected himself. *Ray* got closer. For the sake of his sanity, he had to distance himself. But how do you distance yourself from something that's as much a part of you as your eye color?

He watched the townsfolk milling around, eating, chatting...enjoying the annual Fourth of July barbecue on the grounds of the town church. It was after eight o'clock, but there was still nearly an hour of light left. He found an isolated spot in the shade of an ash tree and scanned the swelling crowd, awaiting Kit's arrival.

Last night had been rough. He'd slammed awake at 3:00 a.m., gasping and drenched in sweat. Ray's memories always came to him in the dead middle of the night, scrolling through his mind like some demented horror film he was helpless to turn off. It was as if Ray were purposely forcing the memories on him...the brutal details of the thing he'd done three decades ago.

And each time the dream came, he saw more of it than he had the time before—the next installment, so to speak. The scenario had been advancing at an alarming rate since he'd met Kit. He used to have the dream three or four times a year, but in the eight days since her arrival, he'd had it every goddamn night.

And each time Ray got closer to killing Anita.

Noah refused to witness that. Refused to feel himself doing that terrible thing to Anita David. Through sheer force of will he'd managed to shake himself awake each time, before the final act could play itself out. Unfortunately, the thing inside him seemed just as determined to see it through to the gruesome end. It amounted to a bizarre clash of wills between his own subconscious and the restless soul of a man who'd gone to his grave before Noah was born.

And the restless soul appeared to be winning.

This battle had been joined two and a half years ago when, as a young family practitioner, he'd given in to wanderlust and followed his gut instinct—for that's what it seemed at the time—to a tiny hamlet tucked into the Green Mountains. Pratte, Vermont. Ensconced in Ray Whittaker's town—in his very home—he'd finally put the pieces together and figured out what had been happening inside him his entire adult life. Or, more accurately, *who* had been happening inside him.

Last night, in his dream, Ray had gotten the now familiar call from a desperate Anita David. *Ray! Help me! I can't breathe—I can't—* And he'd bolted out of the house with his medical bag, driven fast through the dark thinking about the fight on TV and his anticipated winnings from Henry. He squealed to a stop in front of the Davids' house and jumped out of the Fairlane practically before the engine was off.

That part got to Noah. Imagine being in that much of a hurry to do what he'd come to do.

He found her in the kitchen, hunched on the floor near the wall phone. She wore a powder blue nightgown and one satin bedroom slipper. The other lay near her, obviously kicked off in her agitation, her struggle to breathe. The kitchen was spotless, the way she always kept it, except for the remains of a sandwich on the table. Anita always had a late-night snack before retiring. That was one of the things he'd learned about her during their short affair.

Ray was used to these emergencies, when Anita, severely asthmatic as a result of allergies, would need a shot of epinephrine to help her breathe. But he'd never seen her like this. Her face, neck and chest were scarlet and her lips were swollen with a violent histaminic reaction that he knew affected her bronchia, as well. The tubes in her lungs were constricted and filling with mucus. The only sound in the room was her strangled wheezing.

She looked up at him. Any relief she felt at his arrival was eclipsed by the raw terror he saw in her eyes. "Ray..." she croaked.

Anita disgusted Ray. She had almost from the moment he'd finally succeeded in wearing down her defenses. It had been an exhilarating game, seducing his best friend's wife, exhilarating and dangerous, knowing Henry's temper. Ray had used every trick in the book on the tediously faithful Anita. None of his usual smooth lines had worked, so finally he'd let slip how her husband had been messing around behind her back. After that, it had simply been a matter of playing the understanding friend, giving her a shoulder to cry on and a sympathetic ear. The rest had been laughably easy.

Now she stared up at him with those panic-stricken eyes, and he could barely restrain the urge to slap her. He was bored with her, bored with her emotional neediness and the physical debility that yanked him out of his warm bed in the middle of the night. With a voluptuous body like hers, she should have been dynamite between the sheets, but the woman was too preoccupied with sobbing out her undying love to give him the kind of tumble he'd expected from her.

It was time to end it.

Ray opened his bag as he knelt by her. *I'm here, honey, Don't worry. It'll all be over soon....*

Noah had awoken then, his ears filled with the harsh sound of his ragged breathing, his eyes filled with the familiar sight of his own bedroom in the semidark. Ray's bedroom.

He couldn't do anything about the recurring dream, but at least he'd mastered his mind and body enough to keep Ray from emerging while he was awake. The only exceptions were times of extreme physical weakness—exhaustion or illness, usually.

Thirty-six-hour shifts as a medical resident had been a challenge, but nothing compared to the fatigue he'd experienced the day after Andy Kramer's bike accident, when he'd finally dragged his weary butt out of Wescott Community and a marathon session at the boy's bedside. That was the day of Grace Drummond's garden party. The day Jo died.

He didn't remember anything about the party until Henry found him in the solarium. All alone, drinking the treasurer's Glenfiddich. And he needed to remember.

He had to know.

Noah wished Paul Kerrigan hadn't gone on that damn sabbatical. Here he was, at last willing to be hypnotized—to get his answers—and his old friend was climbing mountains in Alaska or some such thing. *Come home, Paul. I need you.*

He continually scanned the crowd for that gorgeous, unruly mop of chestnut corkscrew curls. He smiled, recalling the disdain with which he'd first regarded Kit's "city" look. His smile faded as he thought of untangling his fingers from those silky strands four days ago, in his attic. He'd frightened her then, and he'd frightened himself.

The experience forced him to add one more element to the list of things that made him lose control of the evil thing inside him. Exhaustion. Illness.

Kit.

He'd returned to the house after an aimless two-hour drive to find her gone, and in her place a note stating that she'd called a taxi to take her back to Etta's, and would return the next morning. He was irrationally relieved, when he knew he should have wished that he'd scared her off for good.

In the days since, she'd been a constant fixture in his home, sifting through Ray's belongings several hours each day. Noah had taken pains to be hospitable and accommodating.

And to keep her at arm's length.

They shared meals, long walks with Max and longer gab sessions on the back porch over iced tea and Oreos. When he could spare a few minutes from his practice, he'd occasionally join her in the attic to help sort through all the junk she seemed intent on studying.

Too quickly he'd come to look forward to her easy companionship—feeling let down when she departed each day—and that disturbed him. He had to remind himself of the reason he'd never permitted himself a serious relationship with a woman.

And God knew he couldn't let himself get close to this, of all women. For her safety as well as his own.

As for Kit, she'd acted skittish when she'd returned the next morning—all right, downright jumpy—but had soon seemed at ease in his company once more.

And never once had either of them broached the subject of The Kiss.

Suddenly he spied her through the crowd. He noticed the outrageous hair first, of course, and when she tossed it back, a welcome surprise: a pair of elegant, beautifully shaped shoulders, bared by the wide drawstring neckline of her short-sleeved white peasant top. Completing the outfit was a red denim miniskirt and sexy strappy sandals. This was the most stirring view he'd encountered since moving to

Vermont, and he took a few long moments just to soak it in before making his way toward her.

She was talking to Henry and Bettina David, and all three held cans of soda. Long tables had been set up at the perimeter of the churchyard, laden with food and drink. The sharp smell of smoldering charcoal tinged with lighter fluid wafted on the breeze.

"...no choice but to work two jobs while I was in college," Henry was saying. "Took me two extra years to get my journalism degree, but at least I didn't owe one red cent when I was through. Not like the kids nowadays. Sponging off the government." He nodded to Noah in greeting.

Noah said, "Hey, don't look at me. I just sponged off my folks to get through school. Though I must admit your Horatio Algeresque youth is damn inspirational, Henry." Of course, he doubted any of Alger's stories ever involved marrying into *beaucoup* bucks. He flashed Kit a warm smile, which she returned in kind.

Henry turned to Kit. "I bet you were in the same boat, huh, Kit? Working your way through school?"

"I waitressed nights and weekends," she confirmed. "But I couldn't have scraped by without student aid and a small scholarship. I never thought of it as sponging, though." Her smile was polite but pointed.

Bettina sidled playfully up to Noah. "You and I have to stick together in this, Noah. We're being made out as hopelessly decadent because our families could afford to send us to college."

"Bettina likes to come off as the pampered little princess," Henry said with a proud smile, "but I want you to know she worked part-time while she was in college. Until we were married, that is."

She laughed lightly. "And I would never have lifted a finger if my father hadn't forced me to take the job. To build my character, he said."

"Where did you work, Bettina?" Kit asked.

"Conti-Meeker, one of my father's companies."

"How's that fine retriever of yours, Noah?" Henry asked, snaking an arm around his wife's shoulder and tugging her close.

"Max?" Noah took a moment to mentally switch gears. "Oh, he's hale and hearty, as always. Except he spends too much time in the woods, picking up six-legged houseguests."

"I warned you about that when you moved here with him," Henry said. "Told you to build a dog run, if you recall."

Noah noticed Kit's hand slow as she raised her drink to her lips. Her pensive eyes locked with his. He'd known it was too much to hope she wouldn't notice Henry's offhand remark—her mind was too quick.

"You had Max *before* you moved to Pratte?" she asked bluntly.

"That's right," he admitted. As opposed to what he'd let her believe last week—that he'd acquired him after moving here, and named him for Ray's dog. Max had been Max long before he ever heard the name Ray Whittaker.

Noah felt a firm hand on his shoulder. He turned to see Grace, paper cup in hand, bureaucratic smile firmly installed. She was tall, silver haired and, as always, impeccably attired, in a summery linen dress.

"Noah! Get yourself a beer. There's a keg of Mary Rafferty's homebrew over by Socrates."

Kit's brow knit. "Socrates?"

Henry explained. "That big old weeping willow near the entrance to the graveyard."

"Mary made a nice dark ale this time," Grace said. To Noah she added, "It's not Glenfiddich, Doc, but I think you should be able to choke down a pint or two."

Kit seemed to tense, ever so slightly, and shot a strange look at Noah. His scalp prickled. He tried to find some significance in what Grace had said, but for the life of him, he couldn't figure it out.

Oblivious, Grace eyed Henry's soda can. "Diet Coke? What's *wrong* with you two? Get yourself a beer, Henry!" Apparently the women were exempt from the treasurer's pugnacious brand of hospitality.

A muscle ticked in Henry's cheek. If Noah could have thought up a socially acceptable way to tell Grace to can it, he would have.

Bettina spoke up, her voice flat. "Henry's fine, Grace."

Grace half smiled at Bettina, as if itching to get into a verbal tussle with her. These two had had more than a few go-arounds, Noah knew.

Henry blustered, "I'll try some later, Gracie." He lifted his cup in a mock salute. "After this."

Noah wondered how long Henry would persist in trying to keep up appearances. In years past, he'd tossed back more than his share of anything alcoholic. The town M.D. was probably the only person aside from Bettina who knew why he'd stopped drinking. Henry was just too damn macho to make it public.

"I don't think you've met Kit Roarke, Grace," Noah said. "Joanne Merino's friend from Chicago."

Grace extended her hand, and Kit shook it. "I heard you were here, Kit." She smiled. "No one escapes small-town gossip. I hope everyone's been cooperative in helping you . . . settle Joanne's affairs."

"Everyone's been super."

"It was a terrible tragedy," Grace said. "I called Mr. Merino and told him how sorry we all are."

Henry and Bettina assumed suitably sober expressions. Noah didn't miss the silent exchange between them: *Time to move on.* Now they'd be looking for an opening to do just that.

Kit's pleasant expression seemed forced. "I'm sure Sal appreciated that."

Grace said, "I probably won't see you again, so—"

"Oh, I'll be in Pratte all summer," Kit interrupted, and seemed gratified at the universally wide-eyed response her announcement drew. She met Noah's gaze, and he knew his reaction was the one she cared about. He wondered if her sharp eyes detected the niggling sense of foreboding behind his smile.

Henry and Bettina's unshuttered gazes collided like runaway locomotives. For a split second only, before both directed their eyes to their drinks—just long enough for Noah to wonder if he'd imagined their distress.

Kit explained, "I've been offered a teaching position at the Powell School—just for the summer—and I've decided to accept it."

"Well." Grace quickly regained her magisterial aplomb. "I hope you enjoy your stay here, Kit."

Bettina made a show of waving to someone across the lawn. "Oh, there's Larry, Henry's new reporter. Let's go make him welcome, shall we, love?"

When they'd gone, Kit asked the treasurer, "Did you know Jo at all, Grace?"

"Oh, sure, I saw her all the time at the health club."

Noah could tell by Kit's little smile that she was recalling his assessment of Valkyrie's high-powered clientele. She looked the treasurer in the eye. "Did you like Jo?"

Grace hesitated briefly, her intelligent green eyes studying the younger woman. Something she saw made her admit, "Your friend and I didn't see eye-to-eye on many issues, Kit."

"Issues related to her articles in the *Citizen?*"

"That, yes, and . . . other things."

"Such as . . . ?" Kit persisted.

Grace stared at her a moment, then looked at Noah, and back at Kit. "I suppose you know the real reason Joanne came to Pratte."

Kit seemed to come to attention at that.

"And you're surprised I do." Grace smiled. She looked pointedly at Noah.

"It's okay," Kit murmured. "He knows." He knew she must be wondering if there was anyone in Pratte who *didn't* know about Jo's book.

The treasurer was blunt. "I didn't like her coming here to stir up trouble and make the whole mess public again, and I told her so."

"When was this?" Kit asked.

Grace sighed. "The day before she died. At Valkyrie. I felt I had to try and stop her. You don't know what a sensationalist book like that could do to Pratte."

"The tourist industry," Kit said.

The treasurer bristled. "Yes. Some of us have worked damn hard to make this town thrive, and I'm not ashamed of the tourism dollars we attract. Could you imagine what would happen if that book got published and those trashy TV magazines and movie-of-the-week people latched on to it?"

Noah said, "I suppose that would depend on what kind of spin she gave the story. You know, if she came to any interesting conclusions."

Grace closed her eyes briefly, as if seeking divine guidance. "Good God, that case was laid to rest thirty-two years ago! If it weren't for this true-crime craze nowadays, Joanne wouldn't have bothered with us at all. She was trying to squeeze some excitement out of a nonstory. No one's ever disputed Ray Whittaker's guilt. He even confessed!"

"Only to Henry David," Kit said.

That was true enough. Henry claimed Ray confessed to him, but Ray had officially protested his innocence, even when they exhumed Anita and found curare in her body. Noah could see how an outsider, looking back three decades later, might call into question Ray's guilt. Only Noah knew for certain what the rest of the townsfolk correctly surmised: Ray Whittaker was guilty as sin.

"What does that mean, 'only to Henry'?" Grace demanded incredulously. "Who did Jo think murdered Anita David?"

"I don't know," Kit admitted.

"No one knows," Noah reminded the treasurer. "You heard what happened, Grace. Jo's computer was stolen, and all her notes." Grace nodded.

"Honestly, I don't think she was trying to rewrite history," Kit protested. "She knew Ray killed Anita. I think she just wanted to tell their story. She wanted to get all the facts straight and write a great true-crime book. That's all. She wasn't looking to jazz up the story by pinning the murder on someone else."

Somehow, to Noah, Kit's words lacked conviction. He didn't think she believed them. He could have told her she had good reason not to.

Grace sighed. "Well, I suppose we'll never know exactly what she had in mind, will we?" Her voice softened, and she laid a hand on Kit's forearm. "Don't get me wrong, Kit. I'm horrified at what happened to Joanne. But I'd be lying if I said I'm sorry that book will never get written."

Kit nodded tightly and moved out of the treasurer's light grasp. "How did you find out about it, anyway?"

"Oh. Well, Joanne was very clever at quietly digging up the dirt she was looking for. But you've got to understand, I'm like the hub of the wheel in this town," Grace said proudly. "I know everything that goes on. I caught wind of how she was snooping around, and I confronted her."

"At the health club," Kit said.

"Right. After the locker room had emptied out. Or at least, I thought it had," Grace said, shooting an icy glare across the lawn to where the Davids chatted with a young couple. "As I left, I noticed Bettina David's reflection in a mirror. She was behind a row of lockers, eavesdropping the whole time! I just prayed she wouldn't blab it around town about the book, but it would seem she's kept her mouth shut. Thank God."

If Bettina knew about the book, then chances were Henry did, too, though he certainly hadn't let on when Noah and Kit had spoken to him at his home. Suddenly Kit looked pale and weary, the way she had the first day he met her—as if she'd rather be anywhere else than here, listening to Pratte's town treasurer yammer about how fortunate it was that her dead friend's labor of love would never see the light of day. He took her arm.

"Sorry, Grace, but I promised this lady a tour of the cemetery. Before it gets dark." He shuddered dramatically, and Kit managed a weak smile. In the western sky a froth of clouds hovered over the distant hills, their undersides stained shrimp pink by the setting sun.

"Well, don't go too far," Grace warned over her shoulder as she sauntered off. "You don't want to miss the fireworks."

He escorted Kit across the lawn and past Socrates, the venerable old weeping willow, where a crowd congregated around the beer keg placed under its drooping branches. They continued past the squat stone fence into the cemetery. Timeworn stone markers cast long shadows on the well-tended grounds.

"Thanks," she murmured.

Her quiet melancholy moved him, laying waste to his defenses, and he did what he'd avoided doing the past three days. He touched her, sliding his arm around her back, as if his warmth and strength could somehow seep into her and help ease her burdens. "Tact isn't Grace's strong suit," he said.

"I noticed. I think Henry did, too."

"Henry?"

"When she was badgering him about having a beer. It reminded me of the other day, when we were at his place and he made such a show of offering me Cuervo for breakfast."

"While he had a diet soda."

"Right. What is he, a recovering alcoholic?"

"Good guess, but you're off. Actually, I don't think alcoholism would bother Henry—at least, it wouldn't clash with his macho self-image."

When he didn't elaborate she said, "So? What's wrong with him?"

"Kit, the man's my patient. I can't discuss—"

"Diabetic?" she asked, her sharp eyes gauging his reaction before he could hide it. "I thought so." She nodded. "I figured it was one or the other."

He smirked and squeezed her shoulder affectionately, her skin like sun-warmed silk under his fingers. "So much for doctor-patient confidences."

They strolled in silence for a while, idly examining the older headstones, those from the last century and earlier. Only one other person had had the same idea. Malcolm stood smack-dab on a grave, staring at the headstone, smoking and jangling the change in his pocket. He looked up as they approached.

"Hello, Kathleen. Hello, Dr. Stewart." If he was surprised to see them strolling together so intimately, he gave no indication.

Noah looked down at Kit and mouthed *Kathleen?* She answered with a don't-ask smile. Malcolm gestured with his cigarette toward the stone he'd been studying. Noah watched Kit's eyes widen as she read the name engraved there.

Malcolm said, "Dr. Whittaker was thirty-six years, eleven months and thirty days old when he died."

A long moment later Kit and Noah said, "Uh-huh" in unison.

"If he'd hung on one more day, he would have been thirty-seven." Malcolm shook his head and took a drag on his cigarette, staring intently at the marker, as if, by doing so, he could change the dates engraved there three decades earlier.

Noah couldn't help observing, "But then Ray would've died on his birthday." For whatever that was worth. "You really should try to stop smoking, Malcolm."

Malcolm tapped his ash onto the grave at his feet. "Mr. David and Joanne used to meet here." He pointed to a tall monument near the perimeter of the cemetery. "Right there, actually. After dark."

Noah and Kit exchanged slack-jawed stares. Malcolm didn't seem to notice; to him, his announcement obviously qualified as idle conversation.

Malcolm continued, "I like it here. I come here a lot. Even in the winter. Sometimes other people are here, and they don't notice me."

Noah asked, "When was the last time you saw Henry and Jo here, Malcolm?"

He didn't hesitate. "Twelve-fourteen a.m., May thirtieth. The moon was full, and I saw them clearly."

Noah felt a shiver race through Kit as she glanced at the darkening sky, and he smiled, holding her tighter. She slipped her arm around his waist at last and absently stroked his side through his thin black T-shirt. He suppressed a moan of contentment, wondering if she instinctively knew how sensitive the skin was right there, over his ribs.

Kit beat him to the leading question. "Joanne and Henry saw each other every day at work, Malcolm. Why would they meet here at night?"

"Mr. David was her boyfriend, but she didn't want anyone to know, because he's married to someone else." He dropped his cigarette butt and ground it out on Ray's grave.

Noah had suspected Jo might've been involved with Henry, but he'd never known for sure. He still didn't. This was Malcolm's version of reality, after all. "Were they, um, hugging or kissing?"

"No."

He exchanged a knowing look with Kit. "Well, then," he said gently, "you really shouldn't jump to conclusions, you know. It isn't fair."

Malcolm stared fixedly at him. "I'm sorry."

"That's all right, Malcolm," Noah said with a reassuring smile. "What *were* they doing?"

"They were having sexual intercourse."

Claws gouged Noah's side where Kit's fingers had been. He flinched, sucking in a breath. "Oh," he managed to say, while gently disengaging her death grip. "Uh-huh. I see."

Malcolm said goodbye and strolled toward the stone fence.

"I will never get used to that guy," Noah said.

"Good thing they weren't kissing or hugging, huh?" Kit smirked.

"Well, that answers your question about who Jo was seeing."

She sighed and walked a little away from him, staring off toward Jo and Henry's trysting place. "It answers part of the question, anyway. If you knew Joanne."

Part of the question? "You think she was gettin' it from more than one guy?"

She turned then, her eyes sparkling. " 'Gettin' it'? Why, what a vulgar term for a nice Southern gentleman like you."

"I'd say sexual intercourse in a boneyard at the witching hour qualifies as 'gettin' it.' "

She conceded the point with a tip of her head and looked toward the east, where the deep blue sky had given way to charcoal. Noah warbled an eerie *Ow-oo-oo-oo-oo* to make her smile. She did, but it was a sad smile, and then she came back to him and lifted her hand to his cheek. Her fingers felt cool and soft, and her thumb absently stroked his beard stubble. Her eyes were dark as ink in the twilight. Wide and solemn. They penetrated his, as if she could see his every secret. As if she could see Ray.

"You were the one with her that day," she said, so softly it was nearly a whisper. "When she called my answering machine that last time from Etta's kitchen."

Noah's breath snagged, and he let it out slowly, never breaking eye contact. She'd figured that part out. But how? "Kit—"

Her thumb brushed his lips, willing him to silence, and he closed his eyes. To keep her out. For her own sake or his, at this point he couldn't say. Still he leaned into the caress, ever so slightly. Her hand smelled like her. He parted his lips and gently closed them over the pad of her thumb.

And Ray shook the bars of his cage and threatened to bring down the ceiling.

He forced himself to look at her. "Kit, listen to—"

"I believed you when you told me it wasn't you, Noah. I believed you." Her voice was a tear-choked whisper. An accusation. "She was so scared." She stared at him as if she'd never seen him before. "What did you do to her?"

Dear God, I wish I knew.

He stood mute, and she reached up to his shoulders and tried to shake him. *"Answer me, dammit! What did you do to her?"*

Noah seized her wrists, and she tried to wrench out of his grasp. She fought him wildly, her hair whipping her face and his. He forced her arms behind her back and tripped her legs out from under her, holding her tight as he hauled her down to the cool grass. There he sat, shackling her slim wrists behind her with one hand and pressing her head against his chest with the other. He trapped her legs under his bent knee.

She bucked and twisted, sobbing uncontrollably. Her soft breasts were crushed against his chest, and he could clearly feel her shuddering breaths and the fierce tattoo of her heartbeat.

"Don't fight me, Kit. Don't fight me," he rasped. But she did, with a savagery born, he knew, of her grief and confusion. He kissed her hair and stroked it. Whispered her name over and over.

Ray reached a long arm through the bars of his cage and slid his fingers into the mahogany strands. And Noah pulled him back. Through sheer force of will he held back the thing inside him, trembling with the effort. Her struggles lured Ray out, as if the beast could smell her fear and helplessness.

It seemed like forever until Kit finally ran out of fight and sagged against him, exhausted. He released her wrists and drew her arms in front of her. Tenderly he stroked her disheveled hair off her damp face and tipped her chin up in the fading half-light. Her eyes were closed, and as he pressed a kiss to each soft eyelid, she trembled. He licked her salty tears from his lips.

He cradled her like a child, rocking her gently. "Kit...I hurt for you. God, I hurt for you, darlin'."

Her whisper was so quiet he had to put his ear close to her mouth to make out the words. She clutched his shirt. "She was so scared, Noah. And I couldn't do anything for her. I was too late to do anything for her."

And he understood that her pain came from a sense of her own failure. As did his own. He opened his mouth to utter some banal platitude, then closed it again. How could he reassure her when his own guilt gnawed away at him from the inside?

Instead he said, "I know she was scared, Kit." Too vividly he recalled the way Jo had pretended to laugh off the ransacking of her room, with the bravado she'd spent her short lifetime honing on the rough streets of Chicago. "Jo knew someone was trying to stop her from publishing that book."

She shifted in his embrace, fitting herself more closely against him, and said, "I wish I knew what she'd dug up—what she came to believe about Anita's murder." He rested his chin on her hair and stroked her back. "The thing is," she added, "destroying her work would only slow her down, at best. She'd just start over and redo it all."

He didn't respond. He didn't have to. They both knew that the only way to stop Jo's book was to stop Jo. As obsessive as she'd been about the project, nothing but death would keep her from completing it.

Kit slid her hands over his chest and clung to him; it was the gesture of a lover seeking support. But her next words belied the tender gesture. "You were the one she was afraid of, Noah. She was seeing some guy, she said. Someone 'unsuitable.' Someone who found out about her book. Who knew her schedule and when she'd be out of the house."

Noah knew that in Kit's eyes he fit the description all too well.

She clung tighter to him. " 'We'll pick up a bottle of Glenfiddich after,' she said. She called you 'hon.' That was you she was talking to, wasn't it?"

"Yes," he said quietly.

"You didn't want to share the booze with her. I played the damn tape so many times, I know it by heart. 'Be that way,' she said. Remember? 'I'll just sneak some of yours.' "

Noah let out his breath in a long sigh. He looked to the west, where a thin ribbon of violet still glowed over the hills. "It was her ulcer. Scotch doesn't mix with an ulcer. And she called everyone 'hon.' You must know that." He looked down and tipped her face up again, studying her expression in the semidark. "Would I have been worried about her ulcer if I'd been planning to kill her?" he asked.

She was silent for too long. "Did you kill her, Noah?"

He couldn't tell her he didn't know. He couldn't tell her Ray Whittaker might have killed her, using Noah as a weapon. He looked at Ray's granite headstone a few feet away. Everyone thought the bastard was history, that he couldn't hurt anyone anymore.

When he didn't answer, she said, her voice shaky, "She was afraid of you, but you finessed her somehow. Sometime before she made that last call to my machine. You sweet-talked her, got her to believe she had nothing to fear from you. Convinced her to go to Grace's garden party with you."

"You got it wrong, Kit. She was afraid, but not of me. Never of me." But she should have been. "It was someone else, I don't know who." He looked toward the monument Malcolm had pointed out. "Maybe Henry. He knew about the book, too, assuming Bettina told him."

He looked back down at Kit. "I had no intention of going to that damn party myself—I'd been at the hospital nearly two days straight, and I was wiped out. I tried to talk Jo out of going. I knew she might be in danger there, in a crowd like that. But she was insistent. She wouldn't hide from the bastard, whoever he was."

"That sounds like Jo."

"So I went with her. As her protector. I promised..." It still hurt more than he could bear. But he forced himself to say, "I promised I wouldn't let anything happen to her."

He felt Kit pull in a long breath and let it slowly out. She still clung to him like a lover.

He added, "They tell me I was hanging out alone in the solarium, but I don't recall that. I don't recall much of anything about the party till they brought me to her."

He wondered what she thought his motive was for murdering Jo. Insane jealousy over her involvement with Henry? He decided against asking her. If Ray had indeed used Noah to destroy Jo, he wasn't sure anything so mundane as a motive would have entered into it.

After what seemed an eternity, Kit said, "Jo told me something else, you know. While you were out of the room getting her sunglasses." She met his eyes, studying him intently. "You think the book is gone, that it no longer exists."

"What are you saying?"

"Jo told me she saved the book on a disk." Before he could ask, she added, "She hid it somewhere, and I can't find it."

He watched the breeze ruffle her hair over her bare shoulders, and held her closer. "You wouldn't tell me that if you thought I was the one who broke into her room."

She relaxed against him and slid her arms around his waist. He felt her warm breath through his T-shirt. "I don't know what to think anymore. I just wanted you to know that. About the book." Again he felt her heartbeat next to his, drumming too hard, and knew there was more.

"My room was searched," she said.

"My God," Noah whispered, instinctively tightening his hold on her.

"And my car," she added.

"When?"

"My room, last week. The day I went to the library."

He remembered. The day she talked with Bryan while he took apart Noah's dead birch tree.

"And my car just last night. In the middle of the night, apparently. The trunk was forced open and one of the windows was broken."

"Someone's looking for the disk," he said.

"It would seem so."

"Kit, why didn't you tell me sooner? About your room?"

"I didn't trust you," she said bluntly.

"And you still don't, so why tell me now?"

She shivered, and he heard her answer as clearly as if she'd spoken. *Because I'm alone, and I'm scared.* He wanted to swear a promise to her. *I'll keep you safe, Kit. I won't let you down.* But he knew it was a lie, and the words died in his throat. He'd failed before. He could promise her nothing but pain.

Instead he said, "You shouldn't stay here, Kit. In Pratte. You could be in danger."

She stiffened in his arms. "You think I'm going to run away from this with my tail between my legs?"

A humorless laugh escaped him and he shook his head. "God save me from feisty Chicago street brats."

Noah knew he wasn't the one who'd torn apart Jo's room and searched through Kit's things. If these acts were connected to Jo's murder, then that pointed to Noah's innocence. Someone else might have killed her. The spark of hope that thought gave him was swiftly doused by fear for Kit's safety. He had to convince her to go back to Chicago. He wasn't lying when he told her she was in danger. If not from Jo's killer, then certainly from the evil thing inside him. The thing only she could cause him to lose control of.

He ran his hand over the chilled skin of her forearm. It was almost fully dark now, a moonless night, and the temperature had dropped.

"We should get back," she whispered. He followed her gaze toward the churchyard, and could just make out the glimmer of lights through the trees, and the muted sounds of partying.

She was frightened of him, he knew. And with good reason, though if she ever guessed the full extent of the danger he posed, she'd run screaming from him. While Ray Whittaker's mortal remains lay moldering beneath the grass they sat upon, the corrupt energy that was the essence of the man himself lived on, reborn in Noah Stewart.

Do you believe in reincarnation? she'd asked him. She'd called it wishful thinking. He wouldn't wish this brand of hell on anyone.

He brushed her hair back from her ear and lowered his mouth to whisper, "Be afraid of me, Kit. Don't let me close." But even as he said it, he drew his hand slowly up her side, over the soft fabric of her loose peasant blouse. His thumb sought the underswell of her breast. There was no bra, nothing between his hand and her warmth but a thin layer of cotton.

Her breath caught and her hands slid to his shoulders, shooting a dart of longing low in his body. His long fingers followed his thumb, lifting her soft flesh, stroking her.

Her voice wavered, and he knew she was engaged in an internal battle. As was he. "Noah—"

He silenced her protest, if that's what it was, with his own lips. With all his strength he fought the part of him that wasn't really a part of *him,* but of another man. A conscienceless man who'd coerced and used women. A man who'd killed. Noah had never permitted Ray to influence his lovemaking, and he'd be damned if he'd let him have Kit.

She didn't push him away, but she didn't cling to him, either. He knew he had to break it off soon. He could fight Ray only so far when he was with this woman. She was like a drug that went to the heart of his resolve, undermining his hard-won control. He knew he was playing a dangerous game, tempting himself—tempting *him.* But, God help him, he'd never felt anything like this. The rightness of it. Of Kit in his arms... in his heart. He'd be selfish for a few more moments, then he'd stop.

He brushed his mouth across hers, urging her to open to him. When she didn't, he nibbled her lower lip, gently at first, then not so gently. She gasped, and he took advantage, touching the tip of her tongue with his. She shuddered and went perfectly still for an instant, her eyes wide open, as if she stood poised on the brink of an abyss. In one motion he rose to his knees and grasped her bottom, fitting her against his hips and his throbbing need... pushing her over the edge.

Her arms wound around his neck and she arched into him. He kissed her with a mindless intensity that only made his raw need flare hotter. At last he tore his mouth from hers, panting. Her white blouse glowed like a beacon in the dark, rising and falling with her agitated breathing. He bent her back over his arm and lowered his mouth, unerringly latching on to the hardened tip of her breast through the supple cloth.

Her sharp cry pierced the night and she clung to him, digging her nails into his forearms. Her cries turned soft, rhythmic, as he suckled her with mounting urgency, his answering groan of hunger closer to a growl. He captured the tight bud between his teeth and kneaded it with his tongue, coaxing a strangled whimper from her.

At last he lowered her to the cool, prickly grass. In the dark he could just make out her expression, softly yielding. She reached for him. It was too much to fight. With impatient, trembling fingers he yanked open the drawstring at her neckline and pulled the fabric down below her breasts. The meager light turned her body into an enticing landscape of luminous swells delineated by deep shadow.

With reverence his fingertips grazed the warm satin of her breast. He heard the breath hiss through her teeth, saw her eyes close and her head tip back. Her short skirt had ridden up, high on her thighs. Helpless to stop himself, Noah slid his other hand up her inner thigh and watched it disappear under her skirt. He brushed the backs of his knuckles over the soft feminine mound shielded only by her thin panties.

A moan caught in her throat and she shivered, clutching handfuls of grass. Her hips rose and her legs gently parted.

And Ray slammed into his consciousness with a force he'd never felt before. Noah jerked back. Shuddering violently, he fought to drag the thing back inside of him, deep inside, where it could do no harm. But he'd let down his guard, and the thing had gained strength. It was laughing at him.

Noah knew what Ray would do to her. Use her. Hurt her. Maybe worse.

I won't let you have her, you son of a bitch.

His heart hammering painfully under his ribs, he tried to back off from Kit, but Ray held him fast. The thing reached under her skirt and closed its hand over her, groping roughly.

Kit gasped and her eyes flew open. They widened in alarm when she saw his face, and she started to scoot backward, out of his reach. But Ray was faster. He pounced, digging his fingers into her thigh and her shoulder, forcing her back down.

He took in his surroundings with a quick glance, and chuckled. His eyes lingered on the nearby headstone. It was too dark to read, but he knew where he was. Ray grinned down into Kit's terrified face.

"Home, sweet home."

Chapter Eight

"Noah..." Kit tried to raise her voice above a tremulous whisper. "You're hurting me."

He loomed over her, his fingers biting into her leg and shoulder. He had that look on his face she remembered from that time in his attic when he'd first kissed her. When he'd said, *I'd never let him hurt you, Kit.* This isn't Noah, her mind whispered, though the absurd thought brought little comfort.

Automatically she tried to push him off her, but it was a fruitless exercise, his sinewy arms as immovable as steel posts.

He looked her over, slowly, his eyes lingering on her bare breasts. "Nice." His leering assessment made her feel dirty, where moments before she'd felt only fierce desire, and the sweet anticipation of becoming one with this enigmatic man. Her need for him had overwhelmed her fear and confusion.

But now the fear was back, amplified a thousandfold.

Still gripping her shoulder, he laid his other hand between her breasts. Her heart fluttered against his warm palm like a wounded bird. This tangible evidence of her terror seemed to amuse him and he grinned, his teeth gleaming in the dark like a feral animal's. He spoke with exaggerated patience, as if to a naughty child. "You should've listened to him, Kit. He told you to be afraid."

The Southern drawl was gone, his intonation as Vermont as they come. She swallowed hard, staring at the planes and shadows of Noah's face in the starlight.

She'd read about multiple personality disorder, seen those movies about people with split personalities. It was the only explanation she could think of. Her throat felt dry as dust. "What's your name?" she asked.

His eyes narrowed. He brought his face close to hers, scrutinizing her with chilling detachment, their breath mingling. He wrapped his long fingers around her jaw and tipped her face this way and that, the better to study her eyes.

"No... you don't get it. Not really," he said at last.

She willed the quaver from her voice. "I want to get up now. The ground is cold." She groped for the drawstrings of her blouse.

With lightning speed he captured her arms and pinned them above her head with one hand. He shoved the other hand under her skirt and started yanking at her panties. She tried to scream, but couldn't force a sound out past a throat constricted with terror.

Her rational mind kicked in long enough to register the fact that he had no weapon except his body... and she had no one to rely on but herself. Letting reflex take over, she tucked her leg and shot her foot into his chest with every bit of strength she possessed. Her heel connected like a baseball bat, complete with a satisfying crack. He released her with a grunt and fell back, astonishment plain on his face— a face that, in that instant, looked a little more like the Noah she knew.

But by the time she'd rolled to her feet and backed away a few yards, the stranger had returned, his expression a mixture of fury and admiration as he slowly stood, a hand to his chest. Kit contemplated fleeing, but knew she didn't have a prayer of outrunning him. Already she felt as if she'd sprinted around Lake Michigan.

His low chuckle seemed to echo off the shadowed monuments surrounding them. Never taking his eyes off her, he slipped a hand under his T-shirt and palpated his injury. "I'll be damned. Not one but *two* cracked ribs," he said, wincing. "What a nice surprise for Noah!" His New England accent made her flesh crawl, so incongruous was it with the Noah she knew.

He eyed her warily, as if trying to decide how much pain and suffering she was worth. Finally, with a hint of resignation, he said, "You're gonna give Noah a message for me, Kit. He's a stubborn, strong-willed bastard. I try to show him, but he won't let me."

He closed his eyes briefly and pressed on his ribs, every breath clearly painful. "I can't talk to him. You can. Tell him—" His head shot around as a shrill noise pierced the night. With a thunderous boom, a shower of fireworks burst in the sky, followed by a gleeful roar from the crowd gathered in the churchyard. As if he'd been kicked again, he suddenly doubled over, nearly losing his balance as the air whooshed from his lungs.

In the next instant his head snapped up, his gaze piercing her. The stranger was gone. It was Noah staring at her in the flickering light of the fireworks blossoming overhead amid a barrage of whistles and explosions. He frowned and glanced down at his chest, then gingerly felt his ribs.

He looked up at her, clearly disoriented. "Did you do this?" A Georgia drawl.

Kit could only nod.

After a moment he nodded, too, as if bestowing approval on her desperate act of self-defense. She saw his face tighten with more than pain as his anguished gaze raked her from head to foot. He started toward her. "Kit, did he hurt—"

"*Don't!*" She took a step back, only then recalling her state of undress. Quickly she pulled her drawstrings closed and tied them with hands that trembled uncontrollably. "Don't touch me," she hissed.

Noah stopped. Briefly he closed his eyes, his chest heaving with emotion. He shook his head, his hair glinting silver in the erratic light of the fireworks. "I don't remember what happened," he said. "I never do. Whenever he's... loose."

I don't recall much of anything about the party till they brought me to her. She had the sudden vivid image of Noah jabbing a curare-filled hypodermic into her best friend. Whether he was indeed the victim of multiple personality disorder or just your garden-variety psychopath, Kit had to face the fact that Noah Stewart, M.D., was a very dangerous man.

As she watched him struggle with his pain and emotional torment, she squelched the ridiculous urge to comfort him. She concentrated instead on the soreness in her thigh, her shoulder, her wrists. She'd have bruises everywhere that animal had touched her. *This* animal, she reminded herself. Noah.

"Stay away from me," she said tightly. "Just stay the hell away from me from now on. You got that?"

"Kit." His eyes beseeched her. "Let me explain it to y—"

"*No!* I'm not interested in your explanations." *Save them for the police,* she wanted to say. At least now she knew where to direct her investigative energy. Starting tomorrow, she'd find out who Noah Stewart really was. "You go first," she said, nodding toward the churchyard. She wasn't about to turn her back on him if she could help it.

He stared at her a long moment, his expression unreadable, then turned and slowly made his way toward the stone fence. Kit waited till the darkness had claimed him. Even then she didn't follow him, but stood chafing the gooseflesh from her arms and staring at the spot where she'd last seen him. Only when the fireworks display culminated in an earsplitting finale that turned night to day did she will her feet to move.

THE PAPERS WERE SPREAD out on the floral bedspread, fax transmittals of newspaper articles and police and hospital records. Kit sat cross-legged in the middle of it all, having just reread it for the third time.

Sal Merino had come through for her. At her request, he'd asked his buddy Jimmy Stark—a P.I. who'd been a detective with the Chicago police department until his retirement last year—to look into Noah's background. She knew he'd grown up in Roswell, Georgia, attended Columbia University in Manhattan as an undergraduate and returned to his home state for med school at Emory.

She also knew that after his residency, he'd somehow ended up in Pratte, Vermont. During one of their long, lazy chats on his back porch, she'd asked him about that, and he'd given some throwaway answer about having traveled around till he found the spot that just kinda felt right.

Kit had spent the better part of the day in faculty meetings at the Powell School, whose fax number she'd given to Jimmy along with a request to warn her before faxing anything so she'd be the only one to see it. According to Jimmy, Noah's youth in Roswell had been uneventful—no hint of incipient criminal behavior. During high school he played football and practiced with his rock band, the Puny Earthlings. Her stomach had done a little flip when she'd learned he'd almost died as a result of some kind of diving accident when he was sixteen. He'd never mentioned it.

The real excitement came a few years later. She reread the first headline, from the New York *Daily News*. Brooklyn Man Stabbed To Death. Columbia senior Noah Stewart had been arrested in the homicide of Rick Anders, an unemployed electrician and the father of a fourteen-month-old girl. The stabbing occurred at the apartment of Anders's ex-wife, Tiffany. A note from Jimmy explained that immediately after the killing, Tiffany Anders disappeared with her little girl. Less than a month later a grand jury determined that Noah had acted in self-defense; thus the case had never gone to trial.

He'd killed a man. It was there in black and white. Kit didn't know how much faith to put in the grand jury's finding. Maybe Noah's upper-middle-class family had hired some whiz-bang lawyer to influence the district attorney to withhold evidence from the grand jury. Maybe Tiffany Anders, the only witness, had been "persuaded" to flee so she couldn't testify against him. So many maybes.

Maybe Noah had acted in self-defense.

A part of her wanted to believe it—the part that had spent those few delicious days getting close to Noah. The gentle, funny, sexy Noah. But when she thought about her last encounter with him four days earlier—the soul-numbing horror of having him turn on her like that—she had no trouble believing he'd gotten away with murder eleven years ago. She thought of the victim's baby daughter, fatherless now because of Noah, and felt sick.

She'd called Tom Jordon as soon as she'd digested what Jimmy had sent her. Pratte's police chief, it turned out, already knew about Noah's "troubles" in New York; Doc had told him about the incident himself during the interrogations following Jo's murder. A tussle over some woman, Tom had called it. These things happen, especially in the Big Apple. Thank goodness the mess got cleared up without a trial. And what the hell was Kit doing prying into the citizens' private lives?

She'd opted not to tell Jordon about the strange case of Dr. Stewart and Mr. Hyde in the town cemetery on the Fourth. She could just hear what he'd have to say to that. *You went in there with him willingly? Stayed after dark? Started fooling around and things got a little rough for your taste? Hey, can't arrest a guy for trying, right?*

A sound had hovered at the edges of her awareness for the past twenty minutes, only now registering. A power tool of some sort. She rose and went to the window, to see a familiar head of dark copper hair tied back in a ponytail. The Bad Seed had on a shirt today. If an undershirt with the sleeves ripped off qualified as a shirt. From the second floor she could just make out the hawk quivering on his right biceps as he applied the electric hedge trimmers to Etta's boxwoods.

She shoved the faxes into a drawer and went downstairs. Bryan was just finishing up as she came out the back door.

"I thought you only came here Wednesdays," she said.

"For the lawns, yeah, but Etta needed her hedges done. Where've you been?" he asked.

"Right upstairs." But she knew what he meant. He gave her a look that said he knew she knew. She'd seen Bryan at Noah's off and on for several days while poring over Ray's things in the attic, but naturally she hadn't been back there since before the Fourth, four days earlier.

Four days in which she'd kept busy preparing for her students...and making subtle inquiries around town regarding Dr. Stewart. These had proved less than fruitful. Pratte had been doctorless for four long years before he came along, and the townspeople offered nothing but praise for their savior, Saint Noah.

"You guys have a fight?" Bryan asked, joining her at the redwood picnic set, where she sat on a bench. He set down the hedge trimmer and perched on the edge of the table.

"I guess you could say that."

"Yeah, I figured. He's wound up pretty tight. Even old Max is keeping his distance." He unknotted the green bandanna at his throat and wiped his sweaty face.

She knew Bryan spent a good deal of time at Noah's, sifting through his grandfather's possessions when he wasn't getting the neglected grounds in shape. She worried about the boy's safety. If Noah was as agitated as he'd said, it might not take much to unleash his violent side.

"Does he have a temper?" she asked.

"No way. I've never seen him, like, whacked out, if that's what you mean. Always calm, the doc, no matter what."

"Till now."

He grinned. "Yeah. I've known the guy for over a year, and I've never seen anyone get under his skin like this." He reached over and twisted a strand of her hair around his finger. Kit didn't know whether to be amused or insulted by this pup's cocksure posturing. Ah, the arrogance of youth. "I knew it right away," he said. "It's the hair. You're a wild lady, Kit. Noah doesn't know what to do with you."

Part of him knows what to do with me, she thought, recalling that heart-stopping moment when she was sure the good doctor was going to rape her right there on Grandpa Whittaker's grave.

"Was Joanne a wild lady?" she asked.

His eyes glowed with a sudden intensity. "You gonna ask me next if I knew what to do with her?"

She sighed. "Help me out, Bryan. I'm not very good at dancing around stuff like this."

"I wanted Jo to move in with me."

"In your rented room?"

"No, not that pit. I thought her and me would, like, get an apartment, you know? Our own place."

"She didn't want to?"

"She laughed at me." His jaw worked and he looked away, but not before Kit saw the sudden frost in his gaze.

"Because of the age difference?"

He turned that icy look on her. "*Age* difference? Ask the old man she was getting it on with about age difference. You think that old geezer could keep up with her?"

"Did you keep up with her, Bryan?"

"Yeah." That youthful arrogance was back, with a vengeance. "You wanna know the truth, I was the best she ever had. That's what she told me. The best."

So she was right. Jo was "gettin' it" from two guys.

It came to her unbidden then, more a physical sensation than a memory: the heat of Noah's mouth, of his ravening tongue, searing her through her blouse....

Maybe three guys.

"Jo used to meet Henry in the cemetery," she said, intentionally goading him to gauge his reaction. "Did you know that?"

His face twisted in mingled pain and hatred. "No," he said quietly. "I didn't know that."

"But you knew she was seeing him."

"I guessed it, and she didn't even try to deny it. Like it was nothing. Like it was *her* business who she chose to—" He broke off, obviously trying to compose himself. His arms were ropy with tensed muscle, as if he were poised to spring off the edge of the table at any moment. "I told her Henry was just using her." A mirthless bark of laughter then. "But what the hell. She was using *him,* right? Me, too, it turns out."

"What do you mean?"

"It was all about that damn book of hers. Right from the beginning. Jo didn't give a damn about me—or Henry. It was research. She turned herself into a whore just to get the information she needed."

"About your grandfather."

"Yeah. I found out by accident. A few weeks ago. Slipped into her room one day when I was here mowing. I'd swiped one of Etta's fancy roses and I figured I'd leave it on her bed and she'd come in later and it'd be, like, a nice surprise, you know?"

"You picked the lock on Jo's door?" Kit knew she wouldn't have left it open.

He shrugged. "What can I tell you? I'm a man of many talents."

"And you saw what she was working on," Kit guessed.

"I saw, like, her notes, and some copies of articles and stuff. I figured it out pretty quick." His voice broke. "I loved her. And all along she was just using me."

"That was what you meant by betrayal," she said. "That's what you two argued about right before Jo died." Not jealousy, as she'd first assumed.

"That's right. Jo betrayed me." His tone was suddenly calm.

Jo had been afraid of a man she was seeing—a man who'd found out about her book in progress. And then stole it. Two men now fit that description. No, three, she reminded herself.

Suddenly Kit felt more than grief and guilt over Jo. She felt anger at the friend she'd loved since infancy. The friend who'd taken a no-holds-barred attitude toward her work— her "research." The friend who'd played fast and loose with the lives of others . . . and her own safety. It didn't have to happen. She didn't have to die like that.

Bryan continued, "Jo didn't tell me about the book herself 'cause she knew I wouldn't want her writing that crap about my grandfather. Bringing up the past, all those old lies. She was no better than the rest of them. Just out to make a buck, and to hell with the truth."

She already knew he had his own personal version of the Whittaker-David affair. *I'm not gonna say anything else till I have the proof. Then I'll show everyone.* "I want to know the truth, Bryan." When he just stared sullenly, she said, "I want you to tell me what really happened." *What* you *think happened,* she silently added.

After a moment he said, "Think about it. Why would my grandfather kill Anita David?"

"They said it was because he was having an affair with her, and she threatened to blow the wh—"

"He was having an affair with half the women in Pratte! Why kill Anita?"

"Henry said she'd threatened to report Ray to the medical board. He'd get in trouble for abusing his practice that way...seducing all those patients."

"Aha. *Henry* said." His tone was that of a professor guiding his pupil through deductive reasoning.

"You think Henry David killed his wife." Kit forced her expression to remain neutral. "Bryan, she died when your grandfather gave her a shot of—"

"Don't you get it? His good pal *planted* the curare in Grandpa's vial of epinephrine. Before he went out of town. Henry planned it all out. He knew Anita got these asthma attacks all the time. He was gonna make her next one her last one. And at the same time pay back Ray for getting it on with her, by framing him."

Kit was about to ask why when she remembered something else Bryan had said during their first meeting. "And you hold Bettina responsible."

"No, I hold Henry responsible for what he did, but she's the reason he did it." Bryan absently twisted the bandanna and yanked it taut a few times, as if testing its strength.

"He wanted to be free to marry her . . . for her money?" she said.

Bryan cocked his finger like a gun and touched it to the tip of Kit's nose. "Give the girl a gold star."

"And Ray's confession to Henry . . ." she prompted.

"Totally bogus. Grandpa always said he was innocent." He looped the twisted bandanna around his sweaty neck and loosely tied it. "I figure he must've known it was Henry that did it. So Henry makes up, like, this story that Grandpa confessed, and gets him arrested."

"And then Grandpa comes after Henry when he's out on bail."

Bryan's expression was too cool, too reasonable. "Wouldn't you?"

She bit back her automatic denial, hesitating.

"Yeah," he said, watching her. "You would."

"'Cause I'm a wild woman?"

A slow smile tilted up the corners of his mouth. "You and Grandpa would've gotten along."

"The way you talk, I could almost believe you knew him."

"I feel like I've known him all my life—like he's a part of me. In here." He tapped the sweat-dampened spot in the center of his chest.

She took in his copper hair, his Ray-like features. Just how closely did the grandson take after the grandfather? She didn't believe his theory about Henry. It was too pat, and all the evidence thirty-two years ago pointed straight to Ray.

She said, "You told me Jo was killed by the same person who killed Anita."

"Henry knew about me and Jo. It made him crazy." Bryan grinned wickedly.

"Crazy enough to commit murder?"

"Nah. It was the book. I figure he thought Jo was gonna spill the beans about him in her book."

"Tell the world he killed his first wife," she clarified. He nodded. "But you said you thought she was just gonna publish the same old lies about your grandfather."

"That's what *I* think, but I don't really know, 'cause the stuff I saw, her notes and stuff, it didn't say. And she wouldn't tell me."

Kit thought about Bryan's passionate convictions, about his love-hate relationship with Joanne and his bitterness over her involvement with Henry. Was he capable of violence? And not the losing-it-in-a-moment-of-blind-rage kind, either, but the cold-blooded, meticulously thought-out kind. Joanne's murder was, after all, premeditated. Presumably someone went to a bit of trouble to snare curare and a hypodermic. And the timing! You couldn't do much better than a garden party crammed with a hundred or more potential suspects.

"We may never know what conclusion she came to," she said.

"Not unless her backup disk turns up."

Kit looked at him sharply.

"What?" he asked. "You didn't know she backed it up?"

"Well, *I* knew, but..."

Again that loose-jointed shrug. Kit wondered if Ray had shrugged like that. "Jo was too careful not to. I mean, she was, like, out of control in some ways—" his eyes glowed appreciatively "—but with her work, you know, she'd never take a chance like that. She had to have a disk stashed somewhere."

Bryan knew Jo better than Kit had imagined. Did he also know—firsthand—that the disk wasn't in Jo's room or her car? "Well, I tore apart Etta's basement and her attic and crawl spaces during the last few days," she said. "I was going to search the garage today."

"I'll help you. I've finished with Noah's attic, and it's not there."

Kit's mouth dropped open. "*That's* why you spent all that time up there? Looking for Jo's disk?"

"That and anything I could find about Anita's murder."

"And you came up empty on both counts."

"So far. Come on. Let's do the garage while we still have light."

Together they began exploring Etta's garage, a barn actually, complete with a hayloft—sans hay. To Kit's chagrin, there was even a basement of sorts under the floor where, Bryan informed her, booze had been hidden by rumrunners during Prohibition. It now held the remains of Etta's late husband's wood shop. Decades worth of furniture and equipment was stored on all three levels—it could take days to pick through everything.

"Let's start upstairs," Bryan said, and Kit was relieved he hadn't suggested they split up and work on different rooms. She wanted to keep an eye on him. A flat three-and-a-half-inch computer disk could easily fit in his back jeans pocket.

She could only assume his plans for the disk depended on its contents. If Bryan was right and Jo's book toed the party line by agreeing that Ray was guilty, chances were he'd want to destroy the disk; if, however, it pointed the finger at Henry, Bryan could use these findings to bolster his own pet theory. Now she wished she hadn't mentioned a search of the garage. She couldn't very well keep him from joining her, and what would she do if he found the disk and refused to hand it over?

"Oh, wow," he said in awestruck tones. "Check it out."

She turned to see him wielding an enormous rusty scythe that would have done the Grim Reaper proud. This boy was a magnet for hair-raising implements of annihilation. It was a gift of sorts, she supposed.

"Too cool," he decreed, replacing the thing on the wall.

They threw themselves into the task and worked steadily for two hours. When Malcolm called up to the loft's open window urging Kit to come in to dinner, she declined, saying she'd grab a bite later. Now that she was up to her eyebrows in dust and cobwebs, she was loath to abandon the project, and even more disinclined to leave Bryan out here on his own.

She was glad she'd changed into jeans and a loose, cropped T-shirt after work. This was one grimy job. "My hair's making me crazy," she said, lifting the heavy mass off her damp neck. She sat on the floor in a crowded corner near the window, methodically emptying a plastic milk crate filled with old tools.

"Here." Bryan crossed the room, wiping his hands on his shirt. He squatted in back of her and began gathering the long, curly strands. His callused fingers brushed her neck and ears in the process, and suddenly Kit pictured this eighteen-year-old in an intimate embrace with Joanne, a full decade older. She wondered where they'd made love—in his "pit" of a rented room, probably.

He finger-combed her hair into a high ponytail, then fished a white bandanna out of his pocket and tied it in place. She reached back to check his handiwork. "Thanks." Giving her shoulder a couple of avuncular pats, he rose and went back to the chest of drawers he'd been pulling apart.

She tossed the tools back into the milk crate and rose, shoving the crate into a corner with her foot. At the same moment her other foot flew out from under her as she slipped on a screwdriver she'd left lying out. She landed hard on the crate, howling in pain as something gouged deep into the outside of her thigh. A stream of curses flowed as readily as the blood that soaked through her torn jeans.

Bryan was at her side in a flash. "Take it easy." He eased her onto the floor. "Lemme see."

Reflexively she gripped her thigh directly above the wound as he gingerly peeled back the torn, blood-soaked material to examine the gash. The air whistled through his teeth and he grimaced. "This is one big bad boo-boo." He glanced at the crate. "There's your culprit." The claw of a hammer—rusty, of course—poked through the side of the crate near its top edge.

He pulled the bandanna out of her hair and quickly folded it into a square and applied it to the wound. "Hold this," he instructed. "Come on. Let's get you to Noah's." He helped her rise.

She'd taken two halting steps, pressing the makeshift dressing to her thigh, before his words sank in. *"No!"*

He rolled his eyes. "Yeah, right."

She dug in her heels. "I'm serious, Bryan. Look at me." She waited till he turned to her, exasperation adding decades to his youthful features. "I am not going to Noah's. That's final. Take me to Wescott."

"No way. The hospital's, like, forty minutes away. You need that thing taken care of pronto."

She started hobbling toward the stairs. "I'll drive myself."

"You're gonna *drive* with your right leg like that?" Now it was his turn to swear. "Okay, okay. Get in the pickup. I'll take you to Wescott."

Sitting next to Bryan in his pickup truck, she kept the bandanna pressed to her wound, which was throbbing like hell. It still bled freely, saturating the bandanna and the torn cloth of her jeans. She squeezed her eyes shut and started counting the minutes, praying Wescott Community had miraculously moved a few miles closer to Pratte overnight. Less than ten minutes into the ride she felt the truck head up a rise and heard gravel pelt its undercarriage. This didn't feel like the highway.

She opened her eyes. "You *bastard!*"

Bryan regarded her quizzically. "What, no one ever lied to you before?"

Chapter Nine

Bryan parked in front of Noah's sprawling home and hopped out of the truck. She watched the front door open and Noah saunter out, with a smile for his young friend. He hadn't noticed her yet.

"She's hurt," Bryan said, circling around to the passenger door.

Noah froze, his gaze zeroing in on her. Then Bryan's words seemed to register and she saw his eyes widen. He sprinted to the truck just as Bryan got the door open.

Kit forced her eyes away from Noah's concerned gaze and said tightly, "I told him to take me to Wescott."

"I'm sure you did."

She felt him pry her hand from her leg, then he gently lifted the blood-soaked bandanna. She sucked in a breath as it pulled away from the torn flesh. He ripped her jeans a little more to get a better look. "What happened?"

Bryan gave a succinct account of the accident while they helped her out of the truck. Noah let her lean on Bryan as she hobbled into the house, a concession to his cracked ribs, no doubt. He led her into an examination room and helped her onto the paper-draped table, then dismissed Bryan with a good-natured "Beat it."

"I want him to stay," Kit said.

Both men stared at her. Noah's expression was frigid, Bryan's bemused. "Fine with me," Noah said. "Let's get those pants off." He reached for her fly, with its row of buttons.

"Uh . . ." She stayed his hand, her face growing warm. "Can't you just cut the fabric around the—"

"No." He started working on the buttons.

Bryan leaned against the wall, arms folded, a hateful grin plastered on his face. "Buttons are, like, *so* much sexier than zippers, don't you think? Need some help with that?"

Noah urged her to lie flat and began easing the garment over her hips, his demeanor strictly professional. She'd assumed Bryan would do the gentlemanly thing and turn his back, but she should have known better. He stared avidly as her panties came into view—a skimpy string bikini. Not much more than a strategically placed triangle of ice blue lace through which the dusky wedge of hair was clearly visible. And the cropped T-shirt didn't even reach her navel!

Still, she thought she could handle the boy's presence, till he said, "Lace. Yum."

Her face scalding, she jerked the waistband away from Noah and yanked it back up. *"Out!"* she barked at Bryan. "Get out of here!"

"I thought you wanted me to—"

"Go!"

He shrugged. "I'll go play with the Legos in the waiting room." He ambled out, and Noah closed the door after him. Bryan would probably come up with a Lego flame-thrower, she mused.

"Was he supposed to protect you?" Noah asked, resuming his task.

Anything she said would only make the situation worse, so she said nothing. She lifted her hips to help him slide the jeans down, and even though he took care, when the denim scraped her wound, her entire body snapped taut.

"Sorry," he murmured, tossing the jeans onto a chair. His gaze landed on her left thigh, the intact one. Without looking, she knew what had snagged his attention.

"What happened here?" he asked, sliding his fingertips over the purple bruises. The instant the words were out of his mouth, he knew what he was looking at. She could tell. The question was, did he remember doing that to her? His hand slid down to cover the fading finger marks.

He looked straight into her eyes, and for the first time that day she saw more than a briskly efficient family practitioner. There was an echo of the anguish and regret she'd seen four days ago by the light of the fireworks.

"He *did* hurt you," he said quietly.

"*You* hurt me."

He didn't argue the point. "Where else?" He quickly looked her over, and found the marks on her wrists. He lifted them both and turned them over...rubbed his thumbs over the discolored flesh in a healing gesture. His eyes were sad but sharp when they spotted the edge of another bruise at the rolled-up sleeve of her T-shirt where his own fingers had bitten into her shoulder four days earlier. He pulled up the sleeve and examined it, too.

She yanked the sleeve back down. "They're only bruises," she said harshly. "That's not what I'm here for."

Resuming his doctorly air seemed to take an effort, as if he had to force himself to turn from her and ready the supplies he'd need. He opened cabinets and pulled out items she couldn't see. All she could see was his back, clad in a faded indigo polo shirt. "Was the hammer dirty?" he asked.

She heard the muted click of instruments being laid out on a clean towel, the sound of paper tearing, assorted ominous rustlings.... She swallowed hard and affected a light tone. "Yeah, and rusty." She leaned up enough to squint down at her leg. The sight of her state of dishabille was more disconcerting than the bloody gash on the outside of her right thigh. She let her head flop back and drilled her gaze into the ceiling.

He crossed to the sink and scrubbed his hands, then donned latex gloves. At last he returned to her side with a small plastic basin, some gauze pads, a bottle of Betadine and what appeared to be a turkey baster.

"Heh, heh, where's the cranberry sauce?" she asked in a reedy voice.

He raised her knee and set the basin under her thigh. "Don't be nervous, Kit."

"I'm not nervous." *Hell, no, I always squeak like this.*

Not knowing what to do with her hands, she folded them primly over her waist. It took all her willpower not to clap them over her crotch. Especially with Noah standing right over her, scrutinizing her, breathing on her, blotting her wound with gauze pads. Getting ready to do God knows what with his stupid turkey baster.

A memory assailed her then, of Noah at the cemetery— the real Noah—sliding his fingers up her thigh and higher... dragging the back of his hand slowly between her legs, marking her with a burst of tingling heat everywhere he touched. Now, as then, her body's response was swift and merciless. Kit pulled in a long, slow breath, restraining a moan as scalding heat crawled up her neck and face. She felt suddenly aching and engorged, unbearably exposed under the unforgiving fluorescent light and her inadequate shield of blue lace, her body swelling and blossoming and growing slick with need. Could he see it, sense it? Oh, God. Did he know? If so, his authoritative voice gave no indication.

"This is an irrigation syringe. It's filled with saline solution," he said. "I'm gonna flush out the dirt first." He squirted the salt water right onto the gash. It burned, and she screwed up her face, clenched her fingers together. But she didn't move a muscle.

He flicked a glance at her face, as if to ensure that she'd handled it okay, while he wet a gauze pad with the brown Betadine antiseptic. He began cleaning the wound and the skin around it, his touch gentle, his manner once more businesslike. He seemed oblivious to her near nakedness, as if he hadn't even noticed the screamingly naughty little why-bother scrap of lace and satin that Jo had dared her to buy, so she'd had to get two of every color just to show her.

Guess I showed her, huh?

He removed the basin and lowered her knee, then turned to the counter once more. "Now for the fun part." Kit strained to see what he was doing. She didn't trust a doctor's version of "fun." When he turned back, he was holding a hypodermic needle.

The primitive part of her brain, the part charged with self-preservation, knew right away that something was wrong with this picture, but it took her conscious mind a couple of heartbeats to figure it out.

Look who's about to give you a shot, dummy.

She swallowed a big dry wad of apprehension and said, "What's that?"

"Novocaine." He studied the wound as if deciding where to stick the needle. "You need stitches, in case you hadn't figured that one out."

"Well, uh...wait a minute." She leaned up on her elbows, her wary eyes on the needle. "Don't they use those butterfly things nowadays? Those little bandages?"

"Not for something like this. It's gonna take twelve, fifteen stitches easy. Come on." With a hand on her shoulder he urged her to lie flat again, but she didn't budge. "You won't feel a—"

"I don't want novocaine."

"What!"

Now that she'd said it, she thought about it. How bad could it be, really? She'd read more than one historical novel in which some macho character got sewn up without benefit of novocaine. People used to do it all the time; they had no choice.

An image loomed in her imagination with sickening clarity: Anita David gasping for air, anxiously waiting for the man she trusted—her lover—to administer the shot of epinephrine that would end her suffering. And while Kit knew that Noah couldn't possibly have been responsible for that first poisoning three decades ago, the horrifying fact was, he was the closest thing she had to a suspect in Jo's murder. And it was a matter of public record that, self-defense or not, he'd killed at least once.

"You heard me." She tried to put starch in her words. "I don't want novocaine."

Noah's hard gaze skewered her. His jaw tightened and his throat worked. After a stare-down that seemed to last forever, he said, "I'll show you the vial." His voice was low and raw.

Her throat constricted so tightly she couldn't respond right away. If he was innocent—and with all her heart she prayed he was—she'd just irrevocably severed the fragile bond they'd begun to forge last week. Noah was lost to her, and until this moment, she couldn't have guessed how much that would hurt.

But she couldn't let that sway her now.

"No shot," she said, and flopped back onto the table, inexpressibly weary. "Just do it."

"You don't know what you're—"

"Do it."

He stood there for a long time while she studied the fluorescent ceiling fixture and swallowed convulsively against her trepidation. She heard the slow exhalation that wafted over her seminude body like a warm breeze. At last she felt movement near her leg and she twitched reflexively.

He laid his gloved hand—big and warm and heavy—on her intertwined fingers at her waist, and she felt suddenly calmer, more centered. She became aware for the first time of the tremors that had sneaked up on her, and she took a deep breath, forcing her shoulders to relax, her knees to stop quaking. Still she stared at the ceiling.

"Do you want a sedative?" he asked.

"No." Her voice was a thin whisper.

"I can give you a Valium."

"No." She licked her lips. "Thanks."

He left her side and returned almost immediately. She heard something being torn. A quick peek revealed a sterile packet from which he extracted a curved needle and black suture thread. Oh God.

That's some light fixture, she decided, swinging her gaze back up to the ceiling. *I sure as hell hope it gets more interesting in the next little while.* She lowered her hands to the edge of the padded exam table and gripped it hard.

It took him a few seconds to ready the needle, then he said, "All right, I'm starting."

And he did. She screamed. To her shame, she howled bloody murder. The impulse to wrench her leg out of his reach was overpowering, yet she gritted her teeth, locked her knees and forced herself to lie still while he tied off the first knot. She could feel moisture collecting at the corners of her eyes, and hoped he didn't notice. Her nose was beginning to run.

"Okay, now you've got a taste of it," he said gruffly. She felt his fingers on her jaw, forcing her to look right at him. His eyes were intense. "I'm getting the novocaine."

"No!" He'd said twelve or fifteen stitches. How was she going to go through this twelve or fifteen times? Still she said, "I won't move. I'll try not to be...loud."

His eyes closed briefly. He whispered, "Don't make me do this to you, Kit. It's so pointless."

She closed her eyes, too, to shut him out, to collect herself. She cleared her throat. "C-can I have a tissue?" He gave her a handful, and she blew her nose. Her leg throbbed unmercifully. "Let's just get this over with."

He sighed, shaking his head. "Muleheaded woman," he muttered, his voice more Georgia than she'd ever heard it. "Take slow, controlled breaths. Maybe it'll help. You ready?" She nodded, and he slid the needle into her flesh once more, using an instrument that looked like needle-nosed pliers.

The slow breathing didn't provide relief, but it gave her something to focus on. After the first couple of stitches, the pain seemed to take on a life of its own, like a burning, pulsating energy field hovering in her and over her. The tears rolled out of her eyes and into her ears, but true to her word, she lay quiet and unmoving, squeezing the table edge, with only an occasional sharp gasp punctuating the silence.

At some point she started watching Noah instead of the ceiling, needing someone to cling to, if only with her eyes. He worked with single-minded intensity, his long fingers surprisingly graceful, his movements economical.

She'd counted thirteen stitches when he said, "Last one." He glanced at her, and she nodded mutely. She felt the needle pierce her for the last time, felt him push it through the layers of skin, followed by the thread. A tugging sensation as he secured the knot.

Noah sighed heavily and closed his eyes, bracing his arms on the exam table as if he could no longer support his weight. He looked exhausted, shaken, like a marathon runner at the end of the course. He met her gaze. "You okay?"

No. "Yes."

"God, you're pale."

"So are you."

For some reason that made him smile. He picked up a pair of scissors and trimmed the threads, then bandaged and taped the wound. After peeling off the latex gloves, he slid his arm under her shoulders and helped her sit up. "I'll bring you some Tylenol with codeine."

She groaned, her stomach clenching. "I'll never keep it down. I don't feel so good."

He looked more closely at her face. "You don't look so good. I'm not surprised. Just rest here awhile." He turned back to the counter.

She began to relax. It was over. A lethargic sense of peace suffused her. She yawned.

"When was your last tetanus booster?" he asked over his shoulder.

"Umm...high school...?" *Whoa.* The sudden banging of her heart nearly knocked her off-balance. "Oh. Right. Tetanus..." The casual tone she affected sounded hollow even to her own ears. Her palms grew damp. "Yeah. Now I remember. I had a shot last year."

He turned to face her then, and her eyes flew to the loaded syringe in his hand. The bastard was smiling. "Nice try."

Before she could open her mouth to object, he pushed up her sleeve, swabbed her with alcohol and drove the needle home, holding her arm in a ruthless grip.

"I'm fast," he said. "You gotta give me that."

When she could speak past her blind outrage, she sputtered, "I didn't *want* the damn shot!"

"I suppose you *want* lockjaw! Well, I'm not giving you that option." He dropped the syringe into the red disposal container.

Scowling, Kit examined the tiny puncture mark on her deltoid. She took note of the fact that she was still breathing. Had she really gone through all that agony for nothing?

"I'd carry you into the house to rest in comfort, but..." He touched a hand to his chest.

"You seem to be doing all right for a man with two cracked ribs."

His eyebrows rose fractionally. "How did you—"

"He told me." She watched comprehension dawn on his face. "He told me something else—tried to, anyway." How easily she'd slipped into calling Noah's alter ego "he," as if the alternate personality really were a separate person.

"Tried to?"

"He says he can't talk to you, but I can, so he wanted to give you a message through me."

"And . . . ?"

"And he never got the chance. You came back," she said simply.

He looked haunted, as if he were peering inside himself. "I didn't think I'd be able to. It was only when he got distracted . . ."

"The fireworks."

"Right. That's when I was able to pull him back." He stroked her face, brushed a lingering teardrop from the inside corner of her eye. "I didn't think he could do that, Kit. Get away from me like that. Please forgive me. If I'd known, I'd never have . . ."

"What?"

She saw him struggle to put it into words. "I can control him, except when I'm with you. It must have something to do with . . . my feelings for you. How much you mean to me."

She was astounded. Humbled. After the ugly accusation implied by her refusal to let him give her a shot, here he was, telling her he still cared for her. She remembered how he'd tried to talk to her at the cemetery, tried to explain who "he" was . . . and she hadn't wanted to listen. Well, maybe the time had come to listen. Before she could voice the thought, sharp raps sounded at the door.

"Hey, you guys still alive? You won't *believe* what I made out here, man!"

"We'll be out in a minute, Bryan." Noah reached for her jeans and sized them up. Taking his scissors, he cut right through both legs, above the blood-soaked tear. He stuffed the excess fabric into the garbage can. "Voilà. Cutoffs. *Short* ones!"

He helped her slide off the table and then squatted to let her step into them. The sheer lace triangle of her string bikini was right in front of his face, and he openly stared at it as he slowly pulled the shorts up her legs and past the large white bandage. He rose, smiling suggestively, and slid them over her hips.

"Don't say it," she warned, her face flaming. She felt his fingers graze her belly as he started buttoning her fly. His warm breath stirred her disheveled hair. If he stood any closer, her breasts would brush his chest.

His eyebrows rose, all innocence. "Don't say what?"

"Whatever it is you were going to say about my panties, dammit!"

"I'm a Southern gentleman, remember? We Southern gentlemen do not make rude comments about teeny-weeny little drawers you can see right through." The fingers that had recently displayed such remarkable dexterity with the healing arts now took an inordinately long time buttoning her fly. "I figure I'll let Bryan speak for both of us on the matter of the panties."

Lace. Yum. Kit dragged in a deep breath then, and, sure enough, their chests collided. Noah's eyes were dark... intense. He leaned forward fractionally, tormenting her tingling nipples, his fingers still poised on the top button of her fly. Slowly he lowered his head, angled his mouth to hers....

The door shook under renewed blows. "Are you guys, like, *doing it* in there, or what?"

His lips a hairbreadth from hers, Noah swore quietly and stepped back. "Come on in, Bryan."

Chapter Ten

Kit's palms were slick on the steering wheel as she peered into the rearview mirror for the hundredth time. Even in the dark she knew it was the same car, same driver.

Someone was following her. Again.

She'd first noticed the nondescript gray Pontiac almost a week ago, after leaving Noah's. He'd done a quick wound check two days after sewing her up; she was in and out of his busy office in about two minutes. When she'd driven down the gravel driveway and turned onto the road, she'd heard a car engine start. In hindsight she realized she must have caught him by surprise; he probably expected her doctor's visit to take a lot longer.

In her rearview she'd seen the car pull out from behind some overgrown foliage on the shoulder. Curious, she'd taken note of the driver, a burly youngish man with dark hair and an impressive tan. The Pontiac had stayed a healthy distance behind her on the hilly, twisting roads, allowing other vehicles to come between them. But it had always been there, if she looked hard enough. Only when she got close to Etta's had he vanished.

Then came her first exhilarating, exhausting week teaching at the Powell School, and she'd managed to convince herself the Pontiac was the product of her overactive imagination. Until last Wednesday, that is, when she'd stayed late to give one of her students extra help. Her shadow must have wondered what was keeping her the extra forty-five minutes. Maybe he was afraid he'd somehow missed her.

When she was about to leave the building she looked out Hannah's office window and saw the gray Pontiac—with Tan Man behind the wheel—enter the parking lot behind the school. Kit's Corolla and Hannah's Camry were the only cars still in the lot.

"Hannah, do you know this guy?" Kit asked.

Hannah joined her at the window. "Never seen him. Why?"

Tan Man was already beating a hasty retreat. Had he been checking to see if her car was still there? The hairs on her nape stood at attention. "Well, I've seen him before, in Pratte."

"Is he bothering you? Do you want me to call the police?"

"No... I'm probably just being paranoid. I'll see you in the morning."

Kit kept her eyes open as she drove toward Pratte. No sign of him. Still, something told her she wasn't alone. When a concealing curve in the road loomed just ahead, she followed it around, then abruptly turned onto a private driveway obscured by dense shrubbery, pulled a U-turn and waited. It wasn't long before Tan Man passed in a blur of gray steel, clearly oblivious to Kit in her impromptu observation post. But she was under no illusion that she'd lost him for good. In the days since, he'd faded into the background once more, but she knew he was there.

She didn't even consider going to Chief Jordon with this. He hadn't taken her seriously so far; he wasn't about to start now. No, her only option at this point was to gather what evidence she could, on her own, then drop it in the arrogant cretin's lap as if it were all his idea.

There was no way to know how long Tan Man had been following her. For all she knew, it could have started with her arrival in Pratte three weeks ago. She could almost deal with having her belongings searched. This was a far more intimate invasion, to her way of thinking, an encroachment on her personal space, her privacy. On her sense of security, dammit.

And as bad as it had been to notice this guy in broad daylight, it was infinitely worse to be driving home at one in the morning, on deserted, unlit roads, and suddenly realize she wasn't as alone as she'd thought. Not that he'd been that obvious. But she'd been wary and watchful for so many days, it had become second nature to look for him.

Tonight she'd attended a bachelorette party in a neighboring town for one of the other teachers, after having gone to Noah's to have her stitches removed earlier in the day. That visit, like the wound check, had been a perfunctory, no-nonsense affair; she'd been only one of many patients in the waiting room. Other than those two office visits, they hadn't seen each other during the past hectic week.

Absently she reached for her thigh, and had to force herself not to scratch the healing wound. Instead she wiped her clammy palm on the skirt of her gauzy dress, one eye on the rearview mirror. As she entered the outer limits of Pratte at last, she commanded herself to relax. Her escort would probably disappear as soon as she got near Etta's. Just like that last time. Then she'd be home and safe and—

All alone in that rambling old boardinghouse. She groaned, remembering that the house was empty. Etta was visiting her daughter in Boston for the weekend. She'd taken Malcolm, her surrogate son, with her. In the landlady's absence, there were no other boarders aside from Kit. She barked out a string of curses, her voice sounding unnaturally loud in the dark interior of her car, further rattling her.

She lowered her speed as she neared Etta's, her eyes more on the mirror than the road. True, she couldn't see his headlights at the moment, so she supposed she should be breathing a sigh of relief, but...she couldn't ignore a prickling sense of unease.

As she crested the last hill before Etta's place, she decided to test her instincts with a variation on that little trick she'd pulled last Wednesday. Instead of driving another hundred yards and turning right at the boardinghouse, she swung left at the bottom of the hill, onto a private road leading to a neighbor's farm. An immediate right onto a narrow dirt driveway put her behind a small storage building set close to the road.

She cut the motor and the lights, then stepped out of the car and walked to the end of the shed, where she could observe the road. There were no street lamps, but a fat gibbous moon provided adequate light. Night sounds surrounded her—crickets trilling, leaves murmuring in the breeze, an unseen creature darting out of her path—but she barely heard them over the roar of her pulse. From her concealed location she could see Etta's driveway farther down the road, and just make out the house behind the trees. She'd left the outside lights on.

After a couple of minutes that seemed like a mosquito-slapping, ankle-scratching eternity, she started to turn back to her car when slowly approaching headlights froze her to the spot. She squinted at the vehicle. Yep, it was the gray Pontiac, all right. The car passed her hiding place, then slowed to a crawl when it came abreast of Etta's. Red brake lights glowed, telling her Tan Man was peering into the parking area. The empty parking area. The car stopped. Now he knew she wasn't home.

She'd given him the slip—again—and he wouldn't know what to make of that. She had to be careful; she didn't want him to realize he'd been "made." Somehow she figured she was safer that way.

The Pontiac drove away, and she couldn't tell whether he kept on driving or turned off the road somewhere to keep an eye on the house. How was she supposed to go home now, to Etta's, knowing this guy was probably lying in wait somewhere, watching for her arrival?

He knew she was alone in the house.

She slid back into her car. Locked the doors. Rolled up the windows against the night sounds and the cool, damp night air and the suntanned man in the gray Pontiac. Her decision made in a heartbeat, she turned the key in the ignition.

ANITA STARED UP AT HIM from where she sat hunched on the kitchen floor, her face unnaturally flushed, her eyes glazed with pain and terror. Hideous wheezing filled his ears.

"Noah..."

He knelt next to her and opened his medical bag. "I'm here, honey. Don't worry. It'll all be over soon...." From his bag he quickly extracted what he'd need: syringe, needle, a vial of clear liquid labeled Adrenalin, the trade name for epinephrine.

"Noah, hurry...please...."

An alien sensation tugged at the edges of his awareness as he prepared the needle and began to fill the syringe. Something wasn't right. He looked at Anita.

"I need you, Noah," she said, her voice strangely distant. "Wake up. Come to the window."

His eyes shot open as his chest expanded on a deep, reviving lungful of air. Then he was breathing like a sprinter, hard and fast, blinking at the familiar murky shadows of his bedroom. He started to drag all ten fingers through his hair and stopped short. Anita had called him—

"Noah..."

He jerked upright in bed, his heartbeat drumming in his ears. *That's Kit!* He threw off the sheet and lunged to the window. There she was, on the back lawn, hugging herself, peering up at him. Her face and dress seemed to glow in the moonlight. Like an angel. Only this angel's voice shook, and her wide eyes darted at every noise.

"Thank God," she said. "I need you, Noah."

"I'll be right down."

Since he slept in the nude, he hastily pulled on the pair of running shorts he'd tossed on a chair last night, and raced downstairs. Within seconds he was through the back door and the porch and then she was in his arms, trembling violently. He wrapped himself around her in a bone-crushing hug. Her body felt immeasurably delicate pressed against his own, enclosed in the haven of his embrace. It didn't matter at that moment what had frightened Kit. It only mattered that she'd come to him. That she needed him. *Him.* Never in his life had he felt this way, ferociously protective. The impact of it awed him, shook him to the core.

He buried his face in the fragrant cloud of her hair and whispered a soothing litany of reassurance. She began to apologize. "Shh…" he said, stroking her hair, her back. She seemed to sag against him, as if giving herself over to his care, and his chest swelled painfully with the need to keep her safe.

And with the knowledge that as long as she was with him, she could never be safe.

"Come on," he murmured, steering her toward the porch steps. Max greeted them as they entered the house, tail wagging excitedly, and Noah shooed him away. Kit clung to his hand with both of hers as they made their way through the dark interior of the house to the cozy back parlor with its enormous bay window. Not wanting to turn on a lamp, he led her to the long, wide window seat, now awash in cool moonlight. He propped a couple of tasseled pillows in one corner and leaned back, pulling her down, urging her to curl up next to him. She did, kicking off her shoes and tucking her bare feet under her, her arm sliding around his waist, her head settling on his bare chest.

It felt so natural, so right, holding her like this, feeling the warmth of her body tucked against his, the teasing caress of her breath on his skin. He could almost believe that they could stay like this forever. That she could belong to him forever. It was a bittersweet fantasy.

"What happened?" he said at last.

She shivered and pressed closer to him. "Someone's following me."

His breath snagged in his throat. "Are you sure?"

She nodded against his chest, and he didn't grill her further. If this smart, levelheaded woman said she was being followed, she was being followed.

"How long?" he asked.

"I first noticed him a week ago. I don't know when it started."

Probably about the same time her room was searched, he surmised. "Someone's waiting for you to locate Jo's computer disk," he said. "They hired a goon to keep tabs on you."

"That's what I figure."

His arms tightened around her. "Why didn't you tell me before?"

"What would you have done?" She lifted her head to look up at him.

Make you go back to Chicago, where you're safe. He said nothing.

"That's what I thought," she said, reading his mind. She dropped her head back to his chest.

A low growl of exasperation escaped him. Arguing was pointless. He'd have to gag and hog-tie her to get her back to Chicago before this thing was cleared up.

She said, "If all they want is the disk, I don't think I'm in any danger, really."

Until you find it, he thought. "What happened tonight?"

"I was at a party for Sandy, the first-grade teacher. She's getting married next week. I left there a little after twelve-thirty."

"And you realized the guy was following you."

"Right."

He heard her swallow hard. He thought about her all alone on those dark, lonely roads with some creep after her, and he had to restrain the urge to put his fist through something.

"Who is this guy?" he asked. "What kind of car does he drive?"

"A gray Pontiac. Grand Am. He's kinda young. Dark hair. Deep suntan. That's all I know. I drove straight to Etta's and he was still with me and...and it's empty. The house, I mean. It's just me there this weekend."

"You did the right thing coming here. Did he follow you?"

"I don't think so."

He almost wished he had. Noah itched to drag the bastard out of his car and sic Ray on him. On purpose. Like that time in New York.

He couldn't see her face, but he felt her take a deep breath. "Can I stay here tonight?" she asked.

"You think I'd let you leave?" He was about to tell her she was safe here, in his home, but the words wouldn't come. And she, of all people, would know it for the lie it was. Reluctantly he acknowledged that Kit's seeking sanctuary here, with him, was an act of desperation. An act she probably already regretted.

"I'll give you my room," he said. When she began to object, he cut her off. "It's the only bedroom that's made up.

And there's no way in hell I'd let a woman crash on some dusty old mattress or sofa while I sleep in comfort."

He felt her smile against his bare chest. "The Southern gentleman in you is showing." She raised her head and turned that smile on him. Dear God, she took his breath away. Had she always been this beautiful? Or was it a trick of the moon... of this magic night when she'd come to him and said, *I need you, Noah?* Tenderly he brushed a strand of hair from her face, letting the silk of it whisper through his fingers.

"I can sleep anywhere," she assured him. "When I was growing up, I had to make do with a rump-sprung sofa and a moth-eaten afghan."

"Till you moved in with Jo."

Her bottomless dark eyes softened. "Yeah," she whispered. "Till Jo."

His gaze was drawn to her wide, soft mouth and that fragile smile, fading too quickly under the lash of her memories. So he did the only thing he could. He bent his head and took that smile. Captured it with his mouth and drew it into himself and held it close. And paid homage to her gift with the cherishing caress of his lips on hers. Only when he felt her tentative response did awareness slam into him.

He pulled back instantly. "Damn." How could he have let that happen? He'd made a solemn vow to himself. Two weeks ago, when he'd left her standing alone in the cemetery. Alone and abused and terrified.

I'll never let Ray hurt her again.

If that meant he could never allow himself to touch her, to kiss her, then that's the way it had to be.

He stood and stepped away, putting distance between them. "Forgive me, Kit. I promised myself I wouldn't..." He looked at her then, leaning on her arm now that he'd withdrawn the support of his body. "You know..." he finished.

She was silent a long moment. "Because of him."

"Yes."

"Because you can't...control him when you're with me. That's what you said."

He nodded.

She sat up and pushed her hair behind her shoulder. "Was it happening? Just now? Was he...trying to come out?"

He stared at her, realization dawning as her words sank in. "No." He frowned, trying to remember what had happened inside him when he'd kissed Kit. It was beautiful. Sweet and giving and untainted. It was just *him* kissing her. Just Noah.

But why? Why this reprieve, when every time before...?

She said, "I didn't think so. I could tell." When he didn't respond, she added, "Maybe you can control him better than you think."

He sat next to her, leaning forward with his elbows propped on his knees, rubbing the back of his neck. Thinking. When he'd first come downstairs and he was holding her, crushing her to him...it was just the two of them then, too. No Ray.

Why? What was the secret ingredient that made tonight different from that time at the cemetery? From that first kiss in his attic, for that matter?

He thought about those encounters, how his desire for her had come on sharp and swift, sweeping him up in a tidal wave of raw lust, creating an all-consuming physical need that blocked out everything else. Their surroundings. Her trepidation. His feelings for her.

His feelings for her.

He looked at her, staring back so solemnly in the moonlight. When she'd sought him out tonight in her fear, reached out to him for shelter and strength, it had triggered something in him. Something straight from the heart. From the gut. He'd responded with a soul-searing intensity he hadn't known he was capable of.

Could that be it? Could the power of his feelings for Kit—those tender and protective impulses—be greater than the power of the malevolent thing inside him? Is that what had held it at bay tonight? The strength of his love?

Now that he'd put a label to what he felt for her, he could deny it no longer. Could lie to himself no longer. He wished he could, because the simple fact was, he could never have her.

I love you, Kit. God help me, but I do.

The very fact that she was here, despite everything that had happened, was proof that she cared for him in return, at least a little. He reached out to stroke her cheek, and she closed her eyes and leaned into the caress. Ever so slightly, as if she didn't want to, but was powerless to stop herself.

Could he risk it? If he allowed himself to touch her, kiss her, at some point his body's raging need would take over, and then what?

He dropped his hand. Pulled his gaze from hers.

"Noah?" He felt the tentative touch of her fingers on his arm. "I want to understand," she whispered. "I should've let you explain before . . . when you wanted to. . . ."

"No," he growled. "You owed me nothing. Not after what I did to you."

"But it wasn't you. Not really. I understand that now."

No. You don't.

"Noah . . ." Her fingers tightened on his arm as she tried to make him face her. "Please look at me."

"I'm afraid to," he admitted, with a raw, self-deprecating chuckle, "because I want to do so much more than look."

She rested her forehead on his shoulder. Her gentle sigh stirred the hairs on his arm and sent ripples of sensation skittering along his nerve endings. It was a lonely sound, and far too eloquent for his peace of mind. That sigh said, *What are we going to do, you and I?* It said she shared his pain, his sense of loss.

Instinctively he turned toward her, pressed his lips to the top of her head. She lifted her sad eyes to his, and in that moment he knew that no power on earth could keep him from kissing her again. Her lips felt like warm satin under his. He slid his hand behind her neck and brushed his mouth over hers in whisper-soft strokes. Trying to say with his actions what he couldn't allow himself to say in words.

Her mouth trembled under his, even as it parted slightly. Gently he tugged on her lower lip; her eyes drifted shut and she leaned into him. He flicked his tongue, urging her to admit him. Her mouth closed over the tip and drew it in, sucking it and teasing it with her own.

His body responded immediately, and so did Ray. Just a whiff of him, in his dark corner biding his time, like a carnivore silently stalking his prey. Noah froze for an instant. This was the way it had started the last time. Before he knew it, he'd dropped his shields and the thing had taken over.

But it didn't have to be that way. He'd seen that tonight. This beautiful, responsive woman in his arms wasn't just any woman. She was too good for Ray. *I love you, Kit,* he thought. *I always will.* His heartfelt pledge was a cleansing flame, obliterating all traces of the other man. Purifying his soul. At least for the moment.

Awestruck, heady with his new power, he tore his mouth from Kit's and stared down into her eyes, fluttering open now, her expression drugged. Before that delicious look could evaporate, he tipped his head to hers once more, enfolding her in his arms, crushing her to his chest. This kiss was possessive, demanding, tenderness giving way to hunger. He was instantly hard, his body pulsating with the need to fill her, to claim her completely. And still it was just him—no trace of another man's consciousness burrowing into his own.

I love you, Kit.

When had her hands come up to clutch his shoulders? When had he slid off the window seat to kneel facing her? Still kissing her, he dragged her to the edge of the seat with her legs on either side of him, her dress bunching. Gripping her bottom, he arched into her, driving his throbbing erection against the softness between her legs. She moaned softly into his mouth, and he felt a shudder rip through her. Breathless, she pulled back a little, sliding her palms down to his chest. As he watched, that sleepy look of desire evaporated, to be replaced by something closer to anxiety. He knew what she was thinking.

"It's okay, darlin'," he murmured, smoothing her hair, pressing a tender kiss to her cheek. "You were right...I can control him." Even as he reassured her, he felt unwelcome stirrings from that dark corner deep inside...and effortlessly snuffed them out. Simply by focusing on Kit, and what she meant to him. By allowing himself to acknowledge his feelings for her.

As if freed of a burden, she relaxed into his embrace then, wriggling to fit herself more closely to him. She stroked his sides, his shoulders. Slid her restless fingertips down his back and under the waistband of his running shorts, wringing a guttural moan from him. "Kit, I need you. God, I need you so much." Instinctively he ground against her in emulation of the act they both craved, and reveled in the answering thrust of her hips.

Sighing raggedly, she let her head drop back till it touched the window seat; he slid a hand under her bowed back to support her. The moon painted her with silver highlights, from the rippling halo of her hair, to the delicate bone structure of her face, to her supple body, arched as if in offering. It was an offering he greedily accepted as his fingers and mouth closed over a soft breast.

A hoarse cry broke from her as he sucked hard on her tight nipple through her dress and bra, his insistent fingers kneading her soft flesh, shaping her for his hungry mouth. She writhed against him as he continued the erotic assault on the other breast, her panting gasps coming faster and faster. Her legs circled his hips, and he knew she was close to the edge.

He'd boosted himself off his knees without realizing it, to stay fitted to her, his erection throbbing mercilessly against her softness, the way barred by layers of fabric. Her dark, passion-glazed eyes locked with his and she whimpered, "Noah!" and he knew they'd never make it to the bedroom. "Please..." It was a breathless whisper, nipping at the last lingering thread of his self-control.

He shifted position just long enough to drag off his shorts and her panties. He shoved her dress up, tilted her hips. He rocked against her, nudging her open with his aching shaft, feeling her slippery velvet heat close around the tip. He tensed, practically snarling as he willed himself to slow down, even as his body screamed for a savage thrust and sweet completion. Never before had he felt this blind, raging need. But then, never before had he felt any of the wondrous new things Kit made him feel.

Her eyes were glassy, half-closed. Watching him. Trusting him. He whispered, "Yes, darlin'. Trust me." He lifted her head and pressed his lips to hers, flexing his hips as he began to fill her, inhaling her sharp gasp. She was exceedingly tight, and he stopped short of plunging in to the hilt, afraid of hurting her, groaning with the effort of holding back.

She broke the kiss, breathless and gasping. She thrashed beneath him, strained against him, as if trying to force him deeper. Just knowing she felt his penetration as keenly as he did made his heart swell, and sent him over the edge. Lifting her hips, he drove fully into her, shouting under the impact of it, as if the stark pleasure were a physical blow. An answering sob of fulfillment tore from her throat as her body quivered around his, tightened and released, adapting to the length and breadth of him.

With a harsh growl he withdrew and rammed in again, setting a fast, hammering pace that she matched with equal fervor, each recoil of their hips followed by a thrust more savage than the last.

He murmured things to her then, things both sacred and profane, things he forgot the instant he uttered them. And she whimpered, "Yes...yes..." as her fingers bit into his buttocks and her head whipped back and forth. She sank her sharp teeth into his upper arm, and he smiled. "Noah!" she rasped. Her climax was seconds away, and his would be fast on its heels.

The evil thing inside Noah raised its head...looked at Kit through his eyes...wrapped its malignant tentacles around his mind, squeezing out his will.

No! He went still, shaking and sweating, his heartbeat deafening.

She stared up at him, and he saw comprehension widen her eyes, felt her body stiffen under his. Her harsh breathing filled his ears as she pushed futilely on his arms and tried to twist away. He averted his face, as if, by doing so, he could assuage her panic, and his own.

He fought the thing, but it was no good. Ray was winning, and the son of a bitch knew it. Noah could feel him smirking.

No!

And then he remembered. *That's not the way. That way doesn't work.* He closed his eyes and dropped his face into the silky nimbus of Kit's hair. Drew the scent of her, the feel of her, into himself. Let the essence of what she meant to him fill his mind and his heart. He forced himself to remember her earlier fear, and the overwhelming rush of love it had triggered in him. The need to keep her safe. To make her happy.

He thought about the rightness of this act, the joining of their bodies and their hearts in love. Ray had no place here.

The thing vanished. Blinked out of his consciousness with a suddenness that left him reeling. Noah raised his head and shook it, orienting himself. Sweat sprayed off his hair, but Kit didn't seem to notice. She still stared, with that mixture of dread and betrayal that twisted his gut. *Trust me,* he'd told her. How could he have been so arrogant?

He stroked damp strands of hair off her face, and she jerked her head away. "Shh...Kit..." he whispered, making her look at him, so she could see. "It's me, darlin'...just me. Noah." She studied his face. "I promise...it's just me."

He punctuated the claim with a kiss of exquisite tenderness, his lips lingering on hers, reverently, till he felt her start to relax. He began to move within her once more, but he sensed her distraction. She watched him, her wary eyes on his.

Mentally he cursed Ray. *I won't let you do this, you bastard. You won't take Kit away from me.*

He was determined to reclaim the magic they'd shared moments before. Which meant he couldn't allow her to stare at his eyes, waiting for the thing to return. Withdrawing from her, he gently turned her over, pulling her down till she was kneeling in front of him, bent over the window seat...facing the window and the inky back lawn beyond. Not him.

"Noah...?" She tried to peer over her shoulder at him, but he pressed his mouth close to her ear and whispered to her as he raised her skirt and parted her thighs with his own. Words of encouragement, words of longing, the content less important, he sensed, than the sound of his voice. Noah's voice.

Soothingly he stroked her hip, his hand gliding over the jutting bone to her belly, then lower, into the triangle of crisp hair and the moist folds it shielded. She drew in a sharp breath as her hips twitched backward in reflex, before rolling forward into the caress of his fingers. He took his time, stoking the banked embers, denying himself the sweetness of her body until he was sure she was with him again.

His slick fingers moved higher to circle and stroke the tiny bud, and she shuddered, then rocked her hips to the cadence he set, her breath coming short and fast. He plucked at that most sensitive part of her and she gasped his name, digging her fingers into the upholstery of the window seat.

And still he crooned endearments, not giving her a chance to focus on anything but the pleasure of her body, and her need to join it with his. Only when she squirmed back against his straining flesh, mindlessly seeking him, did he give in. The shock of raw pleasure as he embedded himself in her was as intense as the first time. They drove themselves into each other, moving as one, while his fingers continued their erotic torment, propelling her toward the climax Ray had cheated her out of minutes before.

He lifted her heavy hair and lowered his mouth to the side of her throat in a hungry, ruthless kiss meant to be felt over the pounding of his body into hers. She gave a little start and a whimper of pleasure as his teeth scraped her skin and drew together to nip her. He alternately nibbled, licked and sucked the sensitive flesh until her whimpers turned rhythmic and breathless, testing the limits of his self-control.

"Now, Kit," he demanded. "Now, darlin'. *Now!*"

Her gasping cries reached a crescendo as her body shuddered violently, her release pulsating around him. Still caressing her, prolonging her pleasure, he sought his own then, each fierce lunge bringing him closer to joining her. Then the throbbing incandescence crashed over him, swept him up in its fury, and he roared with the force of it, bucking violently as he poured himself into her.

His last coherent thought as he collapsed against her was *I love you, Kit.*

Chapter Eleven

Why was Etta knocking on her door?

With effort Kit dragged herself out of the haze of slumber. She lay sprawled on her stomach under a light sheet and blanket, her face pressed into the pillow. She inhaled deeply of the scent that clung to the bed linens—*his* scent—and smiled groggily, before her befogged mind put the pieces together and her eyes snapped open. She squinted against the late-morning sunlight flooding the room. Noah's room.

The tapping came again, from the solid oak door. Lazily she flipped over and pulled the sheet up to cover her naked body. She grinned. Foolish modesty, after last night.

Noah's voice was a low, seductive drawl from the other side of the door. "You awake, darlin'?"

She giggled like an adolescent and stretched languidly. *Darlin'.* Dipped in Dixie honey, no less. She'd never get over it.

"Yeah," she croaked, and cleared her throat. "I'm awake. Come on in."

A slight pause. "You're gonna have to unlock the door."

She frowned. Unlock it? She knew *she* hadn't locked the door. Noah had tucked her into his bed last night...well, this morning. After undressing her in the dark and fighting back his obvious urge to make love to her again. Then he'd kissed her and left the room....

"Kit?"

And locked himself out?

"I'm coming," she said, and slipped out of bed, wrapping the sheet around her. She'd wanted him to stay with her last night, to sleep with her. She'd wanted to wake up next to his warm body, her legs tangled with his. . . .

But he'd left her, with no explanation, and she'd been too proud to ask him to stay. His bed had felt cold and lonely as she'd stared at the moon and felt the welcome soreness where he'd made her whole.

She turned the lock and opened the door and swallowed back the little gasp of awe that threatened to escape.

Noah leaned with his palm high on the doorframe, as big and broad and virile as she'd ever seen him. He wore only snug, faded jeans, half-zipped, as if he'd stepped into them about a second ago. A wedge of tawny hair adorned his chest, arrowing into the gaping, low-slung waistband. If he was wearing underwear, she saw no evidence of it. He ran long fingers through his disheveled hair, further rumpling it till the short, fair strands stuck up at odd angles.

His smiling eyes homed in on her, one part boyish charm and two parts potent male animal as his unapologetic gaze loitered on the thin sheet she clutched to her breasts. She didn't know whether to smooth down his hair or throw off the sheet and hurl herself at him.

Nothing in her experience—or her imagination, for that matter—had prepared her for last night. When he'd joined his body with hers, she'd felt him everywhere inside her at once, stretching and filling her to the extreme, testing the limits of her body and her heart. Completing her. And when he'd forced her over the edge into that soul-shattering climax, nothing had existed for her but Noah. He'd been the totality of her universe.

His masterful, no-holds-barred loving had left her emotionally drained and shaking like a newborn kitten. She'd wept afterward, and he'd turned her in his arms and cradled her there on the floor. *Did I hurt you? Did I, Kit?* And when she shook her head no, he held her tighter, held her with a fierce possessiveness that made her sob all the harder, for what they could never have. And she knew he shared her grief.

She'd thought then that their coming together had been as intense—as moving—for him as it had been for her. Gloomily she now realized that if it had been, he'd have wanted to spend the night with her. His rejection still stung.

She tried not to think about the other Noah, the alter ego who'd emerged briefly, terrifyingly, before he'd somehow managed to bring it under control. Just for now, for this one morning, she'd allow herself to pretend that things were normal between them, that her suspicions and fears were as insubstantial as smoke.

That they were two ordinary people falling in love.

"You sleep okay?" he asked.

I would have slept better in your arms. "Fine."

"I have a surprise for you," he said as he absently hitched up the waistband of his jeans, zipped up, adjusted the crotch and fastened the brass button. She couldn't have torn her eyes from the sight if a Sherman tank had barreled through the room.

Noah's fingers stilled, and she groaned inwardly with the knowledge that she'd been caught staring. She forcefully hauled her gaze back up to his face, to find that his potent look had turned downright rapacious. His eyes flicked to the bed.

Hastily she said, "What kind of surprise?"

The boyish Noah returned as he grinned suddenly, then reached up to grasp the top of the doorframe with both hands and execute a couple of quick pull-ups, his lower lip caught between his teeth. She wondered if the exertion was an unconscious way of burning off sexual energy. Still grasping the doorframe, he stood twisting his torso side to side, stretching out sleep-kinked muscles. He was magnificent, all sinew and masculine grace, and the best part was, she knew he had absolutely no idea how damn sexy he was.

She noticed a small scar on the right side of his abdomen. Round and pink. She was about to ask him about it when he said, "I'm gonna take you to a special place I know. For brunch. You'll love it."

"Maybe I should go home and change first."

He shook his head. "No need to get all dolled up where we're going. Besides, I like you in that." He nodded toward her gauzy oatmeal-colored dress, draped over a chair where he'd placed it last night.

"You do?"

"Especially in strong sunlight."

It took her about a millisecond to figure that one out. "You're a perv, Dr. Stewart."

He shrugged. *Yeah, so?*

"You're a doctor!" she said. "People pay you cash money to take off their clothes for you. Why would you want to sneak a peek through someone's dress?"

"I thrive on the challenge. And anyway, it's not *someone's* dress I want to sneak a peek through, darlin'." He smiled crookedly. "Just yours."

"I'm touched. Go away." She slammed the door in his face and called through it, "At least let me get a shower."

"IT'S BREATHTAKING." Kit stood on a rocky outcropping bordering a clear, deep stream the color of Noah's eyes.

"I knew you'd like it. I think of this place as my own private retreat," he said. "Sometimes I bring a rod and do some fly-fishing. I rarely see anyone else here."

She could believe that. This secluded niche tucked into the surrounding verdant hills wasn't easy to get to, even if you knew where to look. They'd had to leave the Jeep some distance away to hike through a thickly forested area and clamber over and around natural barriers of boulders and dense overgrowth. It had been a hair-raising trek at times in her slippery flats—but worth it when Noah gallantly held her hand and gave her the occasional hoist or boost.

Now he turned and began climbing back up the rocky bank—easy for him with his sneakers and long legs. He stretched a hand back to her, and she gratefully took it. Together they picked their way up the tree-studded slope to where it leveled off, and flopped down on the quilt he'd laid in a grassy clearing under a humongous maple tree.

He opened the backpack lying there and started pulling out paper sacks and aluminum take-out containers. The aromas emanating from them made Kit's stomach whine. He'd called in an order to the Thackeray Inn and picked up their meal on the way out of town. Complete with flatware, linen napkins, goblets and a frosty carafe of mimosas, a blend of freshly squeezed orange juice and champagne. Plus china cups and a thermos of coffee, naturally.

"Here you go, Kit. Solid proof that I'm a man of my word. Did I not promise you brunch?"

"At a charming little place with a water view and plenty of atmosphere, as I recall."

"Was I lying?"

"Shut up and feed me."

And feed her, he did. *What a strange and decadent idyll this is,* she thought, watching him pry the lids off their meals and pour the mimosas. Here she was lounging on a blanket in the middle of godforsaken nowhere letting a very dangerous man feed her smoked trout with horseradish sauce, poached eggs Florentine—amazingly intact after their sojourn into the wild—cold asparagus tips, and warm sourdough rolls.

They spoke little during the meal. As she watched him pack up the empty containers, she asked, "So is this the special guy thing you do?'' At his quizzical look, she added, ''Oh, you know. Most men, once they've been dating awhile, develop one particular routine to knock the socks off a woman on the first or second date. Something reliably impressive.''

''Candy is dandy but smoked trout is quicker?''

''Something like that.''

''You wound me, darlin'.'' But he didn't look wounded. He looked amused as he uncapped the thermos of coffee.

''You telling me you've never brought anyone else here?'' She held her breath.

''Well...''

She couldn't help noticing that he avoided her eyes, and inwardly chided herself. *Why did you ask if you didn't want to know?*

''As a matter of fact,'' he finished with a devilish grin, ''Henry and I have slain more than a few trout in that stream. We tried smoking them, but they wouldn't stay lit—''

She flung a sourdough roll, catching him on the ear as he tried to dodge it, chuckling.

''Ow! Ungrateful female. Since you ask, I'll tell you. You're the first woman I've brought here.'' He picked crumbs out of his ear. ''And the last. Damn.''

He poured the coffee, and she accepted a cup. Noah looked deliciously relaxed, leaning on a palm and sipping from his china cup, as mottled light filtering through the tree danced over him. She decided this excessively civilized outing was the perfect time to ask about a decidedly uncivilized matter. ''Noah...I do want to understand.''

She didn't have to elaborate. He studied her face briefly before setting down his cup. For a full minute the only sound was the gurgling of the stream and the chatter of a pair of birds darting from limb to limb.

He said, "And I want you to understand, Kit. I never wanted that before, never wanted anyone else to... know about me. But with you..." He sighed, a heavy sound laden with regret, and looked away. "All I ask is that you keep an open mind."

How much more open could she keep it? She'd given herself to this man, a man whom she feared as much as she loved, a man of stunning contradictions. A man who'd killed at least once and might very well have murdered her best friend. She squeezed her eyes shut against the hellish thought. Keep an open mind? She'd opened herself to him in every way. At this point her mind was the least of it.

He said, "It started when I was sixteen. A swimming party at my friend's house. It was one of these free-form pools that's made to look like a natural pond. Twisty-turny, surrounded by plants and rocks. We were fooling around and I didn't pay attention and I ended up diving headfirst into shallow water."

"My God." This was the accident Jimmy Stark had referred to in his fax. "What happened?"

"Severe head trauma. My heart stopped. They tell me I died."

"Oh, Noah," she breathed.

"'Near-death experience' is the correct term, I guess. They brought me back, but things were never the same after that." He sat up straighter. Rested his elbow on a raised knee. "I started noticing changes. In me. In the way I reacted to things. In the way I felt about things."

"Brain damage?" She hated to think of it.

"That's one explanation, and that's what my family thought. What they still think, I guess. And I bought it at first, but not for long. What was happening was just too... alien. I knew there was something else in there." He looked at her and tapped his head. "In here."

She shivered. "And this feeling didn't go away?"

He smiled grimly. "It got worse. I was most vulnerable during times of physical and emotional stress, it turned out. Like when I had the flu, or pulled an all-nighter studying."

"Or spent two days at the hospital with a medical emergency," she added, thinking about the day of Grace Drummond's garden party.

"Exactly. When I ran into Bryan on my way out of the hospital that day, I was so exhausted he tried to give me a lift—afraid I'd drive the Jeep into a ditch, I guess."

"Bryan was at Wescott Community?" *The day Jo died?*

"Yeah. Said he'd been visiting a buddy of his who'd gone in for exploratory surgery."

She wondered whether Bryan had been at the hospital before or after his big argument with Jo. With a repressed shudder she recalled the ease with which she'd gained access to curare at Wescott. Bryan was an enterprising youth, as skilled at picking locks as he was at chain-sawing trees. Her vivid imagination pictured him tearing off the vial of Norcuron she'd seen taped to the IV bag and stuffing it in a pocket.

Noah broke into her thoughts. "The dream started right after the accident, too." She gave him a questioning look, and he said, "I have this recurring dream. A very disturbing dream."

"About . . . ?"

"Anita David's murder."

He paused, as if waiting for her to mentally trip over that one, and it didn't take her long to oblige him. "Wait a minute. This accident happened when you were a teenager, living in Georgia."

"That's right."

"How could you have known about Anita David?"

"I didn't. Not back then. All I knew was that I couldn't let myself get to the end of this nightmare. It was too real, and it was leading up to something horrible, though I didn't know what at the time. I just knew I had to force myself to wake up each time so I wouldn't see it."

"Did it ever end?"

"Not yet."

"My God," she whispered.

"Dream or no, in the middle of the night, when I wake up disoriented . . . well, that's another bad time for me. A time when my control tends to slip."

The pieces fell into place. "You locked yourself out of my room last night. That's why, isn't it?" To keep her safe from him.

He nodded. "Anyway, I started getting into fights in high school. Instigated them myself. That had never happened before—I'd always been a good kid, decent student but not great. My big thing was art. I was a terrific cartoonist, and that's what I wanted to do for a living, believe it or not. I'd planned to go to art school."

She couldn't picture it. "But . . ."

"But after the accident, it was like that goal had never existed. All of a sudden I excelled in science and math. And I loved it. I went from B's and C's to A-plus in one semester. Aced all the standardized tests. I don't have to tell you how thrilled my parents were when I announced I'd given up cartooning for a career in medicine."

"And your interest in art?" she asked.

"It's like it never existed. I can't draw worth a damn now. Couldn't care less about it."

"So you went to college . . ." she prompted.

"I went to Columbia, premed. Did real well academically. But out of the classroom I was a hell-raiser. Got into a lot of stuff I don't want to think about." His face tightened.

She took a deep breath and said, "I know about Rick Anders."

His eyes snapped to her face. She read surprise there, and sorrow. "What did you do, Kit," he asked softly, "hire someone to dig up my past?"

She swallowed and forced her chin up. "Yes." She watched the play of emotion on his face as he absorbed this, and wanted nothing more at that moment than to take him in her arms and soothe his pain. "Noah—"

"I had no choice. I hope you believe me, but that's up to you. Rick Anders was a dangerous man. I had no choice," he repeated in a hoarse whisper.

She reached over to lay her hand on his arm. "Can you tell me what happened?"

He sighed harshly. "I was involved with his ex-wife, Tiffany. Well, kind of. It was only our second date, if you could call it that, when it happened."

"She had a little girl."

A gentle half smile transformed his features. "Mandy. She was one sweet baby. Just over a year old. Just walking, toddling around. Poor kid deserved better than to live like that, on welfare in a city housing project, with Tiffany Anders for a mother."

That hit all too close to Kit's own upbringing. "But you must've liked Tiffany, if you were seeing her."

His smile twisted. "It wasn't her mothering skills that impressed me at the time. She was a good-time party animal, made to order for a horny twenty-year-old like me."

"Older woman?"

"A year younger, as a matter of fact. I picked her up at an off-campus hangout. That was before I found out about the abusive ex-husband who was heavy into crack."

"But he found out about you," she guessed.

"He showed up, coked to the max, when I was at Tiffany's. Took one look at me and started bellowing and tearing up the place."

"But they weren't married anymore."

Noah shrugged. "Way he figured, she belonged to him. She and Mandy both."

"What did you do?"

"I tried to kick him out. Not easy—this guy had a couple inches and about forty pounds on me. And it was all muscle. But I was holding my own till he grabbed this huge carving knife. Sliced up my arm and my shoulder when I tried to get it away from him. Tiffany was just standing there shrieking. And I...well, I was trying to hold back the thing inside."

"The alien part of you," she said, using his own term.

"Yeah. I sensed somehow that that part of me knew what to do with this animal, if I'd only let it, but I'd spent four years fighting to control the thing. The idea of deliberately letting it loose..."

Something about his expression warned her. "But you did, didn't you?"

Noah's voice turned flat. "Rick got hold of Mandy. Grabbed her out of her crib." His eyes were wintry, his hands fisted. "He held that knife to his little girl's throat and kept hollering about how he was gonna kill both of them. And I knew he'd do it, Kit. Whether I stayed or left."

She felt the burn of tears in her wide eyes. "His own baby daughter?"

"This guy was high on booze, coke and blind jealous rage. He was capable of anything. Mandy was sobbing in terror, and Tiffany just started shrieking louder, saying all the wrong things. So I let it out," he said simply. "The thing inside. Mentally I just kind of stepped back and let it swoop in and take over. I don't remember anything after that till it was all over. I never do," he added softly.

Kit sat mesmerized, trying to imagine the horror that had unfolded while Noah had been deep within himself.

He continued, "I remember forcing my way back to consciousness, like at the—" he shot her a cautious look

"—like at the cemetery. I was standing there gripping the plastic handle of that knife so hard, my hand was cramped up and I couldn't drop it. The knife was covered with blood. It was all over my hand. It had spurted onto my clothes—"

"Noah..." she groaned, watching his eyes lose focus as the horror replayed itself behind them. She shared his pain, a physical ache that burned her chest and radiated into her gut.

He blinked, the sound of her voice seeming to pull him back. "Rick was lying on his stomach, and the blood...the blood was spreading around him. Spreading out on the floor as I watched. And I didn't even know where I'd stabbed him. Turned out it was the chest."

Kit felt the tickle of a tear sliding down her cheek and she swiped it away impatiently.

"Tiffany was still screaming. She was sitting in a corner, squeezing Mandy, squeezing her so tight the poor kid was howling in pain. 'You killed him!' she yelled. Over and over. I'll never forget that hoarse shrieking, or how she looked, bug-eyed and out of control. And I did something then that I'd never done to a woman before. Or since. I belted her across the face. Once. Hard. With my open palm."

Just once? Kit thought, admiring his restraint under the circumstances.

"It did the trick. She started sobbing softly and rocking Mandy against her, and I walked to the phone and called 911." Wearily he scrubbed at his face, as if the telling had taken something out of him. A mirthless half smile arose. "Then I concentrated on trying to let go of that damn knife."

She scooted close to him. Took his hand in both of hers and entwined their fingers. "Have you ever talked about this before?"

"Just to the authorities. My folks. And then to Chief Jordon after Jo was killed. It's not something I like to think about—much less talk about."

"Not exactly church picnic chitchat," she said.

Noah looked at her hands cradling his, then at her small smile, as if amazed that she could stand the sight of him after his gruesome recounting. He squeezed her hands. "No," he said softly, "not church picnic material. Very few people would understand, anyway. Our image of violent death is warped by TV and the movies. The good guys off the bad guys—*bang bang bang!*—and never have a problem living with themselves afterward. It's all cut-and-dried." His grip on her hands became almost painful.

Noah had obviously spent eleven years suffering self-recrimination over what he'd been forced to do. But if his version of events was accurate, she couldn't help seeing him as more of a hero than a villain.

"Tiffany disappeared right afterward," she reminded him.

"Yeah." His expression twisted in disgust. "She'd been in a few scrapes with the law herself. Her knee-jerk reaction to something of this magnitude was to bolt."

"And leave you in the lurch," Kit said, surprised by her own anger at the pathetic woman. "How did the grand jury determine self-defense with no witness testimony?"

"Rick Anders was too damn ornery to die without additional drama. Son of a bitch lived just long enough to mouth off about how he planned to go back and finish the job."

"I suppose that would do it."

Noah lay back on the quilt and stared up into the leaves of the maple tree. "That episode..." He shook his head slowly. "It put the fear of God into me, I'll tell you. I'd been playing with fire, trying to control that bastard on my own."

That bastard? "Rick?"

He looked at her, and smiled, tapping his head. "No. *That* bastard."

"Oh."

"If left to my own devices, I'd never have sought the company of someone like Tiffany Anders in the first place. It was all him." He tapped his head again. "I'd never talked to anyone else about what was happening inside me—I knew they'd think I was crazy—but after Anders... Well, anyway, I had this friend, a graduate psych student named Paul Kerrigan. I confided in him."

"Is that when you found out you have multiple personality disorder?"

His eyebrows rose. "Is that what you think?" When she stumbled over a response, he said, "Paul's heavy into psychic research. The paranormal." Now her eyebrows shot up. "Well, hell, I figured whatever was happening inside me was anything but normal. That only left para."

"I guess you've got a point there." She stretched out next to him on her side. Leaned on an elbow and watched the play of dappled light on his face and his wheat gold hair.

"Paul wasn't able to pin down the source of my problem—demonic possession aside—so he concentrated on helping me develop methods to control it."

"Such as..."

"TM, biofeedback, that sort of thing."

Now she knew where his interest in voodoo medicine originated. "And it worked?"

"Eventually. It took months of hard work before I saw measurable results, and years to refine the techniques."

"Sounds like you were pretty determined."

He turned to lock gazes with her, his own chilly. "Kit, I killed a man."

She drew in a shaky breath. "A man who deserved it, Noah. A man who would've murdered two innocent people if you hadn't stopped him."

Tenderly he reached up to play with a strand of her hair that floated on the light breeze. "I'm not Magnum, P.I., remember? Justified or not, taking a life is still a hell of a thing to have to live with. And who's to say the next time would be for so noble a cause? At that point I'd had four years to get to know this thing inside me. Something told me I couldn't count on it drawing the line at justifiable homicide."

"So you learned to control the impulses," she said.

"By the time my senior year ended, I'd managed to get the thing on a short leash, yeah. Med school passed uneventfully, but I guess you already know that."

He was referring to her investigation. She nodded. "How did you end up in Pratte?"

"After my residency, I took a few months off. Left Max with my folks and just hopped on my Harley and took to the open road."

She blinked. "A motorcycle? Do you still have it?"

"Gave it to Bryan last year."

She'd seen Bryan on that hog when he wasn't driving his pickup, but had no idea it had once belonged to Noah.

"Something drew me to Pratte," he continued. "Like a magnet. It was damn eerie. I knew the layout of the town before I ever got there. Except for a couple of buildings that had been added in recent years. Those were a surprise. Then I drove straight to my house."

"Ray's house."

"Right. There'd been another owner in the interim, but at that point it had been standing empty for four years. I recognized it right away. Then I saw the old sign for the doctor's office and knew I'd come home. When the real estate agent showed me around the place, I was speechless."

"You knew the interior of the house, too." She caught on quickly.

"Every corner, every piece of furniture."

"And the wallpaper," she said, remembering Henry's words.

He smiled. "The wallpaper, yeah. So I snapped up the house that day. Didn't even find out about Ray's past till later. It's not the type of thing real estate agents brag about. But the townspeople clued me in quick enough. And that's when my recurring dream about Anita finally fell into place."

Kit didn't like where this was heading.

He continued, "I can't walk through a room of that house without remembering something that took place there. Dinner parties. Arguments with Ruby. Christmas mornings with Debbie. Not to mention—" he wagged his eyebrows obscenely "—doing the big nasty with an incredible assortment of women. Hell of a swordsman, Dr. Whittaker. Dispensed his healing touch in every corner of that old place, right down to the furnace room. Yesterday I gave a physical to a local grandma, and I had this vivid recollection of ruthlessly wheedling her out of her virginity decades ago on that very exam table."

"So... it was *Ray's* memories you were tapping into all along? Ever since the accident?"

He sat up and leaned on a palm, staring down at her. "You remember when we talked about reincarnation, Kit? I know you don't bel—"

"Noah." She sat up herself then. "You're a bright man, with years of scientific training. You can't really..."

Yes, he can, his expression told her. She bit her lip on further protest. He'd convinced himself he was the reincarnation of Ray Whittaker, and nothing she said was going to dissuade him. All these "memories" of Ray's life had to be the product of Noah's imagination... or perhaps the combined imaginations of whatever multiple personalities inhabited his mind.

She said, "So what you're telling me is, it was Ray Whittaker who attacked me in the cemetery."

"I know it's a lot to swallow, but yes."

It struck her then, and she said quietly, "He . . . he spoke with a New England accent." Noah's expression told her this was news to him. She gave herself a mental shake. Don't start buying in to this nonsense, she warned herself. Get a grip. Trying a different tack, she said, "From what I know about reincarnation, it's not supposed to be like a separate personality overpowering your own."

"You're right, it's not. Normally the synthesis of personalities, of the previous and present beings, is seamless. Undetectable. As it should be. The only thing I can figure out is that when I died and was brought back, the trauma triggered a schism in my personality. Those aspects attributable to my previous incarnation—Ray Whittaker—somehow coalesced and split off." His probing gaze lingered on her face. "You don't buy it," he said, without surprise or rancor.

"But you do," she said carefully. "That's enough for now."

A crooked smile. "You're a born diplomat, Kathleen Roarke."

"I'm a born snoop. Tell me something. Why does your study look like the only lived-in room in your house? Aside from the kitchen and bedroom."

"The visions—Ray's memories—are weakest in that room, so it's easy on the psyche, so to speak. It used to be Ruby's sewing room. He never went in there." He gave a short half laugh. "Well, except for a physical therapy session one afternoon with a buxom brunette named Winifred."

"According to the books I found there, you have a long-standing interest in curare."

"When I realized who I was playing host to in my head, I researched everything that had anything to do with him. Including his weapon of choice."

At the cemetery she'd asked Noah if he'd killed Jo, and he hadn't answered. She realized now he hadn't been able to. Because he didn't know. Whenever his alternate personality took over, he zoned out. On the other hand, she'd bet her life that Noah wasn't the one who'd searched her room and car. Or hired Tan Man to follow her. Logically these incidents shifted guilt away from him, and she grasped at that possibility like a lifeline.

As if reading her mind, he said, "I wish you'd reconsider and go back to Chicago, Kit. God knows it'll kill me to see you leave, but dammit, you're in danger here." He made her look him in the eye. "I'm not just talking about whoever it is that's trying to get their hands on Jo's computer disk. I'm talking about Ray. He's stolen any future we could've had. As long as we're together, you can never be safe from him."

"That's not true, Noah. You can control him. You did it last night." Her face warmed at the memory of the other things he'd done last night.

His expression was heartbreakingly sad. He whispered, "It was a close call, darlin', and you know it. Next time might be different. Anything could tip the scales in his favor. If I'm overtired. If I'm coming down with a cold—"

"No." She couldn't bear to acknowledge the truth in his words. To admit that the alien part of Noah—whatever its true nature—would forever keep them apart. Her chin trembled, and she hated herself for her weakness. "I know you wouldn't hurt me, Noah."

He roughly seized her shoulders, and she saw how painful it was for him, too. "For God's sake, Kit, I *did* hurt you! It could happen again. It could be worse." Abruptly he released her. "I won't take the chance. That's final. I refuse to put you at risk. My God, I can't even trust myself to sleep in the same bed with you! What kind of relationship would that be?''

She had no answer. All she knew was that returning to Chicago at the end of the summer and leaving Noah behind was going to tear her to pieces.

His fingertips stroked her cheek. "I'd give anything if it didn't have to be this way, Kit. Anything."

The indisputable sincerity of his words rocked her, and she lost the battle to contain her grief. He hauled her into his arms and kissed her eyes as the tears flowed. His voice was harsh as he whispered, "I love you, Kit. God help me, I always will."

Chapter Twelve

Noah stretched out on the quilt, pulling Kit down with him to lie snuggled against his chest. He kissed and stroked her until, at last, a languid peace replaced her anguish. She felt the reassuring warm solidness of him, the beat of his heart under his light chambray shirt. She breathed deeply of the intoxicating male essence of the man, lightly overlaid with the scent of soap. Their arms and legs were comfortably tangled, just as if they were sharing a bed. All night. But that, of course, could never be.

Because she knew he was right. They could never hope to enjoy a normal relationship. She'd had too graphic a taste of the dark part of him to kid herself. The terror of that night at the cemetery would always be with her. No matter what else they shared, a little part of her would always be waiting for that thing to emerge.

He rolled them both so she was looking up at him leaning over her, against the backdrop of a living green canopy of maple leaves. "I didn't protect you last night," he murmured, and it took a second to realize he wasn't talking about his alter ego.

"Yeah, I thought about that. After."

"I'm usually very careful," he said. "Hell, I'm *always* very careful. I guess I'd managed to convince myself we weren't going to make love, that I was strong enough to resist." He smiled wryly at his folly. "Last night kind of...snuck up on me. For what it's worth, I know for a fact you won't catch anything nasty from me."

"Same here."

"But as for birth control, well...I'd bet real money you're not on the Pill."

He was right, but she asked, "Why?"

His expression was a funny mixture of tenderness and something else, something that told her this was another one of those things Southern gentlemen don't discuss with a lady. "Well . . . you're awfully small, darlin'. I don't think you've been with anyone else in a long while."

His knuckles brushed her cheek, which, ridiculously, was growing warm. She nodded mutely in affirmation. She could have told him, *You're awfully big, darlin'.* She wasn't very experienced, but she knew that much.

He added, "But even before last night, I figured you for a woman who doesn't give herself easily. It's not in your nature."

How could Noah know so much about her, when he was such a mystery himself?

As casually as he'd packed up their picnic, he started to undo the tiny mother-of-pearl buttons running down the front of her dress.

"Noah!" She tried in vain to derail his busy fingers. A chuckle bubbled up her throat as she whipped her head around to peer into the surrounding woods, though she knew they were alone. "What are you doing?"

"Just a simple wound check, darlin'. Your health is my primary concern." Her dress was now undone to her waist, and he showed no signs of stopping.

"This is nowhere near my wound." She started to redo the buttons at the V neckline as he untied her sash belt. He smoothly captured her hands in one of his without skipping a beat. "Noah, for God's sake, we're in a public place!"

"Don't worry. I never see anyone else here."

"Rarely. You said you *rarely* see anyone here."

"Did I? I meant 'never.' Of course, there was that group of backpacking nuns that one time...." He said this with a straight face as he worked his way down the dress, and she went still, straining her ears for any hint of human sounds. The lilting strains of "Ave Maria," for example.

He said, "Bryan's right about buttons, you know. Sexy as hell." He grinned at her. "I think it's the anticipation. They take so god-awful long to undo."

He reached the hem and the last button, which he unfastened with a flourish. The sides of her dress still met in the middle. She was, technically speaking, as chastely covered as before. Nevertheless, she shivered and her chest rose and fell faster. He released her hands and she let them drop to her sides, making no attempt to button up. The singing nuns would just have to deal with it.

He leaned on a palm, looking her up and down, his hot gaze making her wonder if he had X-ray vision. "I've never seen all of you, you know," he said. "Just tantalizing bits and pieces."

"What about last night, when you put me to bed?"

"Too dark." His fingertip trailed down her neckline and slipped between the two halves of the dress. Slowly, oh, so slowly, it slid downward over her pounding heart and the front clasp of her bra, between her ribs to her abdomen, which quivered at the teasing contact. "You're so soft," he murmured.

She squirmed when his fingertip dipped into her navel and tickled it lightly. In fascination she watched his face, his rapt expression both serious and playful, if that was possible. His finger reached the top of her lace string bikini and lightly trailed along the edge. She breathed a sigh of relief. And regret. This was where he'd stop.

His gaze locked with hers as his fingertip etched a fiery path straight down over the lace triangle and the feminine furrow beneath. She gasped, arching into the delicious pressure as he painstakingly traced the shape of her sex. Her thighs slammed together reflexively and she bit her lip to keep from crying out in pleasure. His heavy, warm palm cupped her then and she groaned, feeling herself swell and pulsate under his hand. At the same moment he seized her mouth with his.

As she felt her arms encircle his neck, she forced herself to pull back from his hungry kiss. She shook her head. To clear it and to make him slow down. "We...we aren't...we can't..." Her tongue was thick, her mind lust-stupid. "We said we weren't gonna do this. Didn't we?"

"Tell me how to stop," he rasped, his eyes glittering like smoked green glass. He took a deep breath. "Kit. Darlin'. Don't expect me to be able to keep my hands off you while you're still within grabbing distance—hell, within the state of Vermont." Some of the glitter fled his eyes as sober reality intruded. "You know I'll try my damnedest to keep you safe—from Ray—but that's not something I can promise. God knows I want more than sex from you, but it's all we can have. And in a few weeks...we won't even have that. If that's not enough, or if you're afraid, I'll understand. I'll leave you alone."

"It's not enough," she whispered, her throat clogged with tears she refused to liberate, "but I'm...I'm not afraid." It was a lie, she was afraid, but her need for him—for whatever closeness they could share, however fleeting—overrode her fear.

She reached up to stroke his cheek and the strong line of his jaw. He captured her fingertip between his lips and kissed it. Then he began to part her dress. "I want to look at you."

He started at the neckline, slowly drawing the fabric apart to fall limply at her sides, working his way down until it lay completely open. His appreciative gaze swept over her before he leaned close to study the elaborate bra clasp nestled between her breasts. Just as she decided they were in for a good long fumble-and-cuss session, the lace cups parted in a blur of nimble fingers and a practiced twist of the wrist. She narrowed her eyes speculatively. He didn't learn *that* in med school. Not in the classroom, anyway.

Wordlessly he lifted her shoulders and slipped off her dress and bra, setting them aside. Now she lay before him in only those ridiculous little panties she was beginning to despise—identical to the ones from the day he stitched her up, only these were lavender.

His voice was an awed whisper. "Darlin', you are so beautiful." He lightly stroked her hip, then hooked a finger under the satin-covered cord that secured that useless scrap of lace. "I do love these little lacy things you wear, though I haven't figured out what purpose they serve. Except to drive me crazy." He pulled them off.

She couldn't resist. "Is this part of the wound check, Doctor?"

"I'm very thorough."

She watched him examine the half ounce of satin and lace that all but disappeared in his big hands. She asked, "You are gonna give those back, aren't you?"

"I dunno. Thinkin' of having 'em bronzed." He twirled the panties, then stretched them between his fingers and let them fly like a slingshot. They hooked on a low tree branch. "Now. Long as I got you nekkid." He peered closely at her thigh and gently touched the wound. "Bet it itches like a son of a gun. Lookin' good, though."

"Good? It's ugly."

''Hey, that's my handiwork you're maligning. Take my word for it. When this baby heals, you won't be able to tell where it was.'' He pressed a kiss to the scar. She felt the healing caress of his firm lips there, felt his warm breath curl over her thighs, and between them. He eased down to lie next to her, his hands roaming in a leisurely perusal as he kissed her forehead, her temple, her ear and throat.

His fingers stroked the side of her breast, following its shape, and she moaned softly. He bent his head and drew her soft nipple into his hot, wet mouth. It puckered instantly with an electric tingle that sent an answering current deep between her legs. Her breath caught and her entire body tightened for one long, delirious moment. Then he settled against her and began suckling lazily.

Kit held him to her, stroking his hair...absorbing his deep sadness into herself, to mingle with her own. She knew that instinctively he sought the solace of her body—drawing on her innate ability, as a woman, to comfort and nurture—and she freely gave him what he needed. She caressed and soothed him, staring up into the shifting pattern of green and azure, watching the sun wink in and out of view, her senses filled with the aromas of growing things drifting on the warm breeze. She'd be content to lie with him like this all day, if that's what he wanted.

But contentment gradually gave way to a languorous yearning as his lips and tongue tugged rhythmically on her sensitive flesh. By the time he turned his attention to the other breast, her breathing had become rapid and shallow, her legs moving restlessly. Her nipple stiffened between his teeth, sparking a deep-throated groan she was helpless to suppress. Noah shifted to lie more fully atop her, pressing the insistent ridge of his erection against her leg. He sucked with increasing vigor, the scrape of his teeth shooting flaming arrows that exploded deep and low. His hands were just as demanding, molding her soft flesh, pinching lightly.

She raised her fingers to touch the place where they were connected, his lips firm and moist and ravenous. Helplessly she writhed against him. Were those wanton cries coming from her? Her entire body strained upward, reaching mindlessly, and she felt her climax begin to gather.

A bird screeched on a nearby limb and she panicked, suddenly cognizant of their less-than-private surroundings, of her nudity and the shameless spectacle she presented. "Oh, God!" She pushed him off her, forcefully, and watched his initial bewilderment change to comprehension as his eyes slowly raked her. She was panting hard, miserably aware of the scorching flush of arousal from her hairline to the pebbled tips of her breasts. She couldn't hide how close she was to release.

His eyes blazed with ruthless determination. "You won't hold back, Kit. I won't let you." Before she could object, he grabbed her wrists with both hands and pinned them near her shoulders, then lowered his head to her breast once more.

He'd taken the decision away from her; she had no choice but to ride out the pleasure he was resolved to give her. As her throat arched and her hips lifted, she felt his hard-muscled thigh push between her legs, parting them, the coarse denim of his jeans unspeakably erotic as it slid against her bare skin. Within seconds he had her once more at the brink. All conscious thought fled as her body surged into his, into the welcome pressure of his leg.

Then the fireball blossomed, consuming her, ripping a hoarse scream from her throat. For endless moments the world receded into pure, pulsating sensation that lifted her and held her aloft. Even after the inferno subsided, aftershocks kept her rocking against him as her own throaty whimpers filled her ears.

Her mouth was dry and she licked her lips, blinking drowsily. Noah swaddled her in his long arms, holding her tight, gentling her with soft kisses and whispered words of love as awareness gradually returned. She felt drugged, boneless, and was vaguely aware of him stretching one arm out toward his backpack and fumbling with one of the outer pouches. She fought her postorgasmic lethargy enough to turn her head and see him toss a small foil packet onto the quilt beside them.

"Mmm...yes..." she murmured, pressing her lips to his throat. The sound of leather snapping as he hastily jerked his belt open. The zipper next. "Uh-uh." She grabbed his hands. Shook her head. "Oh, no, you don't."

Noah gaped. Eyes round, jaw slack. "Oh, no, I *don't?*"

"I mean—" she chuckled "—oh, yes, you do, but not like this." He'd unfastened his pants, but he hadn't touched his shirt or his sneakers.

"Not like what? Tell me!"

"Take off your clothes."

He relaxed slightly; she saw the hint of a smile. "Isn't that supposed to be my line?"

"I will not be the only one out here buck naked!"

"When Sister L.L. Bean comes tromping through, you mean?" Only the top two buttons of his shirt were unfastened when he pulled it over his head and flung it aside. He stood and yanked off his sneakers without untying them. No socks. No underwear, either. He almost tripped getting out of his jeans.

Noah stood staring down at her, his gaze hungry, clearly unembarrassed by his nudity or his powerful state of arousal. He was magnificent. Kit found herself reaching up to him, silently beseeching. He lowered himself to the quilt, but when she picked up the foil packet, he took it from her and set it aside again. He kissed her fingertips, then slid down her body. She felt his fingers open her, his breath a hot feather-stroke on her damp flesh.

His intimate kiss, the firm, leisurely caress of his tongue, stole her breath. She felt a long finger probe deeply... felt the answering clutch of her inner muscles... felt his low moan buzz into her and coax her hips off the quilt.

"Noah." She half raised herself to tug on his hair and dig her nails into his shoulders. *"Noah!"* She needed to be joined with him when the spark ignited once more. And she was so close.

At last he raised his head and grabbed the foil packet, tearing it open. She commandeered the task, sheathing the hot, hard length of him slowly, feeling him twitch and throb under her fingers. From deep in his chest came a low growl as he pushed her back down, fitting himself to her.

She reveled in the size and weight of him... in that glorious moment when he pressed into her and she felt her body open under the delicious pressure. He stared into her eyes and filled her completely in one long, slow thrust. They groaned in unison, and smiled at the perfect harmony of it. She pulled his head down and tasted herself on his lips. He set a gentle, unhurried cadence, in stark contrast to the tumultuous joining of the night before.

Slowly they rocked into each other, melding and retreating, every nuance of sensation keenly felt. And still he kept his gaze on hers. Their breathy sighs blended with the burble of the stream and the whisper of the breeze stirring the leaves.

When she held him tighter and tossed her head restlessly, Noah raised her bottom and angled her hips, forcing himself deeper and more fully against her, each thrust now stroking the tiny ultrasensitive bud, the center of her pleasure. Her cries came sharp and fast, matching the increased tempo of his loving, till she shuddered with the explosive power of her climax.

As her body quieted, she became aware of Noah's hands gripping her hips, holding them still. He bit his lip on a soft half laugh and whispered, "Wait, darlin'...shh, don't move." She felt the throbbing fullness of him inside her and knew he was struggling to make it last. He kissed her, lightly at first, then deeper, a lingering, cherishing kiss. Keeping them joined, he rose to his knees, pulling her up with him, her legs around his hips. His strong hands lifted and lowered her, controlling the rhythm.

She renewed the kiss, tugging hungrily on his mouth, breathing in his harsh exhalations and tangling her tongue with his. Leaning forward, she pressed him onto his back. Raised her head to stare down into his face, curtained by the spiraling tendrils of her hair. His eyes were dark and intense, passion clouded...the cords of his neck taut as a bowstring....

With a slow smile she pulled his hands off her hips and pressed them back onto the quilt near his shoulders, as he'd done to her earlier. Though he could have shaken off her hold at any time, he only grinned playfully and teased, "Be gentle with me, Kathleen."

His playful smile turned smoldering as she moved over him, setting her own pace—a pace he obediently matched until the demands of his body overcame him. Abruptly he yanked his hands away to seize her once more and hurtle toward his own release, his hammering thrusts triggering her fever anew. When his body flexed hard, so did hers. And when his hoarse cry shattered the quiet of the forest, her own voice echoed it.

"ARE YOU FALLING ASLEEP?" Not that she wasn't happy just to sit there staring at him—all of him. For that matter, she was still mother-naked herself. She let the constantly changing pattern of dappled light direct her gaze to every part of him in turn as he lay stretched out on the quilt.

He snorted. "What foolishness. Never heard of a guy falling asleep after sex." His eyes were closed, his head pillowed on his laced fingers.

She trailed her fingernails slowly down his chest, through the crisp hair that gleamed like gold wool. When she got to his abdomen, it tightened in reflex and a chuckle escaped him. He seized her hand and opened his eyes at last. "Witch."

"What's this?" She indicated the little round scar she'd noticed earlier.

"Birthmark. There's a bigger one on my back." He flipped over and there it was, also on the right side, but larger.

"Odd," she said, touching the puckered mark on his otherwise perfect body. "You were born with these?"

He hesitated before saying, "Kit, do you remember those old autopsy reports I showed you?"

"Anita and Ray's? Yeah." She lightly rubbed his back. It was impossible to keep her hands off him.

He rested his chin on his folded arms. "Do you remember the description of Ray's bullet wound?"

Her hand went still, her eyes glued to the scar. The report indicated a small entry wound on the right side of the abdomen . . . and a larger exit wound directly behind. He'd bled to death.

Noah looked at her over his shoulder. He said nothing, and she sensed he was trying to read her reaction.

She licked her lips. "I suppose the scars match up . . . ?"

"You read the report. You tell me."

The scars matched up. Perfectly. She'd pored over every detail of those damn reports, and asked Noah to clarify anything she didn't understand. Apparently satisfied by her unspoken answer, he turned back around and dropped his chin again.

She asked, "Is this...usual? To have markings from a, uh, previous..." Jeez, listen to her. "You know..."

"Incarnation."

"Yeah. Incarnation." She allowed her fingers to touch the odd mark on his back. *Exit wound?*

"Well, the literature includes plenty of cases where people are born with marks that correspond to scars acquired during a past life, but I wouldn't say it's usual. Other indicators of reincarnation are much more common."

"Like recurring dreams. Or knowing the layout of a house you've never seen before." She didn't try to hide the skepticism that infected her tone.

He was silent a moment, as if debating whether to continue. "That's right," he said tightly.

He could talk about "the literature" all he wanted, but it didn't change the fact that Noah was...she hated to acknowledge it...unbalanced in some way. Her armchair diagnosis was still multiple personality disorder, of which she knew precious little. It was way past time he had professional help for whatever was going on inside him. Perhaps then—dare she hope?—he could even be cured and they could be together.

Forever.

She chose her words carefully. "Have you ever consulted an, um, expert on this? Aside from your friend who helped you with the TM and all."

"Oh, I'm still in touch with Paul. He's a well-respected psychotherapist now, in New York. Does a lot of work with hypnosis."

"Is he still into the paranormal?"

"In a big way. He's contributed some important research. In between helping people stop smoking, lose weight and improve their backswing. He's the only person—aside from you—who knows about me. And Ray."

So he did talk to a shrink. A like-minded crackpot who'd probably been encouraging Noah's delusions all these years. Still, if this Paul Kerrigan was an honest-to-God psychotherapist, as Noah said, that had to count for something. She asked, "Has he done past-life hypnosis on you? You know, taken you back to Ray's life?"

His back tensed under her hand. "Paul's been trying to get me to undergo hypnotic regression for ten years, but I won't let him. The dreams are so goddamn realistic. I can feel myself—*me*—doing this terrible thing to Anita. The last thing I need is to relive it all in graphic detail. I'd rather stick to the newspaper reports."

Too bad. Perhaps if he allowed Paul to hypnotize him, he'd find out what his real problem was. And overcome it.

He sat up and faced her. His eyes closed briefly, and when they opened again, she detected a hint of regret. "When you first arrived in Pratte, and I couldn't dissuade you from staying, I decided I had to stick close to you. To keep tabs on what you turned up. And to make sure you didn't—" a muscle twitched in his jaw "—find out too much."

"About you, you mean." He nodded, and she looked away, unable to bear his scrutiny as she thought back to the day she'd shown up in his office . . . and her pathetic gratitude when he'd offered to help her.

He said, "It was an automatic reaction on my part, Kit. Call it an instinct for self-preservation. But at the same time, I realized I had to know the truth. It was looking at your face that did it. Seeing your pain. How much Jo meant to you. That's when I decided to let Paul have a crack at hypnotizing me. Not to go back to Ray's life—never that—but to relive the day Jo died. The part I can't remember."

Grimly she met his eyes again. Drew in a shaky breath. *The part I can't remember.* "You want to find out if you killed Jo," she said.

His expression was bleak. "I have to know."

A weight settled in her chest. And if he found out he was guilty? What would he do? What would *she* do? "But Paul wasn't able to help you?" she asked.

"He hasn't had a chance yet. Been on sabbatical in Alaska since the end of May. Doesn't get back to New York till the end of August. I've left messages for him."

"Isn't there anyone else you can—"

"Trust me on this, Kit. Paul knows my history as well as I do. Knows about Ray and all of it. The guy saved my sanity back at Columbia after I killed Anders. It's him or no one."

Fair enough. "Noah . . ." She laid her hand on his arm. "I think you should let him take you back all the way. To your—" *go ahead, say it* "—previous life. I think it'll help you."

His sad, half-smiling eyes told her he appreciated her paying lip service to his claims of reincarnation. And that he was aware of her ulterior motive. "What you think is that I'll discover I was wrong about Ray and that I really suffer from something much more plausible. And treatable."

Tears stung her eyes. She whispered, "Is it too much to ask you to give it a try?" For both their sakes.

"Darlin', believe me, if I thought there was the remotest chance you could be right, I'd do it in a heartbeat. But the fact is, you're wrong. And deliberately dredging up every repulsive detail of that monster's life can only make *my* life more miserable. And he's already done a damn good job of that."

His words triggered a memory. "Ray said . . . he said there was something he had to tell you," she reminded him, disturbed by how easily she'd slipped into calling Noah's alter ego Ray. "At the cemetery. He said you were a stubborn, strong-willed bastard and you won't let him show you something."

"I'm not interested in anything my good buddy Ray wants to show me."

"Maybe you should let him, Noah. Maybe this message...whatever he's trying to tell you...well, maybe it's something you'd want to know about." And just maybe Noah's reticence was his way of avoiding the truth: that his problems stemmed not from a long-dead murderer but from some sort of mental disorder.

Tenderly he stroked her cheek. "Give it up, Kit. I'm not gonna open myself up to him, put myself at his mercy. 'Cause that's what we're talking about here. And once he sinks his teeth in, who knows what it'll take to make him let go? How do I even know Paul can handle him? He's dealt with a lot in his work, but something tells me Ray just may be a match for him."

Arguing was useless. "Did you sense him when we were..." She glanced at the quilt they sat on, indicating their lovemaking.

His gaze slid away from hers. "Yeah, he wanted to come out and play. That'll never change. But I think I've figured out how to keep a leash on him when we're together. Like I said, I'm pretty sure I can keep you safe."

"As opposed to being one hundred percent positive."

He sighed heavily. "You can back off any time, Kit. I won't press you."

She knew her own eyes reflected the yearning she read in his. As he'd pointed out, there could be no forever for them, just a summer's worth of bittersweet memories. If she'd allow it. She snuggled into his lap and felt his instant response, the hot, velvet-sheathed steel nudging her bottom. She heard his sharp indrawn breath.

"I like to live dangerously," she whispered, pulling his mouth down to hers.

Chapter Thirteen

The short, balding man returned to the counter with Jo's cleaning ticket. "Can't find this. When was it brought in?"

"Says right there on the ticket. June fourteenth."

The man sighed in annoyance. "June fourteenth. Lemme check the back."

Kit looked at her watch. Quarter past ten, and she had a one-o'clock flight to O'Hare. Now she wished she hadn't put off this chore till the end of August. It took a few minutes for the man to return with Jo's plastic-shrouded clothes. She stared at the red linen blazer and navy silk pants.

"Miss . . . ?"

She blinked away the moisture in her eyes and looked at the man, who was wagging a small, fat white envelope in front of her face.

"I said you left something in the pockets. It's all in here."

She accepted the envelope and the cleaning, and returned to the parking lot. An awning of pewter clouds had turned the day murky. The skies would open up before long. Suitably depressing weather for the worst day of her life, she thought. The day she had to say goodbye to Noah. She felt a painful squeezing in the vicinity of her heart. Perversely, the only thing that made their parting more bearable was the knowledge that it was as hard for Noah as it was for her. The last weeks of the summer had been more bittersweet than she'd anticipated, their warm closeness and abandoned loving tempered by the knowledge that this day would come.

She'd gained enormous satisfaction from teaching the troubled fifth graders at the Powell School, and Hannah had offered her a permanent position. But she'd turned her down. Staying in Pratte wasn't an option. Not without Noah. The emotional tightrope they'd walked all summer was as draining as it was exhilarating. He hadn't connected with his buddy Paul yet, and even when he did, there was no reason to think things would ever change for them. The thing that kept them apart would always be there, inside him. Noah would never be hers.

And as much as it hurt to acknowledge it, she also knew the mystery of Jo's death would remain a mystery. She figured the police must have back-burnered the case by now, though Chief Jordon was still as closemouthed as ever. After two and a half months, any leads that might once have existed would now be stone-cold. Kit resigned herself to the fact that she'd failed her friend. There would be no rooting out of the truth at this late date, no avenging her cold-blooded murder. Kit had to go home. Get on with her life. And without the two people who meant more to her than anything.

She opened the rear car door and carefully hung Jo's clothes on the hook over the window, while her rational mind wondered why she didn't simply toss them into the trunk. What would she even do with them? She slid behind the wheel and examined the bulging envelope before slipping a fingernail under the sealed flap. She shook out the contents onto the passenger seat and pawed through them. Sixty-seven cents in change, plus three wadded-up dollar bills. A shirt button with threads hanging off it. A movie stub. Half a roll of mints. A matchbook from the Thackeray Inn. A small key. A scrunchy red satin hair tie. Good old Jo. Didn't she ever hear of carrying a purse?

Reverently Kit touched the three long, dark brown hairs that had caught on the hair tie. Her throat threatened to close when she realized this was all that was left of Jo, the last lingering bit of her corporeal existence, the rest of her having been reduced to ashes. Perhaps Noah was right about reincarnation, and Jo's spirit had already begun a new adventure. Kit's imagination conjured up a toddler pouring Cuervo over her Froot Loops.

Shaking her head on a wry smile, she dropped the hair tie and picked up the key to peer closely at the gold script embossed on its green plastic head. *Valkyrie.* And under it, *49.* A moment for the significance to sink in, then a heated curse as she banged her head back against the headrest. Another stop to make. Jo must have had a permanent locker at the damn health club. Kit started the car and checked her watch again. She was being punished, she knew. This is what she got for leaving everything till the last minute. She hadn't even packed yet!

It took over half an hour to locate Valkyrie, in the next town. After explaining her mission to the pretty young mesomorph at the front desk, she was directed to the locker area.

"Will her stuff still be there?" Kit asked.

"Long as her membership fee was paid up," the woman assured her.

Inside the locker room, she blinked at the bright lights and mirrored walls. The mingled scents of stale sweat and designer hair spray hung heavily in the air. Kit nodded to Grace Drummond, Bettina David and a couple of other well-heeled acquaintances. An aerobics class must have just let out. She hoped no one would strike up a conversation; the last thing she was in the mood for just now was idle chitchat. She let the fact that she was emptying Jo's locker speak for itself. Curious eyes burned a hole in her back as she located locker number 49 and slipped the key into the lock.

The door swung open and she sighed, wondering if the receptionist would be willing to scrounge up a shopping bag for her. Leotards, leggings and crop tops hung from the hooks, along with a sleek hot pink racing swimsuit. Towels, sneakers and athletic socks were crammed in the bottom. The familiar scent of Jo's perfume wafted from the workout clothes. Kit couldn't help smiling. "God, I miss you, Jo," she whispered under her breath. The small shelf near the top of the long locker was crammed with more gear: a shiny gold swim cap and goggles, a clear plastic cosmetic bag bulging with makeup and hair accessories, and an assortment of plastic bottles filled with shampoo, conditioner and lotions.

Okay, maybe two shopping bags. Kit rose on tiptoes to peek into the back of the shelf. A flash of silver caught her eye. Jewelry? She reached in and when her hand connected with the object, her heart slammed painfully into her ribs. Her fingers tightened around the small square as if it might evaporate at any moment. In slow motion she drew out her hand and stared at Jo's computer disk.

The label read, Poisoned Love. Complete June 13.

Complete. Jo had finished her book. Just before her death. She stood staring at the disk. Kit had never stopped searching, and here it was all along, in this pigsty of a locker. She slammed the door closed and dropped the key and disk into her purse. And then noticed how unnaturally quiet the locker room had become. *My, ladies, what big eyes you have.* She spun around quickly and the room erupted into bustling activity and conversation.

Bettina David was closest to her, stepping into a pair of beige raw silk slacks, her dark, shower-damp hair secured in a braid. "Bettina, do you know where I can locate a phone?'' Kit knew her voice was breathy with excitement, but it was all she could do to get the words out.

Bettina smiled and pointed to a corner of the locker room. ''Right over there.'' She pulled on a sleeveless white silk tunic that contrasted beautifully with her sleek, suntanned arms.

''Thanks.'' Kit dug a quarter out of her purse on the way to the phone. Her nape prickled and she sensed Bettina's eyes on her. But when she tapped Noah's number into the phone's keypad and glanced over her shoulder, she saw that the other woman had already left.

Alice's sandpaper voice answered on the third ring, and Kit asked to be put through to Noah immediately. ''It's an emergency.''

She waited two long minutes to hear his voice, harried but concerned. ''Kit . . . ?'' She'd never bothered him during a busy workday, and he wouldn't be expecting to hear from her until lunchtime, when he'd planned to take her to the airport.

''Noah, I found the disk.''

He whispered, ''My God. Where?''

''In Jo's health club locker.''

''Where are you now?'' His voice was strained, clipped.

''I'm still here, at Valk—''

''Go straight to the police, Kit.''

''Noah—''

''I mean it,'' he barked. ''Don't argue with me. You're in danger, dammit!''

''Noah, listen to me! I have to read Jo's book.'' She lowered her voice. ''I have to find out what she dug up about Anita's murder. Lend me your computer, okay?'' She could scan the book and make a copy for herself before handing the original over to the police chief. Maybe she'd have to take a later flight, but right now, that was the least of it.

"Once Chief Jordon gets his grubby mitts on this disk, I'll never get a peek at it. You know that."

"Kit." His tone was softer now, cajoling. "It'll take you a good half hour to get here from Valkyrie, but the police station's practically around the corner from where you are. Your safety's the only thing that matters right now. Someone's been waiting all summer for you to turn up that damn disk. You've been followed—"

"I haven't seen the guy in a few weeks."

An exasperated sigh. "So he's gotten more careful. Or they've gotten a different guy." A pause. "Did anyone see you find the disk?"

Her hesitation was clearly answer enough. She heard him curse, and could almost see his white-knuckled grip on his office phone. She tried to make light of it. "I don't think I'm in danger from a bunch of sweaty ladies in leotards." She loved Noah all the more for his protective impulses— overprotective, perhaps—but at the moment she was too exhilarated by her discovery to humor him.

"Wait for me there, Kit. I'll come for you."

"That's ridiculous. You've got a ton of patients, Noah." His waiting room was always full. "I don't need a baby-sitter."

His voice rose again. *"I said wait there for me, dammit!"*

"No. I'm leaving now. I'll see you soon." She hung up.

NOAH STOPPED SHORT just over the threshold of his office. A bearded man in T-shirt and jeans sat behind his desk, pawing through the box of cheap toys Noah kept on hand to reward his youngest patients.

Paul Kerrigan spared him a glance as he selected a tiny Troll doll with fuzzy purple hair. "If I don't cry, can I have one of these?"

"Where the hell did you come from?"

"Great to see you, too, Noah." Paul stroked his short, dark beard. "Check it out. A whole summer with no razor. What d'ya think? Does it add to my rugged appeal?"

"Paul." Noah slumped into the opposite chair. "I don't know why you're here, but man, am I glad to see you." Kit had called barely five minutes ago, and he was frantic with worry. He knew he wouldn't relax till she walked in the door.

Paul leaned back, frowning slightly, his gray eyes never leaving Noah's. "I got your tapes. Sent my gear on to New York and came straight here from Anchorage. Something pretty heavy must've happened for you to *ask* me to hypnotize you."

Noah propped his elbows on the desk and massaged his forehead. He looked up to find Paul still studying him. "Yeah." He sighed wearily. "You might say that." Where to start?

Alice knocked on the door as she opened it. She scowled at the man sitting in her boss's chair. "That beard looks ridiculous, Paul. Noah, Marie MacIntyre's waiting in—"

"You'll have to cancel the rest of my appointments, Alice. Tell them an emergency came up." It wasn't a lie.

She shrugged and left.

Paul said, "Alice is still the same irrepressible flirt, I see." When Noah didn't smile, he added quietly, "I was sorry to hear about Jo." They'd met a couple of times during the past year.

"There's more." Noah quickly filled him in on everything that had happened that summer, from Noah's possible involvement in Jo's murder to the events of that morning and his fears for Kit's safety.

Paul leaned forward and faced him across the desk. "So you want me to help you go back to the day Jo died. To relive the part you can't remember and find out if you killed her," he said matter-of-factly.

Noah drew in a deep breath. "Yeah, but don't stop there."

Paul's eyes widened as Noah's meaning registered. "I don't believe it. Ten years of nagging has finally worn you down. You're gonna let me take you back to Ray's time."

"Don't applaud yourself. It wasn't your nagging. It's Kit. Somebody's been waiting all summer for her to find that damn disk, and I'd bet my last dime they're watching her till she gets on the plane to Chicago. The hell of it is, she was so excited about discovering Jo's book, I know she's not thinking about the risks."

"What did Jo find out that would make someone go to those lengths to suppress it?"

"If only I knew. Whatever it was, she kept it to herself. Spent eleven months in Pratte quietly turning over rocks." He smirked. "And pillows. Who knows what she found out? Maybe regressing to Ray's life won't accomplish anything but letting the bastard sink his claws in even deeper, but I've gotta give it a try. On the off chance I'll learn something that'll help me protect Kit." He contemplated the unthinkable. "If anything happened to her..."

The idea of regressing past his own birth—of deliberately exposing himself to the evil he'd spent his entire adult life avoiding—brought on a cold sweat and made his stomach roil. But he knew he had no choice. As scared as he was to confront, and possibly empower, the malignant personality that shared his mind, those fears paled next to his overwhelming need to keep Kit safe.

Paul smiled softly, incredulously. "I never thought I'd see it. You really love this girl."

"More than you can imagine. I just hope that when you're through chewing the fat with Ray, you can coax him back where he belongs, that he doesn't turn out to be too much for you to handle. You've never really gone head-to-head with this tenacious SOB."

Paul's response was a confident, steady gaze bordering on arrogance, and a humorless half smile. "He's never gone head-to-head with *this* tenacious SOB."

"The thing is, we've got to do this fast."

Paul was instantly all business. He glanced around the office. "Where?"

"There's only one place I can really relax."

Moments later he was comfortably ensconced on the armchair in his study. Paul brought in a dining chair and turned it around to straddle it facing him, his arms folded over the back. Noah was well acquainted with the procedure, having been hypnotized by Paul many times in the process of learning how to control Ray. That very training now enabled him to enter a state of intense relaxation even before Paul's soothing voice began guiding him. They went through the familiar litany of slow counting while his limbs became progressively heavier. Deeper and deeper he spiraled, descending an imaginary staircase....

OUTSIDE VALKYRIE, the rain clouds had swollen, turning morning to dusk, while the sharp tang of ozone heralded a thunderstorm. Kit climbed into Jo's Corolla and turned the key. The car would stay in Pratte. Noah had promised to sell it for her and send the proceeds to Sal.

The instant she began pulling out of the parking space, she knew something was wrong. The car pulled to the left and made an ominous noise in the vicinity of the front left tire. She *thump-thump*ed back into the space and got out to take a look. The tire was flat. She slumped against the car as the first fat raindrops pelted her. Now what? She'd been driving this car all summer. She already knew Jo hadn't felt the need to carry around such mundane items as a spare tire and jack.

She supposed she could leave the car here for Noah to take care of later, but that still left the problem of how to get to Pratte. She'd die before she called Noah back to come rescue her—

A silver Lexus slowed to a stop behind the Corolla. Kit watched the driver's window roll down, and grinned with relief. "Perfect timing. Mind if I hitch a ride?"

"THREE."

Noah opened his eyes on the count of three to see Paul rising from his chair. His last instruction before ending the session had been, "When you open your eyes, you'll remember everything we discussed."

And, God help him, he did.

Paul said, "I'm coming with you."

"No!" Noah was already on his way out the door. "Stay here in case she shows up or calls." Sprinting down the hallway, he yelled over his shoulder, "And get ahold of Chief Jordon!"

Chapter Fourteen

Noah snatched the telephone receiver away from the young woman at the front desk of Valkyrie. She gaped in shock.

"I'm looking for Kit Roarke." A puddle was forming under him on the lobby's plush green carpeting. He'd raced through the downpour and made it from Pratte in eighteen minutes.

"Who?"

"She came here a little while ago to empty Joanne Merino's locker." The phone receiver squawked in his hand. "Cindy? Cindy, you there?"

"Listen, mister—" She lunged for the phone, but he held it out of reach.

He said, "Her car's still in the lot, Cindy." With a slashed tire. "Where is she?"

Cindy pointed toward a double doorway, her carefully painted face twisted into an ugly scowl. Noah tossed her the receiver and barreled through the doors. A chorus of ear-piercing squeals and outraged cries of *"Dr. Stewart!"* confirmed that he was in the locker room.

He squinted at the labyrinthine banks of lockers and floor-to-ceiling mirrors. "God," he muttered, "this place is a goddamn fun house." He stalked the rows of lockers calling Kit's name, heedless of the sputtering objections of a score of females in various stages of undress. Noah didn't know what they were carrying on about. Hell, he'd done Pap smears on most of these women.

The hurried snap of bra straps and creak of panty girdles accompanied his progress through the room. At the end of an aisle Elizabeth Murray leaned suggestively on her locker, her leathery, overtanned flesh stuffed into a black lace push-up bra and matching garter belt. Mutton dressed as lamb. Though, to be fair, she'd been quite the hot ticket several decades ago when Ray nailed her to his office wall after splinting her broken toe.

"Hi, Liz," he said.

"Hi, Dr. Stewart."

"Have you seen Kit Roarke around here?"

"She that friend of Joanne's from Chicago? The one with the hair?" Keeping her eyes glued to his, she reached into each bra cup in turn to hoist herself a bit.

"That's right."

"She left. I saw her get into a car when I was pulling in to the parking lot."

"Whose car?"

She shrugged. "It was a silver Lexus. I didn't see who was driving."

Noah squeezed his eyes shut on a vicious curse. He was too late. He knew who was behind the wheel of that silver Lexus. Without a word he made his way out of the locker room and the building, pausing next to his Jeep. He blinked into the rain.

Where would Henry have taken her?

He heard it before he saw it, the familiar rumble of a Harley. *His* Harley. Or what used to be his. The sleek, dark silhouette materialized out of the gloom of driving rain, banking hard and reckless on the turn into the parking lot, skating to an abrupt stop next to Noah.

Bryan yanked off his black helmet, heedless of the downpour that had already drenched his black leather jacket and jeans. "I stopped by your place right after you left. Paul told me what happened. Did you find her?"

Noah wondered how much Bryan knew. "No. Henry got to her first. Someone saw her getting into his Lexus."

Bryan hurled an ugly oath, his face a mask of cold rage. He pulled in to the space next to Noah's Jeep and cut the engine, then swung off the bike and hopped into the Jeep as Noah slid behind the wheel. Within seconds they were on the highway.

"Any idea where they are?" the boy asked.

Noah stared straight ahead, determined not to give in to the wave of bleak despair squeezing his heart. "No." His voice was tight and raw. "He wouldn't take her to his home. Not to..." *Not to kill her.* He couldn't say it.

Bryan said, "The cops must've already checked his house. And Paul got Jordon to issue an APB on the Lexus and his other cars. For all the good it'll do." He pounded the dash savagely. "It's my fault. I knew it was him all along. I should've whacked the old bastard after what he did to Jo. If he touches Kit, he'll wish I had."

Bryan was wrong. It wasn't his fault, it was Noah's. If he hadn't resisted hypnotic regression all those years, Henry would have been stopped long ago, before he'd had a chance to kill Jo. His fists tightened on the steering wheel. Before he'd had a chance to get his hands on Kit. She'd told him that in the cemetery Ray had called Noah a stubborn, strong-willed bastard. He'd been right, dammit, and that stubbornness was about to get Kit killed.

It might already be too late.

No. He stomped the accelerator, with no inkling of his destination. All he knew was that he had to get there fast. It wasn't too late. It couldn't be.

"SORRY." KIT WIPED heavy wet strands of hair off her face and lifted her bottom, clad in her red denim miniskirt, to check the car seat. "I'm getting your upholstery wet." Supple ivory-colored leather upholstery at that.

Bettina shot her a conspiratorial glance from the driver's seat. "Relax. This is Henry's car, not mine."

"I really appreciate the lift, Bettina. You can drop me off at Noah's."

"Certainly. I imagine you and your young man want as much time as possible to say your goodbyes."

Bettina's casual reference to her impending separation from her "young man" scraped Kit's already tattered nerves. She hadn't realized the Davids knew she was involved with Noah. Due to the bizarre circumstances and the impermanence of their relationship, they'd taken care not to advertise it. She could only assume it took very little to fuel the inferno of small-town gossip.

Bettina smiled apologetically. "I hope you don't mind, but I couldn't help noticing you opened up Joanne's locker. I hadn't realized her things were still in there."

"I didn't know it myself until today."

"Why did you leave it all?"

"Well...there was too much to carry." Kit cringed inwardly, knowing she could offer no convincing reason for walking out of the health club empty-handed.

Bettina let the subject drop, for which Kit was grateful. She twisted in her seat to drop her purse on the floor in back. It landed next to Bettina's sack-style shoulder bag. The bag had fallen on its side and something protruded from it, something small, shiny red with a silver logo. Something Kit recognized instantly. She turned back in her seat, idly wondering how many accessory gadgets Bettina's Swiss army knife sported. It probably had cuticle scissors and an eyelash curler.

She frowned. It might even have a knife.

Scouring her memory, Kit tried to recall running over anything that could have punctured a tire. Wouldn't she have noticed? She glanced at Bettina, the picture of serenity.

Noah's words echoed in her mind. *Did anyone see you find the disk?* Up to this point, all she'd been able to think about was getting to a computer and reading her friend's book.

The book that got Jo killed.

Kit swallowed hard and averted her face to stare out the window and collect her thoughts. The rain hammered the glass, smearing the bucolic landscape flying past. During the course of her informal investigation, she'd compiled a short list of suspects in Jo's murder, a list she'd been unable to narrow down further. That list included Noah, of course, as well as Bryan and Henry. If Henry was indeed guilty, where did that leave his wife?

Kit jerked to attention as the car unexpectedly turned off the highway onto a side road. "I have to make a quick detour to pick something up," Bettina said, smiling. "I know you won't mind."

"HE'D TAKE HER into the woods," Bryan said, interrupting the rhythmic slap of the wiper blades.

"That's what I figure. Unless he..." Noah hauled in a deep breath, forcing himself to contemplate every possibility. "Unless he took her to a lake."

Bryan grunted in assent. "That's right. Somewhere he could make her disappear."

Any relief Noah felt from the discovery that he hadn't killed Jo was eclipsed by the knowledge that Kit was now in the hands of the real murderer. During hypnosis Ray had shown Noah what had happened back in June, at Grace's party. While Jo had been attacked, Noah was ensconced in the solarium, sipping Scotch and recovering from his exhausting ordeal at the hospital.

When he was called to her side, Ray actually emerged to assist him in saving her, later withdrawing to let Noah perform CPR, a skill he didn't share. Noah now saw the incident as a patchwork of cooperation between himself and Pratte's former M.D. When Henry had reached for Jo, ostensibly to assist in saving her, Ray had lunged to the fore and decked the older man.

Jo's murderer. There'd been no doubt in Ray's mind. It fit the M.O. Henry had established decades ago, when he'd killed his first wife.

And that was perhaps the most startling revelation of all, the knowledge that Ray was innocent of Anita's murder. Noah had finally allowed him to reenact her final minutes, right through to the end. Under hypnosis he'd experienced Ray's horror as the injection he administered to relieve Anita's breathing did just the opposite. Ray could only watch helplessly as respiratory paralysis seized his patient and she succumbed to a hideous death. He stared at the syringe in his hand. At the vial of clear liquid. And he knew.

He poked at the remains of a ham salad sandwich sitting on the kitchen table. Sniffed it. Tasted it. And detected a bit of mustard, to which Anita was violently allergic. Just enough had been added to trigger severe anaphylaxis that might have been enough by itself to kill her. But Henry had taken no chances. That's where the injection came in. Ray didn't know what kind of toxin his old buddy had chosen, only that it looked enough like epinephrine to fool him.

Ray concluded that Henry must have found out about his affair with Anita, an affair he'd been on the verge of breaking off. Ray had known for some time that Henry intended to divorce his wife and marry his wealthy young lover, Bettina Sheridan. Apparently he'd altered his plans to a more immediate and cost-effective solution.

And engineered a diabolical revenge for the good pal who'd cuckolded him at the same time, by making him a party to the murder. As horrified as Ray was at that moment of truth, as he stared at that vial he had to admire Henry's ingenuity.

But he didn't have to sacrifice himself. He picked up the phone and called an ambulance, claiming Anita had succumbed to the asthma attack and he'd been too late to save her. It was simpler and safer than revealing Henry's guilt; toxicology tests might show she was poisoned, but Ray had no proof to connect Henry with the crime. He'd planned it out too well, even arranging to be far away when his wife died, in Montpelier on business. No, Ray would have to take care of his old friend himself.

After the funeral, Ray confronted Henry, who went berserk when Ray mentioned his affair with Anita—as if he were learning it for the first time. He didn't even respond to the accusation of murder. Henry then went to the authorities with a wild tale that Ray had confessed to poisoning her. Anita was exhumed, toxicology tests performed and Ray was arrested. He protested his innocence, but no one gave any credence to his claims that Henry had orchestrated the murder. The minute he was released on bail, Ray made his final fatal mistake. He grabbed his semiautomatic and paid his old pal a visit. The ensuing struggle had ended in Ray's death.

And for thirty-two years the world believed him guilty. Noah couldn't deny that Ray had been a heartless bastard. Predatory and cruel, a manipulating, unrepentant womanizer.

But he was no murderer.

And that's what Ray had been trying to do for so many years, Noah reflected as he raced down the rain-slick highway. To clear his name. Prove his innocence. That was the purpose of the recurring dream, all Ray's attempts to force his way into Noah's consciousness. It's what he'd tried to tell Kit in the cemetery. That he hadn't killed Anita.

Bryan's voice dragged him out of his grim musings. "Henry would pick a real secluded spot...somewhere not too many people know about."

"Damn!" Noah slammed on the brakes and skidded into the shoulder. "That's it. God, that's it," he breathed as he spun the Jeep around and took off in the opposite direction.

Bryan braced himself against the rough turnaround and didn't ask where they were heading. All he said was, "I hope you're right, man."

"DID YOU KNOW your friend Joanne was sleeping with my husband?" Bettina asked in a conversational tone.

Kit whipped her head around to stare at the other woman. Bettina was the picture of serenity as she negotiated the rain-battered back roads they'd been following the past twenty minutes, keeping her speed down for safety's sake. Something about their location seemed familiar. Kit licked her suddenly dry lips. "Bettina, I really need to get to Noah's."

"I figured it out pretty fast, of course," Bettina continued, as if she hadn't heard her. "Men are so hopelessly delusional when it comes to their affairs." She chuckled, shaking her head. "My Henry is, anyway. Always thinking he can hide them. From *me!*" Her tinkling laugh said *Oh, what a scamp that Henry is.* "He forgets, of course, that I was once the 'other woman' myself!"

Pieces of the puzzle were beginning to slither out of the little spaces Kit had squeezed them into and rearrange themselves. The picture that began to emerge made the blood drain from her face. She'd assumed Bettina had been ignorant of her husband's affair with his young reporter. A foolish assumption on her part, for as she'd just been reminded, Bettina had always known her husband wasn't the faithful sort.

"Bettina, where are we going?" Kit asked, an instant before the car turned onto a rutted dirt path that snaked into the woods. Trusting her instincts, she had her door open and one sandaled foot out of the car before the engine was off.

"Don't," Bettina said.

Glancing back, Kit found herself looking down the short stainless steel barrel of a snub-nosed revolver. One elegant French-manicured finger was poised on the trigger. She froze and shifted her gaze to Bettina's face. In that moment she knew this woman had killed before . . . and had no compunction about doing so again. The car door was still open, her right half soaked as rain battered the car.

"Reach into the back—*slowly,*" Bettina said, "and pick up your purse."

Kit obeyed, dizzy with shock and fear.

Bettina took the bag and set it on her lap. Keeping her eyes on Kit, she opened it and dug around with her free hand. It took only a moment for a smile of triumph to spread across her face. "Well. I'd practically given up hope of *ever* locating this thing!" She pulled out the disk, tucked it under her seat and continued rummaging in the purse for another few moments. She withdrew a small can of pepper spray, Kit's only weapon.

"Oh, really . . ." Bettina scoffed. "This is so very inadequate, dear. An attractive young woman like you, wandering around in unfamiliar locales, snooping into all manner of troublesome things . . ." She clucked in disapproval and placed the spray under her seat, then tossed the purse into the back seat. "Now give me my bag."

Kit retrieved the other purse and handed it to her. Bettina pulled a pretty floral silk scarf out of it and tied Kit's wrists together behind her back. Tight. She shooed her with an impatient gesture. "Out."

They stepped out of the car and were instantly drenched. Bettina plucked at her white silk tunic and scowled. "I *would* be wearing something dry-cleanable," she muttered.

Peering into the surrounding forest, Kit realized the car was well concealed from the road. No one would just stumble upon them.

And then she knew where they were.

Bettina wagged the gun. "Walk."

Kit preceded her as they slowly trudged through woods she'd been in once before. But everything had looked so much different on that long-ago day when Noah brought her here for brunch alfresco. Then it had been clear and beautiful, an ideal day for a man and woman to celebrate a new beginning. This gloomy day, on the other hand, was more suited to endings.

Bettina said, "This area is quite off the beaten track. Henry showed it to me. He goes fishing somewhere around here."

As she slogged through puddles and wet vegetation, Kit said over her shoulder, "You have the disk, Bettina. Take it with my blessing. I don't know what's on it and I don't want to know."

Bettina's laughter chilled her more than the rain, now dwindling to an icy drizzle that plopped heavily through the trees. "Well, *I* know what's on that disk. I read the hard copy before I destroyed it, along with her computer and all the rest. Naturally, I had to eliminate the author, as well.

"And please don't insult my intelligence, dear. I know very well you wouldn't simply hand over your dead friend's opus and keep quiet about it. Good heavens, you've spent the entire summer looking for it. As have I. Ironic, isn't it? Weeks of having you followed, and the silly thing is sitting right there in Joanne's locker the whole time. I must have walked past it dozens of times. I'm telling you, you could have knocked me over with a feather."

"That book means nothing to me, I swear." Kit stopped and hazarded a look back. The polished steel of Bettina's revolver glinted in the meager light. She felt utterly defenseless with her hands tied behind her. "No one can connect you with Jo's murder. But if you kill me, they'll catch you. Noah's expecting me. Someone will have seen me get into your car."

Bettina shrugged negligently. "Keep moving."

Kit obeyed.

"You don't honestly think I'm worried about getting caught?" Bettina asked. "It really is shameful how incompetent local law enforcement is." She sighed. "Why, even your feebleminded friend Malcolm Ryder could outthink an idiot like Tom Jordon. Stop here."

She did, and a violent shudder racked her. Whatever Bettina planned to do to her, this was the spot. Deep in the woods, where it could take weeks to find her body. She recognized the enormous boulder next to them, erupting from the earth like a misshapen gray molar. *Keep her talking,* Kit thought. *Stall for time.* Fortunately, Bettina seemed to consider her crime a stimulating source of conversation. "Wasn't Malcolm home when you broke into Jo's room?" Kit asked.

Bettina nodded. "He was in the shower. I hated to leave her room so rumpled, but there you have it. I had to work fast."

Bettina's twisted priorities bespoke a mental sickness that Malcolm's "feeblemindedness" couldn't approach, Kit thought. No amount of reasoning would sway this woman. Something in that pretty head had long ago snapped.

The rain had let up, but Kit was already soaked to the skin and shivering with cold and unadulterated fear. She asked, "How did you find out about Jo's book?"

"I overheard her arguing with Grace Drummond about it, at the health club. I'd stuck fairly close to Joanne since her arrival. I even suggested she join Valkyrie. I didn't trust the little slut, and with good reason, as it turned out. Not only did she intend to rehash that unpleasant business about my husband's first wife, she actually seduced him in her quest for information. By the time I'd found out about it, of course, the silly man had already played right into her hands." She sighed heavily. "After that, it was a matter of exercising damage control."

Damage control? That's how this woman refers to murder?

Bettina continued, "And later, when I found out from Etta that you were looking for your friend's missing computer disk, I realized a copy of the book still existed. It wasn't in your room or car, but I knew that if I kept an eye on you, eventually you'd lead me to it."

That must have been the day Kit had discovered her room had been searched, the day Bettina had visited Etta on the pretext of checking out her roses.

Something dark winked in and out of view behind trees in the distance. It took every iota of mental concentration for Kit to keep her eyes on Bettina's face. It could be a large dog. Too dark for a deer. Were there bears in Vermont? At this moment Kit would have gladly chosen a grizzly over Bettina's little snub-nosed revolver.

Bettina reached into her shoulder bag and extracted a rigid eyeglass case, which she opened to reveal a small hypodermic. Something in Kit's chest squeezed painfully, stealing her breath. As chilled as she was, she felt fresh sweat pop out on her palms, her upper lip, under her arms. Bettina removed the hypodermic and shoved the eyeglass case back into her purse. Had she been carrying that thing around all summer, waiting for this moment?

Don't pass out, Kit commanded herself. *You've never fainted in your life. Don't start now.* That would make it too easy for the bitch.

Keep her talking!

Kit's voice was hoarse. "Henry wouldn't want you to do this."

"*Au contraire,* my husband and I have a sort of tacit understanding about these things. No doubt he's noticed that one of his insulin syringes is missing, but since he's not comfortable with this business—" she indicated the gun and syringe "—I don't bother him with the details. I just do what has to be done." She smiled wryly. "It's always up to the wife to clean up the messes. Don't let anyone tell you different."

She could be discussing balancing the checkbook, Kit thought with a shudder. Trying a different tack, she said, "You know, your actions are...understandable in a way. I mean, you were just protecting your husband when you killed Jo."

Bettina's carefully plucked brows came together. "Protecting Henry...?"

"Well, her book must've implicated him in Anita's murder." At Bettina's funny little smile, the jigsaw pieces squirmed into a tighter fit. Kit whispered, "You killed Anita, too."

"Of course I killed Anita. Good grief, someone had to do something. If I'd waited for Henry to divorce her, I'd probably still be waiting. Never trust a man when he says he'll leave his wife for you, dear." A breezy laugh accompanied this bit of sisterly advice. "Somehow they never *do* get around to it."

"You...but you were only..."

"Nineteen." Bettina raised the hypodermic and tapped it, as if to assure herself it had an adequate load. "But I knew what I wanted. And I was smart enough to do it cleanly and to tie up all the loose ends. It was different with your friend Joanne, of course—more of a hands-on operation as it were—but fortunately, all went well. The element of surprise really does put one at an advantage."

An advantage she lacked with Kit. And that's where the gun came in—Bettina was using it simply to control her. As for the instrument of death, clearly she intended to stick to her weapon of choice: curare.

Kit recalled the day she met Noah, and his reluctant recounting of Jo's torturous last minutes. In that instant she decided she wouldn't make this easy for Bettina. She wouldn't make it "clean." If Kit was going to die today, she swore it would be by a bullet in the back from that little gun—with plenty of "loose ends" for her killer to worry about. She wondered if a bullet removed from her corpse could be traced to Bettina's gun.

"Where'd you get the curare?" Kit asked. "From Wescott?"

"The hospital? Good heavens, dear, they keep substances like this under lock and key! Think of the mayhem if just *anyone* could get their hands on it. No, back when I was in college, I worked in my father's pharmaceutical company, Conti-Meeker. It was shamefully easy to make off with a vial of their curare derivative."

Her stomach roiling in fear, Kit nodded toward the syringe. "This is from the same vial you used with Anita? It's thirty-two years old?"

"Yes, but don't get your hopes up. Curare is an amazingly stable drug. As your friend Joanne discovered."

Kit recalled the frantic messages Jo had left on her answering machine the day she died. *I think it's this guy I'm seeing. That took my book.* Jo must have assumed Henry was doing some of Bettina's dirty work, not realizing the murderess preferred to work solo. Licking her dry lips, Kit said, "Does Henry know you killed Anita?"

"The man's not stupid. When Ray tried to blame her murder on Henry, he knew right away it had to be me. Well, I didn't deny it. Why should I?"

"How did he react?" The dark shape materialized once more, nearer this time. For the briefest moment. Kit bored her gaze into Bettina's face, knowing that if she let her eyes stray even for an instant, the other woman would know something—some*one*, Kit hoped—was behind her.

Bettina smiled. "He was shocked, of course, the dear thing. But he settled down soon enough. Think about it. I'd *killed* for him. Do you have any idea what that does for a man's self-esteem?"

Self-esteem? "What about Jo?" Kit asked, not attempting to hide her bitterness. "Did murdering her also enhance your husband's precious self-esteem?"

Bettina's eyes narrowed. Keeping the gun trained on Kit, she dropped a shoulder, letting her purse slide onto the ground. She took a step toward her, and Kit backed up, struggling futilely with the bindings on her wrists.

"Bettina!"

Kit's gaze snapped to the source of the voice, the dark form now standing out in the open about thirty yards away. Bryan! Startled, Bettina jerked toward him for a split second, long enough for Kit to start running. Instinct kicked in to alter her course abruptly, some primitive brain fold deciding it was time to stop zigging and start zagging.

A fiery pain sliced into her thigh and the next instant she was eating mud. Helplessly she looked up to see Bettina facing her, sighting down the barrel of her revolver. Where was Bryan?

A blur of movement from behind the boulder coalesced into a large, solid force hurtling into Bettina from behind and tackling her to the ground. The gun discharged harmlessly just as Kit recognized Noah. He yanked the gun out of her grasp and tossed it away, then seized her wrists behind her back as he anxiously looked toward Kit lying a few yards away.

"Bryan!" he hollered, but the boy was already sprinting toward him from out of the trees. Noah let Bryan take charge of a sputtering, crimson-faced Bettina, lying prone in the mud. None too gently Bryan shoved a knee into the small of her back and whipped off his belt to secure her wrists.

Noah raced to Kit's side and pushed her skirt up to take a quick look at her wound, then gently turned her and untied her hands. She felt the slight trembling in his fingers, and knew how close she'd come to losing her life. Her leg burned like hell, her skirt blood soaked on that side.

"You're gonna be okay, darlin'," he said, his voice breathless. "Easy now, this is gonna hurt." He wrapped the scarf around her thigh, directly over the bullet wound, and tied it tight.

She stiffened and gritted her teeth against a cry of pain. In the next instant she was in his arms, his embrace so tight she didn't know where she stopped and Noah began. His heart drummed against her breasts as she shivered violently.

"Darlin'...my Kit...my sweet, sweet darlin'." His voice quavered. "I almost lost you." He pressed hard, desperate kisses to her hair, her eyes, her lips. His warm hand closed over her wound. "The bullet missed the bone, thank God. It exited cleanly." Something close to a chuckle escaped him. "Undid all my beautiful needlework, though. Would you believe she hit the same damn spot?"

"I...I was trying to swerve...to make a harder target." She buried her face against his chest.

"That's probably what saved your life."

Bryan called, "What're we gonna do with *her?*" indicating the woman he held pinned to the ground.

Kit felt Noah flinch as if he'd been slapped, felt herself slide out of his loosened embrace. When he spoke, the thick Vermont accent made her heart lurch.

"I'll take care of her."

Chapter Fifteen

Ray welcomed the surge of cold, raw fury that sang through his veins. *His* veins? He grinned. Okay, borrowed veins. Borrowed blood. Borrowed flesh. But the sweet, vengeful wrath was all Ray's. He'd waited a hellishly long time for this, he thought, advancing on Bettina where his grandson held her down.

Bryan stared intently at him, and Ray knew the kid sensed a difference. Kit screamed, "Noah! *Ray! Don't!*" and the boy turned pale.

Ray pulled Bryan off the murderous bitch. Grabbing the full syringe lying in the dirt, he hauled her upright and slammed her back against the boulder, holding her by her throat. She was helpless, her hands tied behind her back. He brought his face close to hers and trailed the tip of the needle down her cheek. Her eyes were round, her pupils constricted to tiny pinpoints. "It's been a long time, Bettina. Thirty-two years, to be precise."

"Noah...?" she croaked.

He gave her a mock pout. "Aw, now, you hurt my feelings, sweetheart. Don't tell me you've forgotten your old friend Ray." He punctuated this with a couple of tiny jabs of the needle. "Maybe I should refresh your memory."

Kit cried, "Ray, don't do this." She struggled to sit up, her face chalk white.

Bryan stood nearby, his stance tense, poised to spring.

Ray said, "Stay out of it, son."

The stark terror on Bettina's face was beautiful to behold. Her eyes bulged as she gaped at him, an ugly flush mottling her face. He said, "Hey, remember all the good times we used to have? Like that Halloween I came across you and Henry balling in the hunting lodge. I put on a Frankenstein mask and knocked on the window, remember? Hell, I'll bet they heard you scream in New Hampshire." He tapped the needle on her nose, with a good-natured chuckle. "God, those were good times."

Her eyes bulged wider, if that was possible. She whispered, "Ray..." He heard Kit gasp.

"Now you're getting it," he said. "I knew you would. Smart girl like you." He pointedly studied the tiny lines around her eyes and mouth. "But you're not a girl anymore, are you, Bettina? No, you've gotten downright haggard. You used to be so pretty. What happened? Oh, yeah!" He grinned, gesticulating with the syringe. God, was he enjoying this. "You got old! Now, me, I never got a chance to get old. And you know why?"

"Grandpa!"

Ray shot his grandson a warning look. "I said stay out of this, Bryan."

"She's not worth it, man. Send her to jail."

"Can't do that, son. There's too much unfinished business here. Isn't that right, Bettina?"

She was trembling so hard that if he hadn't been holding her up with a hand around her throat she'd have slid right down to the ground. He felt her swallow convulsively under his fingers, felt the frantic flutter of her pulse.

She whispered hoarsely, "Ray... it... it was Henry...."

"Well, now, that's what I thought, you know? All that time I figured it was Henry that did this to me. But we heard something real interesting, Noah and me, when we were slipping around this boulder a few minutes ago. We distinctly heard you shooting off your mouth about what you did to Anita." He tightened his hold on her throat, causing her face to contort. "It was real ugly the way she died, Bettina. You know that?" He turned the hypodermic this way and that, staring at it. "Horrible way to go. No one should have to die like that. Except maybe a murderer."

He jabbed the needle into her upper arm, his finger poised on the plunger. She jerked at the impact and howled in terror.

Kit screamed, "Ray! This is wrong." Her voice was choked with tears. "You're not that kind of man, Ray. I know you're not."

"She's right," Bryan said, his voice tight. "You're not a murderer, Grandpa. I always knew you were innocent. Always. Mom and Grandma Ruby, too."

Bettina was sobbing, her eyes squeezed shut. Ray looked at his grandson, at the strain on his young face. And he saw something else. Respect. Love. The boy had never known his grandfather, but amazingly, he'd believed in him his whole life.

Bryan's eyes zeroed in on the needle piercing Bettina's arm. "You're not a killer, man, you're a healer. That's what I'm gonna do. Go to med school. Be a doctor. I wanna be like you."

Ray snorted in derision. "You don't want to be like me, son."

Bryan's lopsided smile said he was under no illusions about his grandfather. "I like it that you never took crap from anyone. But you never killed anyone, either. Don't start now."

Ray glanced back at Bettina. She stared pop-eyed at the needle stabbing her arm. He said to Bryan, "You're wrong, son. I have killed before. Ask Noah."

Kit said, "That was different, Ray. You saved a little girl and her mother. You did the right thing. Let the law handle Bettina. They'll put her away for the rest of her life."

"What about the rest of *my* life!" Ray yelled. "The life I never had! I never got to see Debbie grow up. Never got to grow old with Ruby. This murdering scum deserves to die!"

"Yes," Kit said. "She deserves to die. But you don't deserve to become the thing she is. And that's what'll happen if you go through with this."

Ray looked at Bryan. He was relaxed...confident his grandfather would do the right thing. He looked at the syringe. Bettina's weapon. He stared into her terrified eyes. "Rot in jail, bitch." He yanked the needle out of her arm and dropped it. Her eyes rolled up in her head and she slumped to the wet ground, senseless.

"Ray..." Kit's voice was weak, shaky. The scarf binding her wound was soaked through with blood. "I need Noah. Let him come back. Please..."

Ray was inexpressibly weary. He'd lived a rough life and died a rougher death. And found no peace on the other side.

But it was finished now. He'd done what he had to do. The elation he'd expected to feel was strangely absent; instead there was only a lonely, cheerless sense of closure. But it was more than he deserved, he reflected. He had not been a good man.

"Grandpa." Bryan hesitantly approached him, hand extended. Ray knew they'd never meet again; he'd commandeered Noah's mind and body for the last time. He took the boy's hand and stared long and hard at him. He could be looking into a mirror. The physical resemblance was startling. But that's as far as it went. Behind the sheen of moisture in his grandson's eyes was an undeniable strength of character. Perhaps he'd be the man his grandfather never was.

Ray clasped Bryan's hand in both of his. He cleared his throat, which was suddenly tight. "Make me proud, son."

Noah drew a deep breath, blinking. Why was he clasping hands with Bryan? Why was the boy on the verge of tears?

He took in his surroundings in a flash, from Bettina groggily coming around to Kit lying pale and shivering, watching him intently.

"Noah . . . ?" she said.

"It's me, darlin'." He was by her side in an instant, stroking the damp hair off her face and lifting her into his arms. His lips brushed hers tenderly. "From now on, it's just me and you."

Epilogue

"Why did I let you talk me into this, woman?"

Kit looked up from the wallpaper sample book she was perusing to smirk at her husband's back. Noah was perched on a stepladder, steaming green floral wallpaper—Ray's wallpaper—off their living room walls with a strange-looking contraption he'd rented for the purpose.

"Don't blame me," she said. "I seem to recall a certain sexy young M.D. waxing rhapsodic about how much fun we'd have redecorating this old place by the sweat of our brows." Of course, *she* was more inclined to wax rhapsodic about what happened under those snug jeans as he reached and bent and steamed and peeled.

He threw a sardonic grin over his shoulder. "Is that 'sexy young M.D.' bit supposed to keep me going for three more walls?"

"I was hoping it would get you through the dining room and a couple of bathrooms, too."

Holding her gaze, he descended the stepladder and turned off the steaming machine, laying it aside. The look in his eyes triggered an itch that she knew from blissful experience he was more than capable of scratching. "You'll have to do better than that," he said, advancing on her.

She held up the big wallpaper book as a shield, but that didn't stop him from leaning over her and trapping her between his long arms braced on the back of the solitary old threadbare sofa. Everything else—tables, chairs, carpet, lamps—had been hauled away pending delivery of the modern new furnishings they'd selected.

Noah's mouth closed over hers voraciously, catching her off guard. His long, strong fingers tangled in her hair as his tongue slipped between her lips, darting and receding in a ruthlessly erotic cadence. The itch blossomed and spread, all slick and throbbing, and a hot flush swept over her face and throat. Tearing herself away, she tossed the wallpaper book aside, pulled him down next to her and curled into his embrace.

She said, "I forgot to tell you. Jason Daly called with the publication date. Next December." Jason was Jo's literary agent. In September he'd directed a bidding war among prospective publishers eager to obtain the rights to Jo's book, *Poisoned Love*. The prominent New York publishing house that won out had offered an extremely generous advance, money that would enable Sal Merino to move into a comfortable retirement community.

Noah said, "We have to wait a whole year till it's published?"

She shrugged. "Apparently that's par for the course. But by then maybe the sentence will have been handed down and we can include an afterword about Bettina getting life in prison."

"Doesn't seem much doubt about that."

The trial hadn't yet taken place, but Bettina had been denied bail and the case was clear-cut; it was unlikely her lawyers could successfully plead insanity. As for Henry, he'd been arrested as an accessory to murder. The length of his sentence would depend to a large extent on the skill of his lawyers in distancing him from his wife's crimes. Finding an unbiased jury pool was certain to be a challenge, as the case had captured international attention during the past three months since Bettina's arrest. The world now knew Dr. Ray Whittaker had been unjustly branded a murderer.

The terrifying episode in the woods when Kit had nearly died at Bettina's hand had been Noah's final glimpse of Ray. He hadn't sensed his presence at all since then. At long last, Ray's soul was at peace . . . and harmlessly dormant deep in Noah's subconscious. Noah described it as a profound sense of emancipation. For the first time since his near-death experience at age sixteen, his spirit was carefree and unencumbered. The recurring dream had ceased, as well.

Ironically, by forcing himself to do what he'd avoided all those years—undergoing hypnosis to deliberately tap into Ray's last days—he'd freed himself of the hold the other man had on him. In order to rescue Kit, he'd laid himself open to his worst fears, to the dark, malevolent thing inside, and had not only survived, but triumphed.

Noah said, "Jo's book is pretty amazing. The way she got into Bettina's head. Exposed her whole warped mindset . . . her twisted rationalizations . . . all the details of Anita's murder and what led up to it."

"What's really amazing is that no one had managed to do it before her. Like thirty-two years before."

"No one cared enough. Or was dedicated enough. Or detached enough. Or..." Noah sighed. "I don't know. I just wish to God she'd let us in on what she was digging up, before it was too late."

Kit shivered, and Noah held her tighter. In a sense, she'd achieved her own liberation. She'd discharged her final obligation to her friend, by avenging her murder. It wasn't enough; it hadn't assuaged her grief or filled the chasm in her soul left by Jo's death. But something about it felt . . . complete.

With a lopsided smile, Kit said, "Could you imagine Jo doing that? Sharing her work in progress with anyone? Even you or me?"

He chuckled, shaking his head. "What was I thinking?"

"So, tell me, Dr. Stewart..." She twisted her body to hook her legs over his lap and snuggle closer. "How do the karma points stack up for you now?"

"Karma *points?*"

"Way I figure it, you've racked up a few lifetimes' worth of good deeds. Wrapping up Ray's unfinished business. Foiling the bad guys and all that. The reward comes in your next life, right? You get to be a...megagazillionaire rock star or something."

"Finding my soul mate in this life is reward enough." His warm hand slid up her jean-clad leg, from ankle to waist. She noticed his touch was extra gentle on her thigh, though the bullet wound had healed nicely.

"You mean we were meant to be together?" she asked.

"Can there be any doubt?" His hand slowly caressed her hip, slid under her bottom. "We were probably...I don't know...Antony and Cleopatra."

"I'll go get the eyeliner and the asp."

"I like *this* asp," he said with a pointed squeeze. When Kit's fingers found the buttons of his flannel shirt and became very busy, he asked, "Why do I get the feeling I'm not gonna finish stripping these walls today?"

"First things first," she admonished. "It's time for your wound check." She slipped her fingers inside his open shirt, to burrow through the crisp golden hairs and tease a flat nipple. He sucked in a breath.

"Wound check?" His smiling eyes darkened to a smoky green.

She moaned in affirmation, nuzzling his chest. The scent of him was an aphrodisiac. "Your health is my primary concern."

Noah pressed a hand over hers through the shirt, his voice a low rumble of frustration. "Darlin', this is nowhere near where I hurt."

"Don't worry, I'll work my way around to the spot eventually. I'm—"

"I know, I know," he groaned as her tongue joined the diagnostic arsenal. "You're very thorough."

BRIDE'S BAY RESORT

UNLOCK THE DOOR TO GREAT ROMANCE AT BRIDE'S BAY RESORT

Join Harlequin's new across-the-lines series, set in an exclusive hotel on an island off the coast of South Carolina.

Seven of your favorite authors will bring you exciting stories about fascinating heroes and heroines discovering love at Bride's Bay Resort.

Look for these fabulous stories coming to a store near you beginning in January 1996.

Harlequin American Romance #613 in January
Matchmaking Baby by Cathy Gillen Thacker

Harlequin Presents #1794 in February
Indiscretions by Robyn Donald

Harlequin Intrigue #362 in March
Love and Lies by Dawn Stewardson

Harlequin Romance #3404 in April
Make Believe Engagement by Day Leclaire

Harlequin Temptation #588 in May
Stranger in the Night by Roseanne Williams

Harlequin Superromance #695 in June
Married to a Stranger by Connie Bennett

Harlequin Historicals #324 in July
Dulcie's Gift by Ruth Langan

Visit Bride's Bay Resort each month wherever
Harlequin books are sold.

HARLEQUIN®

What do women really want to know?

Only the world's largest publisher of romance
fiction could possibly attempt an answer.

HARLEQUIN ULTIMATE GUIDES™

How to Talk to a Naked Man,

Make the Most of Your Love Life, and Live Happily Ever After

The editors of Harlequin and Silhouette are
definitely experts on love, men and relationships.
And now they're ready to share that expertise with
women everywhere.

Jam-packed with vital, indispensable, lighthearted
tips to improve every area of your romantic life—even
how to get one! So don't just sit around and wonder
why, how or where—run to your nearest bookstore
for your copy now!

Available this February, at your favorite retail outlet.

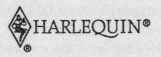

HARLEQUIN®

NAKED

HARLEQUIN®

I N T R I G U E®

Into a world where danger lurks around
every corner, and there's a fine line between trust
and betrayal, comes a tall, dark and handsome man.

Intuition draws you to him...but instinct keeps you
away. Is he really one of those...

You made the dozen "Dangerous Men" from 1995 so
popular that there's a sextet of these sexy but
secretive men coming to you in 1996!

In March, look for:

**#361 LUCKY DEVIL
by Patricia Rosemoor**

**Take a walk on the wild side...with our
"DANGEROUS MEN"!**

Yo amo novelas con corazón!

Starting this March, Harlequin opens up to a whole new world of readers with two new romance lines in SPANISH!

Harlequin Deseo
* passionate, sensual and exciting stories

Harlequin Bianca
* romances that are fun, fresh and very contemporary

With four titles a month, each line will offer the same wonderfully romantic stories that you've come to love—now available in Spanish.

Look for them at selected retail outlets.

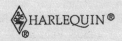

HARLEQUIN®

AMERICAN ✦ ROMANCE®

®

In Name Only

...because there are many reasons for saying "I do."

American Romance cordially invites you to a
wedding of convenience. This is one reluctant bride
and groom with their own unique reasons for
marrying...IN NAME ONLY.

By popular demand American Romance continues this
story of favorite marriage-of-convenience books. Don't
miss

#624 THE NEWLYWED GAME
by Bonnie K. Winn
March 1996

Find out why some couples marry first...and learn to
love later. Watch for IN NAME ONLY!

INTRODUCING...

A collection of award-winning books by award-winning authors! From Harlequin and Silhouette.

Heaven In Texas
by Curtiss Ann Matlock

National Reader's Choice Award Winner— Long Contemporary Romance

Let Curtiss Ann Matlock take you to a place called *Heaven In Texas*, where sexy cowboys in well-worn jeans are the answer to every woman's prayer!

"Curtiss Ann Matlock blends reality with romance to perfection!"
—*Romantic Times*

Available this March wherever Silhouette books are sold.